Antony Cutler is the pseudonym of acclaimed novelist and Renaissance historian Anton Gill. Under his own name he has published a series of thrillers set in Ancient Egypt, and a historical mystery, *The Sacred Scroll*. An English Literature graduate of Clare College, Cambridge, he has been a freelance writer since 1984, and has been translated and published worldwide. He has written a wide variety of historical non-fiction, and previously worked in theatre, radio and television. Anton is married to the actress Marji Campi, and divides his time between London and Paris.

Visit the author online:
www.antongill.com

D1149608

THE ACCURSED

ANTONY CUTLER

piatkus

PIATKUS

First published in Great Britain in 2013 by Piatkus

A CIP catalogue record for this book
is available from the British Library.

ISBN 978-0-749-95922-7

Typeset in Bembo by Palimpsest Book Production Limited,
Falkirk, Stirlingshire
Printed and bound in Great Britain by Clays Ltd, St Ives plc

Papers used by Piatkus are from well-managed forests
and other responsible sources.

MIX
Paper from
responsible sources
FSC
www.fsc.org   FSC® C104740

Piatkus
An imprint of
Little, Brown Book Group
100 Victoria Embankment
London EC4Y 0DY

An Hachette UK Company
www.hachette.co.uk

www.piatkus.co.uk

For
Julian,
who suggested it,
and
Marie-Line & Patrick,
who lent me their flat in Fréjus to write it in.

MORS + ACERBA + FAMA + PERPETUA + EST

(a bitter death means fame forever)

PROLOGUE

ROME, JUNE, AD 64

Two men circled each other in the dusty arena. It was kill or be killed now, though they'd trained a long time together, and sometimes fought shoulder-to-shoulder, in other bouts.

But there'd never been any thought of friendship. Both knew that sooner or later it would come to this. Castor and Pollux were their arena names. Veterans now of fifteen games. Old men at twenty-three.

Castor fought in his preferred role, the Myrmillo. He wore the large crested helmet surmounted by the emblem of a fish, and was the first to strike, feinting with his small shield, then lunging with his sword. Its point flicked off the scaled armour covering the left arm of his opponent, who'd chosen his own speciality, Retiarius, the trident-wielding net-bearer. Pollux stepped back, his left hand grasping his net, the right hefting his trident. His head was bare. The other man could see his eyes calculating. Nothing there but

1

concentration. This was a game, though its end would be no game at all for one of them.

They were scarcely aware of the roar from the crowd surrounding them, surging whenever either made a skilled or savage move. Their job was to play it, act it, give the people what they had come to see. The performance, for the spectators, was free. For the actors, the price was death for one, and freedom, if the crowd was pleased, for the other.

Pollux whirled his net and caught it on Castor's helmet. The helmet, strapped under his chin, wrenched round, pulling his head with it, making him stagger, hurting his neck. He bunched his shoulder muscles and ran in, loosening the hold of the net, shaking his helmet free of it, but he came too close, and too late saw the trident drive into his shield arm, though he yanked it away in time to avoid more than a cut, so the arm was still good.

Then they stood off and the crowd booed. Castor watched Pollux' eyes, trying to guess his next move. Pollux was taller, and had a couple of games' more experience. Castor was stocky, not as fast, but better muscled. And he had the helmet. If he could get the lance to his opponent's unprotected head, above the armoured neck, and make a clean kill there, it'd be over soon.

But not too soon. The act had to be played out and get applause if he were to win his freedom, and be awarded the Wooden Sword.

2

And he had to get in close enough without risk of being caught by the net again.

He licked his lips, gritty with sand. Squinted into the blinding sun. Shit. His opponent was trying to get between it and him. Castor feinted left and the net flew out towards him. He checked and ran to the right. Good. Quicker for once than Pollux had thought. The net lay to the side of him, not yet recovered.

He moved in while Pollux' attention was on the net. Sword raised, aiming for the head. Mustn't get it over with too quick. Struck a blow, not to the eye, to the forehead. Saw blood run, stepped back. Roar from the crowd. Good.

He raised his arms to acknowledge the applause while Pollux wiped the blood away. But he didn't milk it long. His own left arm was hurting from the wound. He and Pollux exchanged a glance. How long would they give it? Five more minutes? End it then.

Sweating in the sun, glistening, conscious of the women enjoying the gleaming muscles and the blood, they faced each other again. Hard to tell who was the favourite.

They circled each other warily, feinting and stabbing with trident and sword to keep the crowd interested. But one feint of Castor's was lucky and gashed Pollux' knee, the point going in deep. This had happened too soon, and Pollux went down, surprised.

Castor had to follow through as the crowd roared again, getting to their feet. His glance swung round them, stopping at the raised daïs where the emperor sat, drinking. Too far away to focus on him through the visor of the helmet, but Nero was showing an interest. The two fighters belonged to one of the best gladiatorial schools, one which the emperor had invested in.

Castor stood over Pollux, Pollux rolling away to get out of reach of the sword, but encumbered by his trident and net. Could he get up again? Castor put a foot on the net, saw it tangled round his opponent's wrist. Pollux, half-risen, fell back again, coughing in the dust. The knee was swelling. Blood there choked with sand. Castor moved to stand over the fallen man, poised his sword, then stopped, looked up, raised his other arm and spread it wide in appeal. What was it to be? Death or Mercy?

It hadn't been much of a fight. He expected to see no white handkerchiefs raised.

He scanned the tiers of faceless people again. Full house. Silence. Not a flicker of white.

He looked down at Pollux, leaning on one elbow, sweating, panting, tired.

He saw the big artery pulsing in the neck.

He drew back the sword. Then struck.

1

'Fuck it,' Nero snarled. 'One of my best men.'

The Legate standing near him nodded sympathetically, though he felt nothing at all.

This was a festive season. How better to celebrate its arrival than in blood?

The unlucky month of May, overcast by the season of *Lemuria*, when the dead walked, was over, and even June was halfway past. Now, the Temple of Vesta had been ritually cleansed. It was safe. People felt free to marry. No one would have done such a thing during the last six weeks, an ill-omened time.

June brides. Nice tradition.

The Legate, Quintus Julius Marcellus, felt for them. Julius, special investigator for VIII Special Cohort of the *Vigiles*, sometimes wondered, though less and less often as the years went by, whether his own decision to get married – in defiance of superstition, just before the scouring of the Temple – hadn't been to blame for his disastrous marriage to dear, blue-eyed Cornelia.

But he called himself rational. He told himself he didn't believe in the supernatural. So they'd married in May. Her parents had made a fuss. It hadn't mattered to him.

In those days Julius was a happier and more confident man than he was now.

He turned his mind back to the present – to the Arena. The Ceremonial Games to mark the opening of the new season had begun, and the Emperor Nero was putting on a big show. Julius, though his job made him no stranger to violence, disliked blood-sports. He couldn't appreciate the finer points. But he had to be there. He was in charge of the emperor's security.

He knew the job, though vital, had been handed to him as a rebuke. His success level in special investigations, which is what VIII Cohort did, hadn't been good recently, and this job was one which a regular security policeman should have been handling.

He consoled himself by thinking that his failure-rate hadn't been his fault. VIII Cohort was efficient, but high-level crime in Rome was too well-protected for him to be able to dig deep enough. He shrugged. Corruption. It was just another fact of life.

But he'd have to watch himself. Any more failures and

he'd be kicked out and sent to some dump in the provinces for the rest of his career.

Julius watched as Nero turned his attention back to the arena. The emperor had bigger concerns than what happened to the career of some policeman. The Games were taking place at Taurus' old amphitheatre, built partly of stone, partly of wood. The place held tens of thousands.

The place worried Julius.

The problem was that wooden stands were old. They might catch fire. They might collapse. Older citizens remembered the big disaster at Fidenae, just north of Rome. Some parvenu ex-slave called Atilius had constructed a wooden arena on the cheap. One day, because the stands were too full, the whole thing fell down, crushing fifty thousand people. The tragedy attracted huge crowds in itself. It took days for all the dying, trapped in the wreckage, to expire. You could see them by daylight, though no one could rescue them – it was just too dangerous. And at night you couldn't sleep for their screams and moans. The stench was the worst thing of all.

Julius remembered people who'd got out, but who could see their loved ones, now just battered bodies twitching under the chaos of wood; and hear their pitiful, fading cries for help.

Along with most Roman citizens, Julius knew all about Nero's dream of a white stone city, his *Neropolis*, which would replace the labyrinth of dirty wooden shacks and tenements out of which the mighty buildings which already existed, the temples and palaces, rose like ships in a murky sea. The Empire was worthy of a greater heart than the metropolis Nero had inherited.

But for these three days of festival, Nero's main aim was to give the public what it wanted. This was Day Two and all had gone well so far. The combats had been well fought, and there had been no need of the attendants armed with red-hot iron wands, there to *encourage* any gladiator who didn't put his back into the fight. As a result, more white handkerchiefs were waved than thumbs turned down. This pleased Nero, who, like Julius, didn't care for more bloodshed than was necessary, and who preferred the theatre anyway.

This was a big event, and to please the mob the emperor had fielded many of his personal gladiators. Good gladiators weren't cheap and Julius knew Nero wouldn't want to see too many of his own men and women die. A few would have to, sure, but most of the combats were staged to avoid loss. Nero's fighters were usually pitched against clapped-out opponents whenever the organisers thought they could get away with it. Otherwise they fought each other, and when the moment of truth came there were enough 'plants' in the audience to make sure that the defeated gladiator was shown mercy. Business is business, after all. But it didn't always work out that way. Pollux had been worth almost a million sesterces.

The first day had been an appetiser. The usual chariot parade, the march-past, plenty of noise from the war-trumpets. Then, after the warm-up men, the *lusorii*, had farted about with their toy weapons, and because you had to give the public something pretty good on the first day, the *bestiarii* staged a hunt, but only killing the cheaper animals – bulls and bears. People loved the *bestiarii*. They thought more of them than the gladiators.

That was something else he'd never understand about the mob, Julius reflected. But he knew all about death at first hand. His body was hard and scarred, and his face and eyes showed what he'd seen in his career. He had no need to be entertained by slaughter. Death had become his business, but he wasn't interested in killing.

It was now late afternoon on the second day. A reconstructed battle of Troy followed Castor and Pollux, though the deaths were real enough. Julius checked the positions of his men around the ground and stood at ease, by the wall behind the emperor's seat, glad of the shade, but thirsty and bored. The emperor's gilded throne was placed on the imperial podium in the centre of the good side of the arena, protected from the sun. Nero took a slug of Laietanian wine, and watched as the arena was cleared of the last act and prepared for the next – the one he was anticipating with special pleasure, as he'd choreographed it himself.

The arena staff were ready to clear the corpses of the

last bout out of the way, but first the shammers were weeded out. Julius watched the smile broaden on the emperor's face as two burly attendants appeared. He knew that this was a part of the games the emperor enjoyed. The man dressed as Mercury, messenger of the gods and sender of souls to Hades, led the pair. He carried a spear tipped with red-hot iron, and poked each body with it as he passed. If it didn't react, fine – it was a corpse.

But sometimes, as – *now!* – it was a shammer. The man squealed and writhed with the pain of the burn, and the second attendant came up. He was dressed as Charon, ferryman of the dead over the River Styx to Hades. He carried a mallet, and with it he smashed in the skull of any malingerer. It happened that if a really expensive gladiator had gone down, and enough money had changed hands in advance, Mercury would simply touch his spear on the sand close by the shammer, and Charon would pass by. The shammer would be dragged out with the real corpses, then, out of sight, be patched up by the arena *medici*, and sent on his way.

Once the corpses, and the severed hands or limbs, had been cleaned up, and the sand raked over the worst of the bloodstains, the *tubae* sounded for the next act. Today's highlight.

The sun was low enough in the sky by now to cast the shadow of the western side of the spectators' terraces across the arena. The packed house was silent as the gates at the northern end opened to admit a ragged bunch of men aged from sixteen to seventy. There were twenty of them, and they were armed simply, with wooden staves and clubs. They were, Julius thought, a poor-looking lot, and no wonder, for they had spent the last three weeks immured in the Tullianum, a place not noted for its haute cuisine, and, half-naked as they were, you could see bruises and weals on their bodies which were the result of beatings in the prison. None of the men was anxious to advance, but attendants drove them forward with whips into the centre. They settled there in a loose group, their backs to each other, looking out at the tens of thousands of people crammed into the amphitheatre to watch them die.

The men turned to cast frightened glances towards the south gate as it opened. The trouble would be coming from there. One of them buckled at the knees, two companions grabbed and supported him. Another, stronger and taller than most, a man of maybe thirty, raised his voice, then dropped it again after he had spoken no more than three or four words; but he continued to speak, and the others followed suit until all of them spoke in unison.

Like an incantation, but there was no chanting; just the voices, low and steady. Round the necks of several of them strange amulets, a fish, a cross, flashed in the sun. Glazed terracotta. Anything more valuable would be long gone.

'Christians,' Senator Sextus Fabius Barbula stated. He was sitting on the emperor's left. Julius cast him a sharp glance. He didn't like Barbula.

'You know your stuff, Barbula,' said Nero, smiling.

'I've studied them.'

'"Know your enemy" – that's always been my motto. You serve Rome well.'

The emperor's steward stepped forward with the wine jug, but Nero waved him away. He wanted to concentrate. Poppaea, on his right, held her goblet up.

'Not bored, darling?' Nero asked her.

His wife smiled, patted the golden-red hair piled on her head, which had set such a fashion in Rome that more than three-quarters of the women in the stands wore their hair the same colour. 'Just hot.'

'It'll soon be over, my pet, and we can go home. But this is special – this I must see.'

'What have they done?'

'Tigellinus's Praetorians caught them handing out pamphlets. Poor stuff, on wax tablets, but you can't be too careful. And I've never liked Christians.' The emperor, sensing the right moment had come, looked across at the Master of Ceremonies, and gave him a nod.

The south gate opened wide. The crowd held its breath.

There was a rattling of harness, the sound of hooves on the sand, wheels crunching. Into the arena drove six two-horse chariots, *bigas*, the most manoeuvrable. The gilding on the casings of each gleamed in the sunlight, as did the saw-edged, polished steel blades projecting from the wheelhubs. They were light war-chariots adapted from a British design. The applause was deafening.

'Beautiful machines, aren't they?' said Nero, as the chariots paraded slowly, nose-to-tail, around the perimeter.

'One of the few good things to come out of Britain, that's for sure,' said Barbula.

'Well, they nearly threw us out five years ago,' said Nero. 'Good warriors.'

Julius watched the people surrounding Nero on the podium. You could smell their anxiety. Not one of them dared say anything. There was Petronius, Nero's artistic advisor, forced out of his daytime hibernation for once, pale as death, smiling, drunk. And Tigellinus, Co-Prefect of the Praetorian Guard, close-faced, standing as close to the emperor as he could get. A survivor in the choppy waters of court politics, and a man who never let his conscience get in the way of his ambition. Poppaea lounged, languid and bored, and drunk or drugged, but not so very much today. She looked aware of her beauty, but there was a sadness in her, as if she were aware that it was beginning to fade. How long, Julius wondered, would the emperor give her? Nero wasn't noted for long-term fidelity.

'They did! They nearly kicked us out on our arse!' continued the emperor. 'Luckily General Paulinus kept his nerve, and that bitch of a queen of theirs overreached herself. Pity they didn't capture her before she killed herself. They should have brought her back here – I'd've liked to meet her.' But he was watching his charioteers now, and his voice trailed off.

They'd completed a first circuit of the arena. Now they made a second, faster, their long hair flying around their strong faces, for they wore no helmets, just kidskin masks to cover their eyes, hide their identity. Their leather tunics were short and sleeveless. Most of the men and some of the women in the crowd gazed avidly at the bronzed legs and arms, the strong shoulders and slim hips, the hint of firm buttocks where the tunics fell short of covering them.

Julius had seen the girls once before, at a distance, but as they were from Nero's private gladiatorial school and worked with their own exclusive *lanista*, and as they were worth four or five times the value of average gladiators, it was no wonder that the emperor usually reserved them for private performances, only giving them a public outing on rare occasions.

'Designed the tunics myself,' Nero said. 'With a little help from Petronius. Made a couple of modifications to the chariots too.'

'Where are they from, your charioteers?' asked Barbula.

'Dacia. Warlike people. Make good bodyguards.'

'How –?' began Barbula, but the emperor, watching his charioteers with all the attention now of a director watching the stage at curtain-up on a first night, interrupted him with a gesture, stood, and dramatically raised his right arm.

The charioteers, having completed their second circuit,

14

spread out at equal distance from one another, and wheeled their chariots to face the knot of men, who had drawn together in the centre of the ring. They transferred their reins from both hands to one, and drew swords, longer and lighter than the *gladius*.

Nero, his arm still raised, smiled his approval. He glanced over again to the *editor*, who in turn gave a signal, and the *tubae* sounded their strident note.

Nero let his arm fall.

The chariots moved forward.

Nero sat down and turned to Barbula. 'Now watch my little fillies play.'

The Christian victims had fallen silent. A few dropped to their knees. Others tensed, bent their legs, gripped their hopeless weapons with both hands. The majority simply stood there, watching the chariots. Then a man let go of his cudgel and ran, breaking away from the group, making for the high wooden side of the arena, as if he intended to escape that way. Vain hope, and he didn't get far. Julius watched coldly as one of the charioteers, the nearest, spurred her horses and chased him down. As the steel spurs projecting from the hubcaps of her vehicle cut his legs, she leant forward and slashed at his neck with her sword, severing his head before he fell under a fountain of blood. A good clean kill. She wheeled away and raised her sword high, but there was no triumph in her face.

The crowd roared with delight. Nero turned and smiled

at his entourage, who smiled back, clapping their approval. Only Petronius seemed less than interested, and Poppaea was too busy with her drink.

In the arena, the men broke and scattered, except for five who stood fast in a tight knot, their backs to each other, ready to go down fighting.

Five charioteers drove after the Christians, but the sixth was in difficulty. Her horses reared, she was unable to control them. They bucked, came back down heavily, and careered around the arena, only by a miracle failing to collide with one of the other chariots. At last the driver brought them under control, to the shouts of the crowd, who thought this was all part of the act.

Julius watched carefully. He wasn't sure.

The others were working in cold unison. They pursued the running men like cheetahs, their chariots twisting and swerving, sending sprays of sand from their wheels as one by one they caught up with their targets and cut them down. It lasted no more than ten minutes. The crowd screamed with delight, right through.

Nero, whose brow had furrowed at the mistake one of his team had made, now saw that it had increased the excitement, and was appeased. No harm in departing from his direction a little, provided it added to his glory. He decided to forgive the girl, though she was out of the fight now, riding round the edge of the arena, calming her horses.

The floor of the arena was littered with fifteen bodies,

most of them dead, though four still lived, clawing the air and trying to drag themselves out of danger. The emperor focused his attention on the survivors, who held their ground in the centre. The brave ones, thought Julius, there were always a few brave ones.

There was a lull as the five chariots still in the game regrouped. But now came another surprise. One of the five men – the big guy who'd led the prayer earlier – called out – what? – a name? An insult, perhaps, which was followed by a short string of words. Not in any language Nero or the spectators recognised or could understand, but it had an effect on the girls. It made them angry. One more than most. She pulled at her reins viciously, then drove her horses forward, alone, directly towards the small mass of men.

Julius could see the fury on Nero's face. The haze made it hard to make out the faces of the girls.

Now at last the men scattered, or she would have driven her horses over them. But Julius knew from long experience that you should never attack in anger. As they fled, the same man who had uttered the strange words and flung out the challenge, turned and threw his pathetic bit of wood at the passing chariot. It was a chance in a million, but the stick caught in one wheel's spokes, and, instead of snapping, lodged. The chariot kicked into the air, throwing its rider out of her foot-grip, and, crashing onto its side, dragged the horses back and down. The upper wheel spun wildly, and onto its spinning, saw-toothed steel cutter, the rider fell. It cut deeply into her side, and a fresh torrent of blood pumped onto the sand.

The crowd stood in shock, everything fell silent. The other chariots stopped. Apart from the laboured breathing of the horses, it was so still that you could hear distant birdsong. Then a curious thing happened. The men came up to the wounded girl, stood round her, cudgels still in hand. But then they dropped them, stopped the still slowly-turning wheel, lifted her gently off the steel spike, and laid her on their meagre cloaks, spread on the ground.

The silence continued, and Julius watched the shadow of evening continue its slow march across the sand. Somewhere in the middle of the unshaded side of the arena, too far away for anyone on the podium to see who it was, a man rose. He was just some anonymous punter, but, though judgement had not been bidden, he raised his white handkerchief. It worked as a signal. Within seconds the whole side turned white with fluttering bits of cloth, reflecting the last of the sun and dazzling Nero. And it spread, until the whole auditorium was signalling mercy.

Nero, who, Julius could see, was still furious, rose to the occasion. He stood, smiling as if this had been his intention all along, and generously acquiesced. The crowd roared.

The emperor left the podium quickly then. Julius followed him.

Once in his private room behind the royal box, Nero

picked up a small onyx table and hurled it at a slave-boy who was standing nearby. The boy leapt to one side, the table smashed to pieces against the wall. Then Nero, too, roared.

But he recovered fast, and summoned the Master of Ceremonies.

'Those five Christians we've just spared?'

'Yes, Lord?'

'Have their throats cut.'

2

The charioteers wheeled out of the arena to applause and cheering, but it wasn't as enthusiastic as it should have been.

The charioteers did not acknowledge the crowd. Their heads were bent. Their wounded companion had already been carried ahead of them on a stretcher, her body wrapped in a white cloth through which blood was seeping fast. A third of the surface of the cloth was red by the time they'd got her back through the south gate.

Attendants had run in to unshackle the frightened horses from the damaged chariot – a tough business, with the beasts ducking and plunging. Others came in with oxen attached to hurdles, and dragged the corpses onto them, pausing only to kill off the four wounded men, still moaning where they lay.

The show was over, and the crowd made for the *vomitoria*,

packing those exits tightly as they made their way out into the darkening city. Today's highpoint hadn't gone as planned, some of them thought; but it hadn't been bad, and anyway, there was always tomorrow.

Among the first to leave, quitting their seats early to avoid the crush, were two Semites. The first, a big man of maybe sixty, was sunburnt and tough, with a peasant's muscles and gait, white curly hair and a stubble beard. He wore a faded blue tunic like a fisherman's, and he was angry. His companion, about fifteen years his junior, bearded too but balding, had finer features. He might have been a senior house-steward or a librarian. He was trying to placate the fisherman.

'Be patient, Petrus,' he said. 'Our time will come.'

'I wanted to see their faces.'

'Forgive them. They had no choice. If they had not obeyed, they would have been killed.'

'Better to resist and die than commit evil.' Petrus paused. 'One of them tried to show mercy.'

'We must concentrate on building our Belief. We must seek souls to bring into the Brotherhood. Those who died today are now in the arms of the great Nazarene.'

'Paulus, you saw how they died.'

'Some showed mercy, and the emperor spared them.'

The fisherman was still angry. 'Spoken like the Roman that you are.'

'Calm yourself. Build. In numbers is our strength.'

★ ★ ★

Nero's charioteers had their own dressing-room on the cool side of the Taurus Arena. They waited there for news of their sister.

The news was bad. The doctor told them they'd tried to save her, but it was impossible. Too much blood lost, ribs broken into her lungs, smashed legs. He didn't tell them Claudia had died in agony, in too much pain even to scream.

'She would have died there on the wheel if the Christians hadn't moved her,' the doctor said. 'She stood a chance then. But by the time we got to her it was too late.'

Miserably, bearing her body with them, her sisters returned under escort to their quarters on the northern fringes of Rome.

They weren't pampered there, and their *lanista*, a tough thirty-five-year-old veteran of the ring, kept them on a tight rein; but she was fair, and the girls enjoyed better conditions than most fighters. But that didn't make them any less unhappy, less homesick, or compensate for the loss of their freedom. That, they felt most keenly of all.

According to the rites of their country, their sister would be burned on a pyre at sunrise on the day following her death. The School made the necessary arrangements, in the Roman manner, swiftly and efficiently. Claudia would go to join her ancestors at dawn.

That night, they kept watch over her.

They prayed to their own gods that she would revive before the dawn robbed them of all hope.

3

Their vigil was interrupted by a visitor. Shrouded in a black cloak, underneath which a golden tunic glinted, Nero arrived unannounced, and accompanied only by Petronius, Tigellinus, and five of the Praetorian Guard. At first the girls thought their last hour had come. But Nero sensed their fear, and swept it aside.

'Never mind about today's show,' the emperor said benignly. 'I am sorry about your sister.' Privately, his blood boiled at the further money he'd lost by Claudia's death.

'An accident, Lord,' one of them replied.

'Who was the man who brought her down?'

The girls hesitated. The man had been spared, hadn't he? Hadn't he been questioned?

'I was hasty,' Nero continued, guessing what was in their minds. 'I was angry. A foolish thing to be. I could have asked him myself. But now . . .'

'A Dacian, like us,' volunteered the eldest.

'Go on.'

'Our cousin, Lord. He was brought back to Rome with us. He escaped. We hadn't seen him again until today, but we'd had news of him. He'd joined the Christians.'

Nero wandered about the large dormitory which was home to the girls, looking for a drink. A slave hastened to provide something. Some Falernian wine and a small dish of deep-fried dormice with a dash of *garum*. Nero nibbled and sipped. He was very calm.

'Interesting. Continue. This wine is warm. Fetch ice.'

Two slaves scuttled away.

'A Dacian. Like you. Brave souls. I wonder if we'll ever manage completely to liberate your people. Bring them into the family of the empire.'

The girl didn't answer. She didn't know what to say. She thought of the dead man, and her heart grew hard.

'Come on,' Nero said impatiently, as the slaves reappeared with a beaker riding in a basin full of ice. 'What caused Claudia to upset my choreography?'

They'd all been given Roman names. They hated it, but what could they do? The Romans couldn't get their tongues round Dacian.

'He insulted our father. He cried his name aloud and said it was a mystery to him that such a fine dog could have sired such bitches. Claudia was the youngest.'

'I know.'

'Forgive me, Lord. Claudia was our father's pet. She couldn't control herself. We are fighters.'

'Daughters of a chieftain,' simpered Nero. 'And yet — brought to heel by an emperor.'

'Lord,' the girl said submissively, avoiding her sisters' eyes.

Nero sipped and nibbled. The dormice were too rich. What he really needed was some grappa, to settle his stomach, but there was none.

Didn't matter! He'd made his decision; that was why he was here. He'd get it over with. 'It's late, and you must keep vigil for Claudia. So I'll be brief.'

He paused, and gathered his cloak about him theatrically. 'I'm taking you out of the ring for a while. I have a mission for you. It will be dangerous, but the wages of your success will be your freedom.' Nero paused again. 'You will be able to go home.' He raised his hand. 'I know! You are thinking of the personal cost to me. But am I not emperor?'

The girls looked at one another. The eldest sister said, 'Lord, what is your desire?'

'I have a project planned. It involves the Christians, who murdered your sister before your eyes.'

'Lord.'

'The price of your freedom is this: I want you to live in the town. I have apartments prepared for you in my best blocks on the Esquiline and the Caelian. I want you to go among the Christians. I want you to join them. And I want information. You will report to Tigellinus here. When you are settled, his agents will brief you further.'

The girls looked at one another. The eldest spoke again for all of them. 'Lord, will we be separated?'

Nero smiled. 'You wish to discuss terms with me?' His eyes flashed. 'Yes, you will be separated, but don't worry, my little doves. Five of you remain. I am putting two pairs of you in two flats, and the last – you –' he said, pointing at the girl who'd lost control of her horses – 'Alone. You'll be watched, so don't try anything. But,' and here he made a magnanimous gesture, opening the cloak to reveal the gorgeous tunic of cloth of gold beneath it, 'I grant you permission to meet – discreetly. As I said, Tigellinus will keep an eye on you, but at night we'll leave you alone. Who knows? I myself may wish to visit you then.' He beamed. 'My dear children. How muscular you are. How fine. You could almost be boys.'

He popped the last dormouse into his mouth, crushed its little bones in his teeth, swallowed, dribbled, and took another swig of Falernian.

'Got warm again,' he said. 'Disgusting when it's warm.' He looked at them with shrewd eyes. 'Don't let me down, my little butterballs. You'll have to give up your finery, of course, but it's a small price to pay. Remember what you were like when I found you.'

The girls were silent. They remembered well. The battle. The defeat. Their dead companions. Their father, dead.

Nero's tone hardened. 'I want information about the Christians. I want something I can *destroy* them with. I have a project in mind which won't be popular, and I need a scapegoat. It's that simple. Succeed, and you will have your freedom.' He wrapped his cloak around him again, but not before a body-slave of his had slunk up with five fat leather purses on a golden tray. 'These are for you. But take care. Step out of line and you will die a death undreamed of. Christians are the enemy. Of your gods and ours. Never forget that.' He turned. 'Tigellinus, I leave these beauties to your care. And now I must go. Petronius and I have dresses to design for Saturday's pageant.'

Nero swept out.

4

A month later, the world changed. A fire raged in the Imperial City for a week, and by the 24 July, Rome was in ruins.

The wood-built districts, with their twisting alleyways, their shops, bars and brothels, their fishmongers and poulterers, their bakers and tailors, their cake-shops and restaurants, their crumbling tenement blocks, all lay in black wreckage.

Poor, ruined Rome, thought Barbula. It was now autumn, in the tenth year of Nero's reign.

And, to the Christians, the sixty-fourth year since the birth of their Lord.

Sextus Fabius Barbula was true to his claim. He knew a lot about Christians. His career had taught him that any group of subversives, however small, needed watching and understanding. And, by the gods, the time he'd invested had paid off. Here he was, vice-chairman of the committee investigating the causes of the Fire, with a good stipend and four *lictors*, as well as his own private bodyguard, to escort him round town. Now that summer was giving way to autumn, he'd bought a red cashmere *laena* to throw over his tunic, which itself was made of the best Egyptian cotton, cooler and smarter than linen, and far more comfortable than the toga he had to wear in the Senate.

He'd done well. He thought to himself, I might be fifty but I'm still not bad. Not bad at all.

Barbula patted his paunch contentedly. Rome might lie in smoking ruins, but a phoenix would rise from those ashes, and meanwhile only the poorest spirit would fail to mine the opportunities which disaster created. His own transport company was making a fortune carrying rubble from the old city to fill the western marshes; and when they'd been transformed into solid land by the process, land prices would rise. He'd borrowed hard to buy as much acreage as possible before they did. He'd clinched a new deal that very day.

And now, he could afford a little treat. Even if it meant crossing the dangerous city centre. But what of that? Barbula was well protected.

Nevertheless his thoughts turned to reports of killings in the *Daily Acts*. The news was overshadowed by glorification of the building of the New Rome, but any other time, they'd have made the headlines. The gods knew, they were horrible enough, and the victims were prominent citizens.

To think of such people being pulled apart, their limbs torn off, their guts ripped out, was appalling.

He'd left his office on the Esquiline Hill later than intended – always too much paperwork, and especially now – so that by the time he'd set out, the light was fading. He had the curtains of his litter left open so he could see what was happening as he passed. His destination lay on the other side of the city, on the Capitoline, so his path ran between two unravaged points, but to reach his goal he had to cross the centre, where the Fire had done its worst. The middle of the city was gone – the labyrinth of little streets and even the Forum had been reduced to ashes. Total destruction, the Last Days of the Gods, had visited the Imperial City.

The *Daily Acts* said the deaths were owing to attacks by wolves. It was possible. In the days following the Fire, parts of the city had quickly become a jungle ruled by looters and disease. For the first time in years, wolves had appeared on the streets. At first, no one would go into the centre at night. Even now, there was no lighting, no one about.

It had been a terrible fire, thousands had been ruined by it. The litter lurched as his bearers reached a broken part of the road and had to pick their way, but the senator didn't yell at them. Barbula was thinking of nice things to keep his fear at bay, though he was sure that no one would attack such a large number of armed men. He closed the curtains of his litter at last, and turned his mind to the triumphant conversation he'd had with the emperor a few weeks earlier.

He knew Nero saw him as his creature, and he'd played a good hand getting his nominee made Prefect of the police, the *Vigiles,* at the end of June. Talk about perfect timing. The only problem was the emperor's own unpredictability. Anyone else, you'd have their eternal gratitude. But with Nero, the scorpion could turn and sting at any time.

But Barbula knew how badly Nero needed friends in the Senate. More than ever now, with the rumours that Nero had started the Fire himself.

His thoughts returned to the audience the emperor had given a month ago, in August. The date that marked Barbula's ascendancy.

5

Barbula remembered the vast assembly room, draped with pink and yellow silks and satins. Nero perched on a golden throne with scenes from the Rape of the Sabines carved on it, a monument to theatrical bad taste, draped with red and green organdies.

Nero started the meeting on a high note. How the little man loved performing, Barbula had thought.

'The Senate blames me. Bastards! They've started a rumour half the damned aristocrats and politicians in the city are fanning.' The emperor paused, a tear in his eye. 'Only the plebs support me. As if it wasn't them who suffered most.'

Barbula had inclined his head, a nice touch, and it hadn't gone unnoticed. 'Then we must scotch the rumour, Lord. Show it for what it is.'

'I shouldn't have sung that *song*. I know that! But I was moved, damn it all. By the gods, can't an artist be allowed to express himself? I tell you,' Nero went on, addressing the gathering at large, though Barbula principally, who kept as close as possible. 'I tell you, I felt like bloody Priam. I felt it was like Troy, that the king was dying – dying! – with his city!'

'Lord, may *you* never die!'.

'Thank you, Barbula,' said Nero, pressing his arm. Barbula looked down at the spotty young man and held his breath against the body odour.

'No one present and hearing you sing your "Fall of Troy" could have thought you had anything but sympathy for your city,' he said. 'And your performance was masterly. Your lyre-playing alone –'

'As if I hadn't rushed back here to Rome from Antium,' muttered Nero, his eyes black with rage. 'You know that, Barbula! Overnight! Without a thought for my own safety! As if I hadn't set up hospitals and refuges for my poor people, victims of the flames! As if I hadn't saved Rome at the eleventh hour! And now they accuse me of indifference – and worse! They accuse me of starting the Fire myself!' The emperor's voice rose to a shriek. 'Well, I know who my enemies are, and by Jupiter I swear that as Rome burned, so will they!'

Whoever *had* set the fire had done a good job. Two-thirds of the town was rubble, or close to it. Only three districts survived intact. Four had been laid waste so utterly that not a trace of them was left. The other seven were still uninhabitable. A good thousand private mansions were gone, together with maybe thirty thousand apartment blocks.

How could the Senate take it upon themselves to blame Nero? The emperor's own palace had gone up in flames, as well as the Temple of the Vestals and the Temple of Jupiter Stator. Barbula shuddered at the memory. He'd come back from Antium with the emperor and the sight, as they approached, had been frightening. People screaming and running, some abandoning, some helping each other, some rooted to the spot as the flames engulfed them, others trying to protect their children, others still casting their bodies between the flames and their possessions. And the destruction, the confusion! People clogging the roads; carts, screaming animals; lost infants, muddied and bawling by the edge of the road.

After the *Vigiles* had finally started to pull down buildings in the Fire's path, leaving nothing for it to feed on, and it had petered out on the seventh night; after that came the rumours. Everyone knew that Nero had set his heart on a gigantic new palace, and it was the first building work started on after the Fire, right in the centre of town, *and* he'd marked out one hundred acres for it. It was said, too, that he had plans to replace the ruined Forum with a shopping mall. The people loved the idea. Why should senators hog the city centre?

On the other hand, no one could deny that Nero *had* set up first-aid centres and refuges in his own gardens on the Esquiline Hill, and on the Field of Mars, and in the Vatican Gardens near the Circus of Nero and Caligula, all of which by the mercy of the gods were far enough out to have remained unscathed.

'There are people,' Nero was saying, 'who say that men *in my pay* roamed the city, preventing the fire brigades from doing their job, and even *killing* anyone who tried to put out the flames. These people also say that my men not only impeded the *sparteoli* but threw torches into buildings which otherwise might have escaped. I want the people responsible for this sedition found. I'll make torches of *them*! I'll illuminate the entire fucking *Vatican* with them! Barbula!'

What now? Sweating, the Senator cleared his throat. 'Lord?'

'You're our authority on the Christians? What do you think?'

'Lord, I —'

'True, isn't it, that, despite our tolerance of them in our midst, they hate us, they regard us as the New Babylon, that they see this world ending in fire and some kind of dreary moral judgement as soon as possible?'

'Well, Lord, the lunatic fringe, perhaps —' Barbula had to tread carefully. Everyone at court knew that his wretched philosopher brother — though no Christian — was a notorious dissident, though luckily, like most dissidents these days, harmless.

35

'The fanatics!' Nero swept on. 'Yes! But the worst are buried deep within the Christian community. They all look alike – long hair and beards, and the women with their headscarves – how do you suggest we should root out the troublesome minority? Surely Christians are accessories after the fact, even if the moderates didn't want to torch the city which has given them succour and comfort?'

'It isn't against the law to be a Christian.'

'It *is* against the law to be an incendiary!'

Barbula knew this was no time to argue. 'Lord,' he said, submissively.

'Quite right. *Lord*.' Nero paused again, then, affecting modesty, he asked, 'What shall we do?'

'Arrest the leaders?'

'Good idea.'

Barbula recognised irony when he heard it. 'Kill them all!' he said firmly.

'That's more like it! *Kill them all!* Make an example of them!'

Why was it Barbula sensed Nero already had a plan?

6

The litter lurched badly as one of the bearers howled in pain. Barbula, brought back to the present, drew the curtain. The man had fallen and was writhing on a bed of broken stones.

This was a bad place to stop.

Barbula lost his temper. Luckily one of the attendant slaves quickly took the weight of the litter on his shoulder. Barbula looked at the young man's face. He'd remember it with gratitude. But night was falling, that made him nervous.

'Get going!' he snapped at his head slave.

'Sir.'

'Well?'

'What'll we do about –?'

'Leave the useless sack of shit!'

'Sir!'

'Move, fuck you! I'm already late.'

Contented as he felt, pleased as he was at the thought of what awaited him, Barbula didn't like the dark. Especially now. But there was the comforting presence of his guards, his *lictors*, and his slaves.

The battered terrain gave way to proper roadway just as the final glimmer of sunlight in the west gave way to evening. Barbula was glad to see soldiers up ahead putting torches to streetlights, bulky things high up on poles.

The screams that came from those lights were quickly swamped by flame and smoke. Luckily for him, Barbula was windward of them. He knew what they were.

He tucked his chin into his neck as he passed the twisting lamps. He didn't look up. He looked at the shadow cast by his litter on the street. He thought, I'm nearly there. I'll be safe. But he shuddered.

Christians. I'm to blame. But somebody had to carry the can, so why not them?

Barbula put such thoughts behind him. To give himself a boost he rubbed his hands. What a coup! He was in the inner circle of the emperor, his profits were up, and he was about to enjoy the most delicious courtesans money could buy. Twice divorced, now alone, rich – he could take his pick, and he was he glad of it.

His performance was a worry. He drank too much, which diminished his prowess. He'd taken Spanish Fly to help; bought it directly from Locusta, who, the world knew, was

Nero's poison-maker, though that was only one of the branches of her pharmacy. Please Priapus he hadn't taken too much.

He shook himself. He felt fine. He felt ready for action. So why this sense of foreboding?

The litter-bearers set him down. Was it just the motion over the rough ground that made him feel queasy?

He clambered out into the street, breathed in and out, slowly, to settle himself. Down the broad avenue behind him the torches had all, long since, ceased to cry out, and the dead bodies, fuelled by their own fat, burned steadily. With their pitch-daubed shirts, they would last till dawn. The wind bore the smell away.

Up on the Capitoline the air was fresh. Barbula filled his lungs. He looked down on the wreckage of the town, but knew that the New Rome would rise from the rubble before he had turned sixty. Well before then, if he played his cards right, he'd be – what? – Consul?

Better late than never. Some bastards made Consul at thirty.

He put the thought away. Pleasure now. He looked at the portico. It was his first time at this brothel. It had been highly recommended. Discreet too. No wonder the prices were high. He looked forward to shagging a couple of teenagers! Girls, he thought. He'd never been much of a one for boys, and, as far as *he* was concerned, let fashion go hang.

But he was glad of the bright lights in the portico. He told his bearers, his *lictors* and his private and official bodyguards to stay close, but to stay outside. The house would be safe, he was sure, and he entered it alone.

Inside, the lights were lower. Dark curtains shielded details of the interior from view, but Barbula noticed with approval several tasteful statues in Carrara marble; men and women, despite their poses, too cold for anyone to want to fuck them. The lighting was theatrical; the statues a tease.

How generous of Nero to have suggested this house to him!

And now for the girls.

7

The plump redhead with curly hair and green eyes who led Barbula to his couch had already aroused his interest; but when she drew back the emerald plush screen to reveal her wares, he was riveted. The only problem was which and how many to choose. Six of them, and they all looked delightful.

He couldn't see any other clients. Was he the only one? He drank a glass of wine.

'I suggest,' cooed the redhead, 'Number Six. She's new. A little vixen.'

The girl was maybe 18 years old. Athletic-looking, strong thighs rising to tight buttocks under the short *chiton* she wore. Tanned too. Hard to say where she might be from. Not Roman, unless from the north the country, the mountains. Too blonde and bronzed to be a local. And extraordinary eyes, pale blue, the colour of duck eggs.

Barbula's throat was dry. He glanced along the line of other girls again, to be sure; but he felt inclined to go along with the Madame's choice. The Nordic girl was quite something, and he liked her shy but knowing smile. He had an erection already, may Apollo calm him, and he was sure she'd noticed it. For a moment he wondered if she didn't find him ridiculous, but he put the thought out of his head. This brothel was top class, but the girl was still a whore, doing her job, and what did her opinion matter?

He followed her down a long corridor. A young male slave stood near a torch in a sconce every ten paces. They obviously matched discretion with high security in this place. Wall-hangings from the distant east completed the sense of luxury.

And yet a thin voice of caution continued to sound at the back of Barbula's mind.

He'd wait until daylight to return home.

The girl paused at a curtained door and smiled again. She hadn't yet spoken, but as the attendant standing nearby came forward and pushed the door open, she leaned in to Barbula and took his arm, inclining her head so that he could see the long brown curve of her neck with its heavy crown of golden hair, and smell a scent of honey and roses.

Inside, the large bed stood against the middle of one wall. It was scattered with rugs and cushions, and there was an oil-lamp on a low marble side-table either side of it.

There was another table against the opposite wall, on which

stood two silver basins decorated with erotic scenes which challenged even Barbula's imagination, flanked by elaborate ewers. Large towels hung nearby, with silk gowns in the same pale shade as the bed-linen. A large, mullioned window, almost completely obscured by crimson and dark-green curtains, gave onto a velvet night pierced only by distant torches, and silent as the grave. Under it, two gilded chairs and a long, low couch were arranged.

She still hadn't spoken, but the smile was inviting. She gestured first to two golden carafes on a tray with goblets. Barbula wondered if another drink wouldn't hurt to begin with. He walked over and sniffed the contents. One carafe contained *mulsum*, the other a good Falernian. He chose the latter, unadulterated wine, and poured them both a drink.

He sat in one of the chairs, and she came to him, the *chiton* riding high up her thighs as she straddled his lap and took his goblet, taking a little wine into her mouth and then pressing her lips onto his so that with the soft kiss and the embracing tongue the warm wine invaded his throat.

Barbula was excited, but he was taken aback as well. He hadn't encountered this kind of enthusiasm in a prostitute, even a good one, before – the best offered an imaginative range of skills, but they applied them with such professional efficiency as to rob them of their edge.

And the other thing was, this girl was strong! She had

muscles – and she was using a variety of them now – like an athlete. Barbula had a strong desire to get out of the chair. He felt trapped.

At last she allowed him to. He wanted to ask her name at least, but her deft hands pulled away his clothes and now they were delicately caressing his prick and his balls. Before he knew it he was sprawling on the bed, in a kind of ecstasy only tempered by his resentment that all this was going too fast, and he couldn't control it. The girl was naked now, teasing him with her lips and tongue, now advancing, now retreating – playing with him, running the show.

His anxiety returned; he wanted to stop, drink a little wine. He thought he might lose his erection and cursed himself. As if she had read his mind, the girl's right hand snaked down and massaged his manhood back – her hands felt as if she had oiled them – but when would she have had the time? Her body, too, slithered over his as if it had been oiled like an athlete's. He wished he had retained the flat stomach and firm muscles of twenty years earlier. He needed to master the situation but when he started to get up, he found he could not.

Instead he heard her voice for the first time in his ear, a clear, strong, whispered couple of words in an accent he couldn't place but whose tone was unmistakably that of command:

'Lie still!'

'I want –'

'Let me give you what you deserve.' Now the voice was cajoling, the tongue worming in his ear. Had he misheard her? Hadn't she meant 'desire'? But she wasn't a Roman. Foreigners sometimes confused words.

Now, with a fluid movement, she mounted him, gripping him with the muscles of her vagina. He caught his breath with pleasure and wanted to respond until he realised she was holding him fast. He saw her smile flash close to his eyes and caught the odour of honey and roses, as she let him move again.

'Don't want to frighten you,' she said, almost to herself.

He smiled to himself and put his arms round her, trying at the same time to roll her over onto her back. He didn't mind her being on top – some women preferred it that way – but as this was his party, she should dance to his tune.

But he couldn't move. He was held fast.

'I've had enough of this,' he told her hoarsely. 'I want to get up. I want some wine.'

'Don't be frightened,' came the voice in his ear again. Why did the tongue which grazed it feel firmer and rougher? Imagination, surely. But Barbula was beginning to panic.

Suddenly he knew he was very frightened indeed.

He ran his hands over her back. Somewhere he would find a place to get hold of her and fling her from him.

His hands reached down her body as far as he could. Was it his imagination or was it more slippery? His hands

45

slithered over the surface, and then he knew that what he was touching was not skin, but scales.

Other things had changed. Not only was he pinned down by a body which was becoming both heavier and more sinuous, but he could scarcely move at all. His arms had been thrust away, and he could feel ragged nails – no, *talons* – digging into his back and into his thighs, holding him firm.

He thought of the slaves outside. Whatever this was, they could kill it. He opened his mouth to yell.

And immediately her mouth was on his. Her mouth had become bigger, and felt rough, and covered his own completely – he could scarcely breathe as its muscular wet lips obscured his nostrils. This must be like drowning, he thought, though he could scarcely think any more, and his mind began to scream silently as he felt the tongue, like a living being which had invaded his mouth, thrust his own aside. It was no human tongue – it was thin and narrow, and ended in a sharp point.

Then he knew.

It was a tube.

He felt it glide down his gullet towards his stomach.

The smell of honey and roses was overpowering, sickly, like something rotten, like a loud noise. It was the only thing, apart from the pain yelling in his head, that filled the last moments of his world.

8

Julius looked down at the body – if you could call it a body. His assistant, Mercurius, had left the room, his face the colour of moonstone, the same colour as the face of the local Cohort centurion who'd waited for him to take over, and whom Julius, after questioning, had dismissed, swearing him to secrecy.

Julius had handled some tough cases in the five years since his promotion, but none before at the direct instigation of the emperor, and none like this. His job was specialised, like all the members of VIII Cohort, and he was the senior legate, but now he was being asked to investigate a murder calling for more expertise than the other seven conventional police cohorts put together could muster.

But he was relieved. This was like a vote of confidence from the highest level. Maybe Nero didn't know much about his dismal recent track-record. He'd have to make the most of his luck. He was tough. He knew how to roll with the punches.

VIII Cohort was a special branch, smaller than the others, and separate from the Praetorian Guard, controlled by Tigellinus, and the Secret Police, who dealt with spies, and whom *no one* was supposed to know about.

Few knew about VIII Cohort, so Julius was in elite company. A good family and a good military and political background had got him where he was, but to be ushered into the direct presence of Nero just as dawn was lifting her skirts in the east was something he hadn't been prepared for. Nero had been nervous and angry. News had reached him – all this in great confidence – of the murder of a favourite senator, in unpleasant circumstances, in one of the most exclusive brothels in town. Julius was aware of the weight of responsibility on his shoulders as he looked down at the shining floor of the room on the Capitoline, and the mess that spewed onto it from the bed. The Senate knew about it already, in that way it had, and as the emperor was still under suspicion for starting the Fire, he'd had to react quickly. Not that anyone would ever *openly* blame Nero, but he had established a reputation for removing people who stood in his way, and he was eager to deflect this from himself.

But it was more complicated than that. This senator had been one of the few close to the emperor.

Julius would have to tread carefully.

He went over what he'd already established. Whatever had happened must have occurred towards midnight. There'd been a girl in the room, Justina. Nice girl, new to the job, working there part-time. Never any complaints. Best possible references too – though now no one seemed able to trace their source. But that wasn't unusual for a woman in her profession, even at the top of the range.

Julius made himself look at the mess again, running his eyes over what remained of the man – he didn't feel up to getting too close yet, still less to touching any of it – to see if any clue presented itself. It didn't. Julius had seen some things on the battlefield; but never anything like this.

Mercurius returned, still pale, but his composure restored. He'd been sick. Julius guessed he'd cleaned his mouth with water and a beaker of *mulsum*. Just as well. Julius would need him. Five years his junior, Mercurius, at 25, had been with him for the last eighteen months, appointed from VII Cohort, which managed the Ninth and Fourteenth Districts.

Julius decided to send him away from the crime scene but at the same time make him feel useful. He could see his Number 2 was turning pale again. Some tough guy Mercurius was turning out to be. But he'd never been to war, he'd never seen anything.

Julius walked over to the window and looked out. The house was built on a slope and the window overlooked

49

gardens falling steeply away and densely planted with cypress. He breathed in the remains of the night air.

'Go over to Number VII's headquarters,' he said, turning back. 'You still got contacts there?'

Relief showed itself immediately on Mercurius' face, but he was guarded when he said: 'Wouldn't I be more useful here?' Mercurius was an ambitious man, didn't want anyone to think he wasn't up to the job, but Julius knew all about the three unpleasant killings – violent even by the standards of this city – which had taken place recently. Two of them had happened in districts covered by Number VII.

'I'll deal with the people here. Where have you put them?'

'In the atrium, with your duty scribe. He's doing the preliminaries now.'

'Everyone from last night?'

'All there – except the girl who was with Fabius Barbula.'

No one knew what had happened to her. She'd disappeared.

'Some of the clients are kicking up,' Mercurius added.

Naturally. A brothel like this would have clients who'd hate publicity, wouldn't want to be missed either, from home or work. 'Get onto your friends at VII. See what you can find.'

Julius didn't hold out much hope that there'd be a link between this and the other killings, but if there were, it'd be a start.

After Mercurius left, he took a breath and turned back to the body. He didn't think he'd ever forget a single detail.

The first problem was how the thing had been done. The man was naked, his legs spread-eagled on the bed. What was left of his torso hung down over its edge, arms flung back in an attitude that reminded Julius of crucifixion. There were deep gouges in the man's thighs and, when Julius could bring himself, eyes averted from the face, to lift the body, he also found further gashes in the shoulders, where something like knives had dug in so deeply as to rip chunks out of the flesh when they were withdrawn.

But it was the body itself which caused him to breathe hard and deep. It was almond-white like a lot of corpses with the blood drained out, sure, but there was something else – *there was nothing of it.* The rib-cage stuck through the skin and there was no bulk in the abdomen at all. The skin hung like a cape, draped on the bed around the cadaver.

He had been emptied.

Julius noticed something in the dead man's mouth which looked like fat worms. He looked more closely. When he recognised it, nausea overcame him once more.

The remains of the dead man's entrails.

He got to a basin in time to vomit, pulled himself together, washed, cleaned his mouth, and made his way to the atrium where the brothel staff and clients were gathered. One look told him he'd never be able to interview them all, here and now, in any depth, but he installed himself at a desk with his duty scribe in a room just off the atrium.

'How many of them?'

The scribe consulted his notes, reeled off the list. 'Eleven girls – not including the one who –'

'Get on with it!'

The duty scribe cringed. 'Half a dozen clients – it was still early, and business hasn't been so good. People don't go out at night much any more. The Madame – Dorcas – and Fabius Barbula's official guard. His private bodyguards ran off after they found out what'd happened.' He gave Julius a look. 'Hard to get re-employed if it gets about that the man you've been guarding's been done in.' Julius glared at him and he hurried to the end of his notes: 'House slaves, about twenty of them, but the only one who's got anything to say is the head steward, Drogo, who discovered the body.'

'Let's deal with the clients first.'

'What about the body?'

'I've seen all I need to. Get it cleaned up and tell someone to notify his family.'

'Don't think he had one.'

Julius looked at him angrily.

'I'll get them to contact his household.'

Julius spent the next half-hour ticking names off the scribe's list, and beginning to wonder if he'd done the right thing in sending Mercurius away. Two heads are better than one when an investigation starts so badly, and Mercurius wasn't a fool.

But Julius wasn't keen to let Mercurius too close to the core of the inquiry. Mercurius was an ambitious bastard.

★   ★   ★

None of the other clients knew anything – they'd been busy with their own sex games in other parts of the house when Barbula had met his end, and hadn't learnt about it until afterwards. The brothel was spacious – that was why it was so expensive. Privacy and silence were guaranteed.

He knew one or two of the men by sight, others by reputation. There was the obese owner of a quarry, and the confident director of a large concrete factory, both of whom were good-natured and sympathetic, and could afford to be, since Nero's immense building programme was making them richer than ever; but both were concerned with keeping themselves out of the pages of the *Daily Acts*. Neither was any help, nor were a blustering and florid vintner from Pompeii or the pompous and spindly son of a minor senator – the first anxious that his wife shouldn't find out where he'd been, the second worried about his father discovering how he'd been spending his allowance.

Last of all were the two Julius knew from Nero's own entourage. Vatinius, the cobbler and *scurra*, with his hideously deformed nose, would have to be handled with kid gloves for the simple reason that, as everyone knew and no one would admit, he'd gained his present position by acting as the emperor's personal informer. But even Vatinius, who would, Julius knew, soon root out as much as he could about what was going on here on his own account, seemed eager to get away now.

The other man was Petronius, charming and pale, who had

turned indolence into a fine art and who boasted that he hadn't voluntarily seen daylight since his adolescence. He, too, was close to the emperor, and trusted by Nero on all matters of taste. Julius would have to tread carefully there, too.

Not that any of them, Julius felt sure, had had anything to do with the sucked-dry corpse currently being packed into a box by slaves with pegs on their noses and gloves on their hands.

Their partners of the previous night were equally unhelpful. The girl who'd been picked by Petronius was drunk or drugged or both, and she was still out of it. The slim little thing of maybe fourteen who'd been with Vatinius had an unpleasant bruise on her neck, and another on her thigh; but the injuries were slight, and when Julius questioned her about the injuries she shrugged them off as something that went with the job.

Barbula's own people, the *lictors* and the official bodyguard, had remained outside by the front portico, had been given bread and beer, but had seen and heard nothing.

No one wanted Julius to interview the slaves, but he insisted. None of them had seen or heard anything either.

The fat redhead who ran the place, Dorcas, had missed her vocation. She should have been on the stage. With a full accompaniment of hand gestures and eyelid-fluttering, she said: 'Look, sir, captain, whatever, the slaves posted along the corridors have orders *only* to disturb the clients if they hear sounds of *real distress*. And they know how to tell the difference between that and what the girls put on.' Dorcas looked like she was in real distress herself. 'I run a good business,' she told Julius fretfully. 'A clean house, with a regular clientele.' She looked at him. 'How much of this needs to come out?' Julius guessed she'd send a runner to Nero as soon as he'd left, and wondered how much attention the emperor would pay her. Shit, what a mess.

'What about Justina?'

Dorcas' eyes filled with tears. 'We've no idea. We've looked everywhere. There's no trace of her. Whoever killed Senator Barbula must have taken her with them. By Venus, what can have happened to her?'

The chief slave, Drogo, had discovered the body. Plump, genial, bald, what hair was left shaved close. Late fifties by the look of him. Good opinion of himself.

'When was that?' Julius asked him.

'About three hours after Justina and the senator went in.'

'Why then?'

'He'd given orders. Seemed nervous.'

'Why do you think that?'

'No idea. Just a feeling. You get it sometimes in the job.'

'Nervous because he mightn't have been able to get it up?'

'Maybe.'

'So why did you go in then?'

'He'd given orders. Not to check up on him, just to keep the food and wine coming. And he said he might have had enough of Justina by then, might feel ready for some group action.'

'Where are you from, Drogo?'

'Athens.'

'Really?'

'What's it to you?'

'Not a very Athenian name. You don't look much like a Greek to me.'

Drogo shifted his feet. 'It's been a long night. Mind if I sit down?'

'Yes.'

Drogo remained standing.

'What did you do after you found it? Were you sick too?'

'I closed the door and posted two men outside it with orders not enter on any account. I told the Mistress. Quietly. The Mistress sent two others to the *Vigiles*. She knows the local centurion. No one else was disturbed at first, and then very discreetly. Nothing like this has ever happened here before.'

'What did the centurion do?'

The man spread his hands. 'Sir, he decided to refer the matter . . .' he hesitated. 'Elsewhere. He posted guards, and then you came with your own men.'

'And no one saw the girl?'

Drogo looked grim. 'Poor kid,' he said.

Julius' duty scribe returned. 'Seal the place,' Julius told him. 'Search the gardens as soon as it's light.'

'It *is* light.'

Julius hadn't noticed that the sun had risen. His mind had stayed in that accursed room. 'Then do it now,' he snapped.

9

VIII Cohort's HQ had by the grace of some god – Nero himself perhaps – escaped the Fire. It stood at the southern end of the Via Piscinae Publicae in one of the less seedy quarters of the Aventine district, a dirty-looking stone building with a dingy hall. Beyond the hall, however, the offices were white-painted, clean, had modern furniture and a big staff of scribes and clerks. Behind its high walls, the courtyard contained stabling for thirty fast horses and a dozen light, two-wheeled *cisia*. VIII Cohort was well bankrolled.

Julius sat in his room with his back to the window, feeling the sun warm him. His desk was littered with papers and scrolls, and his personal scribe sat nearby, taking notes. Thank Minerva that here was someone he could rely on.

Nothing, not a trace, not a footprint, had been found in

the garden. Julius listened as Mercurius, seated across the desk from him, made his report. He prayed there might be a few scraps in it for him to throw to his own chief when the time came. His chief, a Barbula appointee, was not easy-going.

'The legate of my old Cohort let me go through the case-notes on their two murders. He's having copies made,' Mercurius was saying.

'Any results?'

Mercurius shook his head. 'He's not keen on the idea of us taking over the investigation, either.'

That didn't surprise Julius. Communication between the different police districts stank. 'What've we got?'

'Two businessmen, one in grain import from Egypt, the other a contractor on the aqueducts; wealthy, quite a lot of leverage. Both cremated now, but from the descriptions I got it seems they were ripped apart, arms and legs torn off, and . . .' Mercurius hesitated.

'Yes?'

'Had the blood sucked out of them.'

Julius breathed deeply. The palms of his hands were sweating. 'Same kind of perpetrator, then?'

'Not exactly the same kind of death.'

Julius thought fast. 'There was a third body. Anything on that?'

'Yes. It was found in the Third District – near the Esquiline. My people got some notes from II Cohort, in case there was a connection. But the third body had been in the sun for days before it was discovered, so it was hard to tell. And it was so badly mutilated they couldn't tell what sex it was. They found out *who* it was from the rings on its fingers.'

'And?'

'Bloke called Curtius Verus.'

Julius raised an eyebrow: '*The* Curtius Verus?'

'Yes.'

'Hell. Someone must have reported *him* missing.'

Mercurius shrugged. 'Didn't have any family. Split up with his boyfriend a few months ago. Lost his house in the Fire. Started to drink. Couldn't find work any more. You know what that's like for an actor.'

Julius didn't, but he did remember seeing Curtius in some old comedy or other by Plautus. The actor had been furious when someone had run into the auditorium and shouted that the Games had been announced. That would mean poor houses in the theatre while the Games were on. Well, you couldn't blame the citizens. The Games were free.

Sometimes Julius wondered about his countrymen, his fellow citizens. Practical, civilised, effective soldiers, yet they'd flock to see other people hack each other to death, or get torn apart by animals. But of course he didn't appreciate the finer points.

'So, apart from Curtius, we've got three leading citizens –'

'I wouldn't say *leading*,' Mercurius said. 'And the grain-importer was Greek, started life as a slave.'

No one liked the Greeks. They were always busy worming their way into key positions in society, they were too clever by half, and they were favoured by Nero.

Julius raised a hand. 'Prominent anyway.'

'No connection between any of them that we've come up with.'

'Give it time.'

'I don't see that there need be one. Rome's like a barrelful of snakes. Would *you* go down the far end of the Circus after dark alone?'

'What are you saying?' growled Julius.

'I think it's obvious. These might have been pretty vicious murders, but it's not as if they're uncommon.'

'Uncommon? You were throwing your guts up over Barbula a few hours ago. And now you're such a tough guy?'

'You know what I mean,' said Mercurius, but he was backing down, looked apologetic.

'You think Barbula's death *wasn't* out of the ordinary?' Julius shouted.

'I didn't say that.'

Julius leant back. The sun on his back had become unpleasant. He stood up, turned to the window, drew a blind across it.

In the gloom, both of them were silent. They saw

themselves as rational men, by nature and by training, but there was never any knowing what the gods might cook up. What if the gods were angry? They'd sent famine and disease before. What if this was the start of some fresh plague, which neither the VIII Cohort, the Praetorian Guard, nor even the emperor himself, could control?

Neither spoke of this shared fear, but it was there in the room. They knew there was a menace walking the town which it might be beyond them to combat.

'There's more,' Mercurius muttered.

'Yes?'

'Probably nothing to it.'

'Go on.'

'After I left this morning, I remembered having dinner with a friend who owns a couple of farms on the outskirts, a little way out into the Campania. He got them from his father, managed by a handful of good freedmen – reliable people, I mean, not superstitious peasants – and slave labour, of course.'

'Yes?' Julius was getting impatient.

'I tell you this because the sources are dependable.' Mercurius paused briefly. 'Thing is, a few of the other guests had farms too. One or two of them happened to mention that they'd lost more livestock than usual over the last few weeks. More than feral dogs or the occasional wolf would account for.' Mercurius paused. 'They'd all had the same experience.'

His tone was serious. Julius sat again, elbows on the desk. The scribe bowed over his paper.

'This might not be worth setting down yet,' Mercurius told him, but Julius motioned the man to continue.

'What sort of animals?'

'Pigs, goats.'

'And?'

'Something had sucked up their guts and blood from the inside, through their mouths, and there were gashes on the bodies.' Mercurius shrugged. 'They all had the same story. One of them even lost one of his guard dogs, and you know what they're like. I've known gladiators avoid them. I sent a runner over to my friend's house with a message while I was at VII's HQ and he sent word back to say it'd died down. He said he'd ask the other farmers.'

Julius was silent for a moment. 'Wolves?'

'Have you ever known wolves kill like that?'

'No.'

'Might have been people,' said Mercurius. 'Lot of people homeless, on the loose.'

Julius made a dismissive gesture. 'No! Nero reduced the price of grain to a fraction of its value after the Fire, gave vast amounts away, organised temporary housing – you know that. And people don't turn into beasts after a disaster, not unless there's no succour at all. If anything, they're cowed.'

'Some aren't.'

'Who do you mean?'

'The pagans.'

'Oh, I think they are cowed now.' Julius knew what Mercurius was talking about.

He glared at his assistant. Tall, bronzed, dark curly hair, muscular. Intelligent eyes set a tad too close together above the aristocratic nose for him to be absolutely handsome, but a powerful face, strong chin. Thick iron citizen's ring on his finger. In his dazzling white tunic and soft brown sandals, matching the soft brown leather of his arm-purse, he already looked as if he were dressing for the job he hoped to inherit.

Well, to hell with him. Men like Mercurius, who preferred the company of other men to the company of women, always took better care of themselves than ordinary blokes anyway.

Julius himself was without company. He'd drifted through a handful of affairs since his marriage, but no one had struck sparks from him, and he had struck none either. He had his career to think about; he was fine on his own.

He concentrated on the investigation. What about the pagans? Most people couldn't tell them apart as far as their appearance and rituals were concerned. The Jews, who enjoyed the favour of Poppaea, kept to themselves; but the Christians, a new religion, were active in pushing their beliefs.

He knew one or two Christians, decent people. Their

prophet, sent here to be one of them for a while, took a more forgiving line than his heavenly Father, the same one the Jews worshipped, though *they* didn't buy the Christian prophet as their god's son. It was complicated. The Son, a guy called Jesus of Nazareth, died on a cross in Judaea about three decades earlier, by order of the provincial governor, who'd had complaints about his revolutionary talk.

Maybe in time the Christians would end up having as many gods as us, thought Julius. If they last long enough. Or none at all. Who took the gods seriously these days?

'. . . need to stamp out extremism,' Mercurius was saying. Julius hadn't been listening.

'Well, we're certainly doing that,' he agreed.

'Do you think there's a group out there that's taking revenge for what we've done to them? It'd only need a handful of people to terrorise even a town this size.'

'You're barking up the wrong tree,' said Julius. 'Look, the emperor has made it clear that he thinks the Christians are to blame for the Fire. We all know that. Maybe they asked for it. They're a secretive sect, they have weird rites, and for all I know some of them thought this Fire was the one they see as the Great Purge. *I* think the Fire started by accident. But I also know the *sparteoli* were called out late, and I know all about the rumours of gangs of firesetters going about.'

'The Christians are suspicious, they're secretive,' said Mercurius.

'Yes, and not many people like them. Who would? As for their leaders, Paulus has only been here for a couple of years, and, sure, he's more aggressive than Petrus; but he's a writer, not an incendiary. As for Petrus, he's been here twenty years, and in all that time he's caused his followers to do nothing more than affirm their faith and try to spread it – but not by terror.'

'Paulus is a political agitator. We should have locked him up instead of keeping him under a loose guard – it's so lenient it hardly counts,' said Mercurius, angrily.

'Get real. This kind of killing – the kind we saw last night – that isn't like the work of *any* . . .' Julius stopped.

They both let the silence hang in the air. Humans were capable of greater cruelty than any animal, and Julius had, Mars knew, seen enough of it in his career; but the method . . . to suck a person dry? To pull the entire guts out through the mouth?

In his mind's eye Julius saw Barbula's spread-eagled corpse again. He knew what was coming next, though he tried to turn his focus away from it: the sight of those worm-like objects drooling from the senator's gaping mouth.

The animals had been sucked dry through their mouths.

The animals had had gashes on their bodies.

But that spate of killings was over. Or so it seemed.

Had that been some kind of *learning process*?

And there was the question of the deaths of the grain

importer and the contractor. Torn apart rather than eviscerated.

Rehearsal again?

A pity, he thought, that they hadn't been able to see the bodies, but the weather was still hot, and last month the heat had been tremendous. Julius toyed with the idea of the impossible luxury of having enough ice available to keep a corpse fresh long enough to examine it. But that'd be too expensive. Hadn't Nero – or possibly Petronius – invented a non-alcoholic cocktail which had become hugely fashionable among the mega-rich, since its basic ingredient was snow? If he was approached in the right way, might Nero organise ice for him?

Unlikely.

He turned back to his problem. How he was going to solve it he didn't know, but he and Mercurius were going to have to interview those farmers, and everyone who'd known the four dead men. Fast. Well, he didn't feel much like sleep anyway.

He was too afraid of his dreams.

He'd started to parcel out the work ahead with Mercurius when they were interrupted by the arrival of a police runner. The scribe met him at the door and there was a whispered conversation. The scribe turned to them.

'They've found the girl.'

10

They'd covered the corpse with sacking, and, by the grace of Pluto, she was lying in the shade, on a large oblong block of trimmed marble waiting to be put to use by the workers who were rebuilding the temple of Jupiter Stator, reduced to ruin by the Fire. All around them, men were lashing wooden scaffolding poles together and pushing up fragile towers to encase the salvageable parts of the building. A handful of them watched the small knot of policemen out of the corners of their eyes, but turned away quickly if any of the cops looked up at them. Julius was well aware of what the average Roman thought of the *Vigiles*. The cops still carried the nickname *sparteoli* – little bucket carriers – from their older function, doubling as firemen.

But something – or someone – was working in their favour. It happened that the building contractor for the restoration work was visiting the site that morning. He was a client of Dorcas' House, and when the body was discovered, he'd been called over. Thinking the girl's face was familiar, he'd sent one of his men to Dorcas, who'd sent him back with Drogo. Drogo had identified Justina, and alerted the local Legate of *Vigiles*, who'd uncharacteristically contacted VIII Cohort. So much for secrecy – but in this case the lack of it had worked to their advantage. In this case, the police had to hang together – everyone else hated them even more than they hated each other.

'I'll do it,' Julius said, and twisted the sacking away.

Justina lay on her back, arms at her sides, her left leg bent at the knee. She was naked, and evidently had not been dead long. Her eyes were closed, and she looked as if she were asleep. The sunlight caught and glinted off the fine golden hairs that grew on her forearms and the great mane of dark golden hair, which cradled her head. Her eyes and lips were closed, and her face had an expression of deep peace. Of course they'd been told what to expect, but Julius was still unable to stifle a gasp of astonishment.

Her body was without a blemish.

What in Hades' name was going on?

'Take her to Opimius Decula's hospital. Have him look at her,' said Julius, and gave the necessary orders.

He looked at Mercurius; Mercurius was still looking at the corpse.

★   ★   ★

The doctor thought she'd died of shock, enough of a shock to stop her heart; but, as Julius could see, Opimius really didn't know. Who had placed her there, and when, and why, they had no idea, though her discovery had tied up one loose end, and very quickly. Very quickly indeed, thought Julius.

The sun was past its zenith. No one knew what to do with the corpse. They sent another messenger to Dorcas. Drogo arrived soon afterwards.

'My mistress makes no claim to the body,' he said tonelessly. 'The girl had only worked for us for a few weeks, part-time. Therefore, the expense . . .'

'So you'll do nothing for her?'

'She was just an employee. We have no responsibility.'

Julius thought, I might have known. No funeral pyre, or even a slot in a columbarium for poor Justina. He turned to Opimius. 'Can one of your people make the arrangements?'

'Yes,' said the doctor, then hesitated. 'Where shall I send the bill?'

Julius looked at him. 'Public Treasury, idiot.'

The doctor sniffed. 'Very well. So the body – we send that to one of the *puticuli*, I suppose?'

'Nothing else to be done.' Julius, thinking of the public burial pits reserved for the destitute with no one to care for their remains, reached into his arm-purse and drew out three coins. 'For her eyes and her tongue.' He wished he could afford to give her even a halfway decent funeral, but he couldn't. And what was it to do with him, anyway? What had it to do with anybody?

'I'll attend to it.'

Julius was fairly sure the coins would never accompany Justina into the grave, but he felt sorry for her. The thought of that lovely body being thrown into a public burial pit and covered with quicklime . . . But she had been spared Barbula's fate. For some reason.

What in Hades was he up against? What creature would kill so barbarously and then abduct a girl, to leave her as if she had not died at all?

He took a last glance at the body. It was hard to believe that it wasn't still alive.

11

Justina had gone to the grave taking her secrets with her. Julius got nowhere with the farmers, who added little to what Mercurius had already learned. Julius had been hoping for reports of tracks perhaps, churned earth, anything that might have left a trace of the killers. But there was nothing.

'What next?' Mercurius asked.

'I'll start talking to the friends and relatives.'

'Big job.'

'Yes.' Julius knew what Mercurius wanted, and knew he'd have to give it to him. But he didn't like it.

'Want me to take some of it on? Or don't you think I'm up to it?'

Julius had Nero breathing down his neck already. He had to make the most of time, even if that meant risking

Mercurius' snatching any glory a chance advance would bring them. 'Good idea,' he said. He selected the interviewees least likely to give any joy and gave the list to his assistant.

It soon became clear that few friends or relatives were willing to acknowledge the fact that they had been connected to the dead men, and those who had no choice, because connections could be proven, had nothing to say, and seemed to be hiding nothing.

The dead men had all been powerful in life, and powerful people have enemies. But the worst enemy a man could have, Julius reasoned, would scarcely be able to inflict an end so horrible as that visited on these people.

He felt terror enter his heart as he imagined again what Nero would do to him if he failed. He hoped he'd get enough warning to leave Rome fast before Tigellinus' guards came to tell him to top himself. He'd better get a break soon or he could at best look forward to spending the rest of his life in the remote provinces, some shithole like Londinium, and that didn't appeal.

Three days passed. Then death raised its head again.

News travels fast in the Campania, though that is where country news usually stays. Not this time. The animal deaths had broken out again, though few, and all at farms not far from Rome. Sheep. Pigs. Goats. And whatever beast had killed the first animals had also killed these, by the same method.

But it was the new *human* victims who robbed Julius of what little sleep he got.

12

There had been three new killings, all within one of the three districts unaffected by the Fire. After a lull of three days.

All influential people.

And all three – one on the Caelian Hill, one on the Capitoline, and one to the north on the Quirinal – took place at the same time. So there wasn't one killer, but three, at least.

Aulus Carvinius was a wealthy merchant whose family's vast acres in the Campania had been providing food and timber for the palace since the time of Julius Caesar himself. They found Carvinius with his bowels ripped out, spread-eagled in the middle of one of his own fields, and, by the time the local *Vigiles* got to him, what had been left of him already half-eaten by crows.

By his side lay his two mastiffs, tough dogs and a match for most creatures, but sucked dry like their master.

'They loved him so much,' said his grieving wife, leaning on the arm of her young house steward and giving it the occasional, reciprocated, squeeze with her beefy hand. 'They would have defended him to the death.'

'I guess they tried to,' Julius said, looking around angrily for any sort of clue, but there was nothing, except the method in which the killing had been carried out.

There was one lead: Nero owed Carvinius money. Carvinius had provided the wood for the poles on which the Christians were being burned.

But Nero owed plenty of people money, and all but the biggest fools among them realised they'd never see their money again, that the loans were insurance against greater losses in the form of imperial requisitions; so why would Nero bother to kill off his creditors, as long as they were useful to him?

Julius kept such thoughts to himself, but he knew he couldn't keep the killings secret forever. However hard the official *Daily Acts* news service tried to suppress them, rumours spread about the murders in Rome as fast as the Fire had, and, with them, panic. And with the panic, pressure.

He had nothing to get a grip on, and his time was limited. Nero's eye was on him. Tigellinus hated him. Mercurius wanted his job. But he wasn't someone who gave up. If this was the work of dark gods, and it'd take a lot to convince him of that, he'd take them on. What had he got to lose?

Carvinius was joined in death by a Greek copper dealer who'd romanised his name to Manius Gellius. The shopkeeper on his way to work before dawn who first found him, in the middle of town, on the Via Sacra, thought it was an ordinary mugging and ignored it, so it wasn't until daybreak that a peddler, drunk from the night before, stumbled and cursed, then went white at the sight of the messy sack he'd tripped over.

Manius was another of the emperor's creditors. But he was one of those Greeks who stuck to his own country's gods, and, although romanised, had remained less tolerant of the gods of others. One of the rare birds who still took religion seriously.

Jewish business competition had evidently bothered him. The few friends he'd had told Julius that perhaps he'd confused Jews for the other major pagan sect in Rome, the Christians. But there was nothing for Julius to build on. This didn't look like a contract killing by a business rival, Jew or Christian.

Too many deaths, panic rising, fear rising. Julius badly needed something to chase other than shadows.

The third victim was different.

The third was a woman. The second female victim, but, unlike the whore Justina, this lady hadn't been let go gently.

77

Her name was Sexta Fannia Decula. Julius knew of her by repute. A pale, slim, pretty blonde of sixty-odd, empty dark-brown eyes, dimpled chin, slight overbite, pretty nose, neat tits and nice legs, hair always tied in a black ribbon. Looked as if butter wouldn't melt. But rotten to the core.

She was a businesswoman. Her business was specialised. She'd run a brothel, but a different type from Dorcas' joint.

Mercurius brought him the report. 'This woman really deserved to die.'

'What do you mean?'

'She was evil.'

'Not many people *deserve* to die. Something you'll learn.'

'Do you know what she did?'

Julius nodded, but Mercurius didn't notice, and went on. 'Listen to this.' He consulted his tablets. 'Sexta catered for men and women whose taste led them to children and animals. She had available, at any time – can you believe this? – half-a-dozen children, from about four to ten. They were abandoned, picked off the streets to the south of the Circus Maximus, earning their bread by scavenging and begging. They didn't last that long, they got damaged, some survived but had to be let go, for obvious reasons. As for the animals – dogs and chimps were popular, donkeys cost more for a session. Off-duty, unlike the kids, which could be replaced more easily, they were treated well, kept in trim. When Sexta died, the place was closed down, and the animals and children were turned

78

loose, but no one knows what became of them. I guess the attendants found employment elsewhere. There are two other brothels, on the edge of the city, which run to that kind of clientele.'

Julius paid weary attention to his junior. Officially, Sexta had been on the *Vigiles*' books for years; but they'd never been able to close her operation because Nero saw himself as a liberal in all matters sexual. That wasn't the only reason.

'A lot of shit has come down the drain this time,' continued Mercurius. 'Sexta didn't merely run the place as a business; she participated. Had mules fuck her in front of an audience. And she bumped up her income as a police informer for IV Cohort.'

Julius leaned forward. IV Cohort covered poor districts, where most of the less privileged Jews and Christians lived; and it was in those districts that Sexta had preyed. Whistle-blowing on clients who didn't pay up, and on the competition, helped everyone. The *Vigiles* got their arrest quotas and Sexta got a clear playing field.

'Give me the file.'

Once he'd read it, Julius put it at the bottom of his pile. For once, the killers preying on his fellow-citizens had done Rome a favour. But he'd see what he could dig out of IV Cohort, the bastards.

One detail stuck in his mind. Sexta had lost a finger. From the report, it had been bitten off. One of her little fingers, as heavily be-ringed, no doubt, as the other nine.

Why?

He went to look at the body, already rotting. But it told him nothing, except that Sexta hadn't been thoroughly eviscerated this time, and there were traces of vomit nearby. He looked closer, disturbing the flies. Maybe Sexta hadn't tasted so good.

It worried him that he was getting used to the sight of such corpses. What also worried him was that Sexta, repellent though she'd been, didn't fit the shaky pattern they'd been building.

Apart from Sexta, most of the victims were from the top two classes – patricians or knights. But how many killers were there?

He had at least three creatures to deal with. But what were they? Furies sent by a god? And if so, which one? Juno was the most vengeful. But she reserved her spite for her husband's many lovers. Julius shook himself free of the thought. He was going crazy. Who believed in the gods anyway?

But there was something other than human at the source of all this. Except that there couldn't be. Demons didn't exist. Did they?

Rome had already withstood plague, fire, and a financial crash. The gods were angry. The leaders of society had been exposed as weak, inexperienced, and bloated with self-importance. The *Daily Acts* could only tell what Nero let it, but the rumours and the terror were spreading. No one felt safe. The horror was throwing its shadow across Rome like nightfall.

Julius took the sheaf of papers from his scribe, a good friend, normally dispassionate, who'd had a hard time recording this investigation.

He went to seek help, some of it from people he didn't want to owe favours to, but he was desperate. He arranged an audience with Tigellinus, a man he hated, in his office at the *castrum* of the Praetorian Guard.

He knew Tigellinus well. Vain enough to cram himself into a corset under the lightweight dress armour he affected, he'd used his fortune (his father had had to leave Sicily, where he'd grown up, for "health reasons", but took his stash with him), to build up a position of strength within the Roman *nomenklatura*. But there had been moments when he'd sailed close to the wind – he'd slept with both Nero's mother and the emperor's aunt, when Nero was a baby and that psycho Caligula was on the throne.

Tigellinus had also been a client of Sexta's.

Tigellinus' office was overblown, full of expensive marble and too much gilding; a décor that made you think of fat tarts at the theatre, flashing their tits.

The Co-Prefect lolled at his desk, scratched his balls, didn't stand up. But he did sit up and draw his chair in. Julius had the emperor's mandate, and Tigellinus knew it.

'Dear Julius. How can I help you?'

'You know what I'm doing.'

'Of course.' Tigellinus made a little pyramid of his finger-tips. 'And you're not doing well, are you? The emperor is impatient.'

'That's why I'm here.'

'You want help?'

Julius squeezed his fists together hard behind his back. 'Yes.'

Tigellinus studied his fingernails. 'We don't have anything for you. Not our case.'

'But the people involved. The victims.'

'Yes?'

'Some of them were close.'

'What do you mean?'

'Were creditors.'

'Oh dear.'

'What I'm getting at is, could the killers have been enemies of Nero? Given that the victims were his friends?'

'I thought you said they were his creditors?'

'His supporters, then.'

'Hmmn.' The pyramid again. How irritating Julius found that. 'I'd hardly like to think that you are suggesting that Sexta fell into that category?'

'Naturally not,' replied Julius drily.

'Good.' Tigellinus paused briefly.

'Tell me what you know.'

Tigellinus looked at a silver paper-knife on his desk. The

haft was shaped like a penis. 'More than you already know? But it's your investigation.'

'We need leads.'

'You'll find them.'

Julius placed his hands on the desk, arms bent, leaning forward.

'My commission is from Nero.'

'I know that.'

'Don't block me, Tigellinus.'

'Are you threatening me?'

'Yes.'

Tigellinus looked at him lazily. 'If I could help you, I'd have to. Even if I didn't want to. You know that. But I don't know any more about who's committing these crimes than you. I repeat: if my people had information I'd help you – I would already have offered. The emperor speaks highly of you.' He paused, then said, gently, 'Perhaps in time you might like to join us?' He looked at his impeccable finger-nails again. 'More money and better quarters. And no more problematic Mercurius.'

Julius knew that Tigellinus was reading his thoughts.

'I'm sure Nero would approve of your help.'

Tigellinus leaned forward. 'Are we dealing with demons?'

'Demons?' Julius sneered.

'What do you think?'

Julius looked at the cold eyes. They were nervous.

* * *

He didn't get any further with the Secret Service. The man there, who, Julius knew, had bought his way in from the insurance business, made Tigellinus look like the High Priestess of the Vestals. Another fat, slippery bastard, this time with boils the size of goiters on the back of his greasy neck. Little eyes, smug grin, what hair he had cropped close on a round skull. Another useless piece of shit in this foundering administration, thought Julius.

No help at all. Julius toyed with the idea of getting out, dropping the job, leaving the whole mess to Mercurius. But he couldn't. His *Parcae* – the Fates watching his every move – wouldn't let him. And he didn't like living with the suspicion that someone out there was blocking him.

He returned to his office. And went over the paperwork again. But once more he was frustrated – what use was paperwork? Wasn't he simply going through the motions? And the head of his Cohort was after his balls. Sooner or later, he'd be summoned by the palace to explain himself. He desperately needed some trail to follow.

He left late, and as he made his way home he kept looking over his shoulder. He'd fought many battles in his time, but this was the worst.

13

If he didn't come up with something, it would only be a matter of time before Julius was arrested for negligence. As if he needed anything else to prevent him from sleeping. Now, he'd been summoned into Tigellinus' office again. But he wasn't about to knuckle under to that bastard.

Work on the rebuilding of the city went on relentlessly, and Nero's achievements were being trumpeted on every corner. But under the surface, rumour and horror were rife. Even the whores at the south-eastern end of the Circus Maximus only plied their trade after dark on a race day, when it was certain that there would be plenty of people about, and the streets were well lit. But as soon as the crowds thinned, even the area around the Porta Capena and the Appian Aqueduct was deserted. Of course nobody, not even the most outspoken senators, spoke of the cloud that hung over the city publicly, but it was in everyone's minds. The poor were unaffected by it; none of them had yet been attacked. They knew what was going on, though, and only the homeless were left on the streets after sunset.

'The emperor wants more cops on the streets at night,' Tigellinus told Julius grudgingly. 'He's granting you extraordinary powers to co-opt men from every Cohort of *Vigiles* in the city.'

'About time.'

'Watch your mouth, Julius Marcellus. Nero wants a head on a plate soon, and if you're not careful, it'll be *yours*. As it is, I've suggested the job's taken away from you and given to the Praetorian Guard. We'll soon flush these bastards out.'

'I'd like to see you try.'

'It's the fucking Christians. They failed to bring the city down with the Fire, now they're trying terror.'

'How troubled is he?'

'The emperor? Troubled?' Tigellinus leant forward. 'I told you – watch your mouth. You're in enough shit.'

But Julius was left alone. And that was the way he preferred to work. He rustled up some more cops and had night-patrols doubled, but he didn't think it'd do much good.

Life at court went on as if nothing was happening. Nero preferred being an actor to being an emperor, and he had one big advantage over his fellow-thespians: no one, however good, could stand as his rival; no one, however talented, could win any prize against him. Music, poetry, singing, acting, racing – the emperor always scooped the pool.

But that wasn't enough for the stunted young man who ran the city and the empire. Nero hungered for approbation so much that he had to organise it. A big theatre was one of the first buildings to go up after the Fire, and as soon as it was ready the emperor was performing in it, either masked and holding a baton, or wearing a wig of golden locks and strumming a lyre to one of his own compositions. He was always centre stage and stage front. And well lit.

Nero, Julius thought, had come to believe that his power proved his talent. As no one challenged him, there was no end to the degradation of Rome. Brothels and taverns were established in the woods planted next to the Naval Lake, and everyone who wanted to get on in society was obliged to attend them. The too-old and the too-young, and anyone who needed bringing into line, had to fight in the Games, and senators' wives had to spread their legs if they knew what was good for them.

All this amused the emperor.

It made Julius sick. What kind of system was he serving?

But the horror still lurked in the shadows, and no amount of pzazz could drive it from people's minds. It was a storm cloud over the city.

And in the midst of this, thought Julius bitterly, was Nero's troop of *Augustiniani*, who went about their business as usual.

They were fun, the *Augustiniani*, but they aroused Julius' suspicion.

The original lot were a bunch of Alexandrian sailors who'd captivated Nero by their rhythmical way of applauding his recitals, and those men had formed the nucleus of a full-time professional fan-club which grew and grew, and included tough guys, girlie guys, and secret policemen who sat in the audience to make sure no one nodded off, passed a remark, or tried to leave – even to take a piss. And some of those performances were *long*. Julius remembered a friend of his managing to get away after three solid hours by shamming a fit; and even that was followed by an inter-rogation. No direct action was taken against him, but the friend found that the number of invitations to attend Nero's shows suddenly doubled, and there was no way he could wriggle out of them.

This band of personal supporters, most with just enough brain as a swallow needs to fly north and south when the seasons demand, and there were five thousand of them, were Nero's core audience.

They were close to their boss, and it was a lucky break for Julius when he interviewed one of them about the murder of the concrete-factory owner. Turned out the kid was the dead man's nephew.

Despite his bulk, the man had an effete air, and Julius could smell rose-oil before the man had entered the room. This brawny, thick provincial was ill-at-ease in Julius' office, though Julius had taken the precaution of placing his scribe out of sight. Julius wanted this interview to seem as informal as possible.

Once he'd got through all the usual questions – like, what kind of person was your uncle, did he have any unsavoury connections that you knew of – Julius became more interested in the man himself. Such a person, approaching a bovine stupidity, interested Julius, who was beginning to think that the killings, however savage and random they seemed, might be under some kind of central control. To put up with being an *Augustinianus*, you didn't need brain. Brain was the last thing you needed because the job was so *boring*. What you needed was to be greedy and obedient. And not past doing whatever was necessary to protect your privileges. Julius needed to lull this guy into feeling secure, relaxed. 'So,' Julius said, 'What do you do exactly?'

Murcellus was nineteen, running to fat, and dressed like a hand-me-down version of the emperor. He replied: 'Clap.'

'What?'

'I clap.'

'Oh, right,' said Julius, humouring him, and reining in his impatience. Keeping the investigation going, even this close to home, would keep his neck off the block. If Nero questioned him, he'd say he thought there were infiltrators within the privileged ranks of the Royal Applauders. A risky strategy, but not bad as a last throw of the dice.

'Go on.'

Murcellus knitted his brow. 'What?'

'Tell me about your special skills.'

On any other face the expression would have brightened. Here, it was just a clearing of the odd cloud. 'Oh. Yeah.'

'Go on.'

'Yeah.' Murcellus took a breath. 'I'm a flat-tiler.'

'Really?'

'Yeah.'

Julius waited for the man to go on, but he just sat there, like a block, his heavy eyebrows drawn together over a great cliff of a nose. 'Tell me about it,' said Julius.

There'd been another killing the previous night in the Via Latina, not far from the theatre – one in which Nero had recently given a benefit for people the Fire had rendered homeless, and which had been paid for by Murcellus' uncle. Any connection, however slight, needed to be explored. But first Murcellus – suspicious, scared, and one of the emperor's pets, had to be put at ease.

'A flat-tiler,' said Julius, smoothly. 'What's that?'

Murcellus looked at him, amazed that anyone could be so ignorant. 'My lot are called that because we clap the emperor's performance with our hands flat against each other.'

'I thought everyone applauded like that.'

Murcellus warmed to his theme, a sad little professional light in his eye. 'Oh no. No, no. Not at all.' And lapsed into silence.

'You're having me on,' said Julius.

'There's quite a skill to it,' said Murcellus, leaning forward. 'The other lot, the hollow-tilers, they clap with their hands *cupped*, like this.' He demonstrated. 'It's quite different. And then there are the Bees –'

'What do they do?'

'They hum. Or buzz, depending on what's most effective for the acoustic. People think we're a load of wastrels paid for arsing around at the theatre and doing fuck-all else, but they're wrong. It's a responsibility, keeping Nero happy, and if he's happy, Rome's happy, the empire's happy, everyone's fuckin' happy.'

'I don't think your uncle's very happy.'

'Well, you can't win 'em all.'

'Are you happy that he's dead?'

Murcellus spread his hands. 'We weren't close. Didn't see much of him. Dad was in the army. We travelled a lot when I was a kid.'

'Did he leave you anything?'

'I wish!' Murcellus shrugged idly. Julius knew how rich the *Augustiniani* could become. Each section leader got 400,000 sestercii per concert, and if that wasn't enough, the influence you had, and the fact that being a member automatically made you a member of the *eques* class, more than put you in a position to make up for it.

'Nero's not too happy, in fact,' said Julius, changing tack. His voice hardened. 'The killings are terrorising the people.

No one goes out at night.' He paused. 'Apart from anything else, that's bad for business. We need help, and if we find that anyone's been withholding it . . .' He let the sentence hang.

Murcellus studied his fingernails. 'Don't know much about that, mate.'

'There are a lot of you *Augustiniani* aren't there?'

'Good few, yeah.'

'And you're all loyal?'

'Goes without saying.'

'And you look out for each other?'

Murcellus thought about that. 'S'pose.'

'But you do what the emperor tells you.'

'Don't we all?'

You flabby fuck, thought Julius.

'He panics a lot,' said Murcellus, after a nervous pause. 'He gets stage-fright. He's scared of the judges when he competes with other singers in competitions. He dropped his sceptre the other day in mid-lyric, and boy, did we have to applaud to cover for him. Of course he won anyway.'

Julius pondered this. What a fucking mess it all was. The rebuilding of Rome was going on around him at a staggering rate, but the banks were empty, taxes were rising, the rich knew better than not to leave half their estate – at least, half of what they hadn't secretly invested abroad – to the emperor, for fear of having the lot confiscated; the poor just stayed where they always had been, and nobody lifted a finger to criticise or rebel.

All Romans were *Augustiniani*, Julius thought, because they were so *craven*. The only people, it seemed to him, with any sense of integrity, were the Christians, who didn't even have the privilege the Jews had of enjoying the protection of Poppaea; or the Greeks, adored without qualification by Nero.

No wonder Nero hated the Christians.

'What else is he scared of?' asked Julius.

Murcellus was silent.

'The Christians?'

'No.' Murcellus laughed. 'He's got them sorted.'

'What, then?'

Murcellus looked crafty.

'Look, whatever you tell me, it won't go any further. And I'll make sure no one bothers you over the death of your uncle.'

Now Murcellus looked uneasy. 'I had nothing to do with that.'

'Of course not.'

'He only left me a crummy farm near Ostia. Costs me more to run than it fetches.'

'Let's trust each other. I won't say anything about this conversation, as long as you don't.' Julius paused. 'But you've heard the rumours.'

'Yes.'

'Is he bothered by them?'

Silence. Julius knew he was on thin ice. 'Some of the people who've copped it – your uncle for instance – well, their deaths haven't been exactly inconvenient.'

'Nah.' Murcellus dropped his voice. 'But the boss can have anyone he wants iced. Who'd bat an eyelid?'

You don't know the mood of some of the senators, thought Julius. But Nero does.

'That's true,' he said smoothly. 'Even so, if our dear emperor wanted to be a bit secretive . . .' Julius let the suggestion hang, then shrugged. 'Look, I'm only after a bit of advice, really.'

That worked. Murcellus was flattered. He was also relieved about being let off the hook over his uncle. Innocent or not, he wouldn't welcome an investigation. 'I'm not that close to dear Nero,' he said slowly. 'But I'm around him enough. Something's bothering him.'

'Like what?'

Murcellus thought. 'As if he'd lost something and can't find it.'

14

After the youth had left, Julius called Mercurius in.

'What next?' Mercurius said, after Julius had filled him in. He was wearing yet another new outfit today and Julius felt distinctly shabby and unfresh. It irked him.

'Go and talk to the section leaders of the *Augustiniani*.'

'Nero's not going to like that.'

'I know.'

Mercurius looked doubtful. 'What do you think we'll get out of it? Those guys have influence – and money.'

'Nero pays them enough. They might know more than Murcellus. Use what we've got from him and build on it.'

'What'll you do?'

'I'm going to talk to the Christians.'

Mercurius looked at him. 'Good luck with that.'

He knew it wasn't an easy task. Although the savagery

of Nero's purge had slackened since the days following the Fire, Christians were still arrested and dragged off to torments in the arena, or on the Cross, or at the stake. The community which remained in Rome had turned in on itself. Few now admitted membership of the sect. It was still officially legal, but it had gone underground.

They couldn't disappear completely. They had to buy food and drink, they had to pay rent and taxes. The best they could do was pretend they weren't what they were. They had their signs and symbols, their secret codes and their hidden ceremonies. If they could hold out, they knew that, with time, as the new Rome rose from the ashes of the old, memories of the Fire would fade, and they would stop being in the front line of persecution.

VIII Cohort had little to do with the Christians, but Julius knew that when they wanted to keep something secret, it stayed that way. He had a few contacts of his own among them, and decided that the best way to play things now was to get to talk to the chief men.

'It's not possible,' his friend Titus told him, over a cup of Falernian in a noisy bar just north of the Gardens of Maecenas.

'Doesn't have to be official, I just need some information.'

'Word's spread about these murders. You're not hanging them on us, like you did the Fire.'

'You know that wasn't my doing.'

'Still work for Nero, don't you? Word is, this investigation's a personal commission.'

'It's my *job*. And it needs clearing up.'

Titus shrugged. 'There hasn't been a *Christian* victim yet.'

'Nor a Jew, so you're all under suspicion.'

'The Jews have nothing to worry about. They've got Poppaea.'

'Are you sure? If Nero chose to, he could snap Poppaea's neck like a twig.'

'Fuck off, Julius.' Titus was a recent convert, a Roman citizen and a rich entrepreneur with plenty of pull in the Senate. There'd be no going to the Arena for him, no being pulled up on a pole wearing a shirt daubed with pitch. But he and Julius had been friends since boyhood when their fathers, both *Praefecti Castrorum,* had sent their sons to the same tutor. Titus had gone into the army, risen fast, made good contacts.

Now he relented, and turned the conversation to a subject close to his heart. 'Julius, I wish you'd join us.'

'I don't believe in anything. What we have is here, and that's it; we only own the present moment, and *that's* like trying to pick up mercury.'

'It isn't meaningless. Not this.'

'Give me one reason why your people *shouldn't* be under suspicion.' Julius was losing patience, but tried not to let it show. He didn't want to antagonise his friend.

Titus paused. He'd had an idea, Julius could see that. But

he was shying away from it, as if it were too risky. Still, it wouldn't let him go.

Julius, sensing an opportunity, waited. Titus was still wrestling with himself, and Julius wondered if he needed a shove, when his friend reached the decision which saved him the trouble.

'It might be possible for me to arrange something.' Titus looked at him. 'But you must keep an open mind.'

Julius returned the stare. 'I need to ask questions. For information. No arrests. No strong-arm stuff.'

'It'd do you no harm to do some *listening* as well.'

'It'd do *you* no harm to have a Christian legate in your pocket.'

Titus didn't smile. 'Like you? Perhaps. But I'm not promising anything.'

The bar was smart, with a sundial in its small atrium – an unusual luxury, but the place was frequented by people for whom knowing the time was important. Titus stood up and consulted it. 'I must go. Can you meet me here tomorrow, about the seventh hour? I'll buy you lunch.'

'But will you bring news?'

'God willing.' Titus grinned at last, though his grin stayed tight. 'You might show some gratitude.'

'Oh, I will.'

The rest of that day Julius spent looking at the reports Mercurius had prepared from his interviews with the bosses of the Bees, the Flat-Tilers and the Hollow-Tilers. They had nothing to say, didn't know the actor who'd been murdered because they were too young to remember him, and didn't know anything about the murder outside the theatre in the Via Latina – or so they said. But Julius no longer believed the gang of vicious murderers he was after came from the pampered, perfumed and powdered ranks of the *Augustiniani*. Whoever was committing these crimes, he thought, was either supernaturally determined and inured to the risks, or was driven to commit them by a force greater than themselves. He shook himself at that last thought. Hadn't he just told Titus he believed in nothing but what was here? People said they'd seen ghosts, demons, but you never saw one *yourself*. Still, he was uneasy.

The following day, which was hot for autumn, he arrived early at the bar. He found Titus there already, and on his second beaker, by the look of him.

'Quick drink then we'll go,' said Titus, his smile broader today but still nervous.

'Go?'

'I'm taking you straight there. Maybe we can get a bite afterwards.'

Titus poured him a cup of wine, and Julius noticed Titus had chosen a bottle from Chalkidike – and if they were drinking Greek wine, he must have something important to celebrate. Julius was in a hurry. He drank the wine more quickly than it deserved.

His friend led him through streets of new stone-built houses, golden in the sunlight, which thinned to gardens and villas as they worked their way northwards along the Esquiline. They turned east along an unmade country road, and then north off it, until they reached a farmhouse of wood and thatch, so low-built that it blended with the countryside around it. It must have ceased to function as a farmhouse, for the yard was neat and tidy, and there were no dogs, no other domestic animals, and none of the mess and clutter you always get on a working estate.

They had been walking for half an hour. Titus was tired. He was sweating and he looked grey. The booze had taken its toll.

'We're here,' Titus said. 'Go in.'

'What?'

'Go in.' Titus' voice was strained. Julius felt for the hilt of his dagger.

'What about you?'

'You're expected. This is a big favour, Julius. You don't need me to introduce you. I'll wait outside.' Titus made for the well in the middle of the yard. Late-summer flowers covered its low, yellow guard-wall. The air was still. Julius could hear the song of invisible birds. 'Don't waste his time,' Titus said over his shoulder, and jerked a thumb in the direction of the dark entrance.

After the bright sunshine it took Julius a moment to adjust to the gloom, and he stood immediately to one side of the door-frame as soon as he had entered, so as not to be silhouetted by the light. He didn't want to make an easy target. He'd known Titus most of his life, but he wasn't sure how much his new loyalties outweighed the old.

The voice which welcomed him was deep, and somehow kind. That unsettled Julius somehow.

'Come in, sit down. There's a chair by the table. Forgive the lack of light. These old places . . .'

Julius found the chair. Across the coarse boards of the table he saw a seated figure opposite him, outlined in faint light from the window behind him.

'You know why I've come?' Julius said.

'Titus explained.'

'I'm investigating the killings.'

'Rome is a violent city.'

Julius ignored that. 'Who are you?'

'My name is Petrus.'

Julius was surprised. Titus certainly did have influence if he'd organised an interview with *him*. Or was the fact that Petrus had agreed to meet an indication of the Christians' own anxiety? 'Everyone has an interest in tracking these killers down,' said Julius.

'Yes.'

There was no way he could pick his words carefully, so Julius went on. 'No Christians have been harmed.'

Petrus frowned. 'Oh, but they have. In the Arena. On the stakes.'

'Don't talk about that,' warned Julius. 'I can arrest you, and I will.'

'Arrest me, then.' The voice had grown harder.

'That wouldn't help me,' Julius said.

Petrus raised a hand, placating. Julius recognised less aggression than nervousness in him. 'The killings, from what I know of them, are cruel.'

'Very cruel.'

The old man looked thoughtful. 'I wish I could help you. We are not interested in destruction. We abhor war, violence. That is the basic tenet of our Creed.'

Julius ignored the preaching. 'What do you know?'

'Nothing.' Petrus looked thoughtful. Julius was thinking too: this man is going to do anything he can to exonerate his followers.

Petrus continued, as if remembering something. 'It seems to me that forces have been unleashed beyond the imagination of . . .' He paused. '. . . most mortals.'

'What are you talking about?' Julius was losing patience with this drivel.

Petrus spread his hands in the gloom. His head was lowered and it was impossible to read the expression on his face. 'We can only pray this scourge can be averted.'

Julius wondered if that amounted to any kind of confession. 'We know you harbour extremists in your midst. If you know who is responsible for the killings, tell me.'

Petrus said, 'I will do what is in my power. But from

time to time even a dog, however well trained, will turn on its master, or return to the wild. None of us lives very far from the savage within us. And we can be weak, even when we try to be strong. Moments of weakness can unleash forces that pass out of our control. We all have our weaknesses, and we must live with them and combat them all our lives. Mine is anger.'

Julius wondered where this was leading. He thought about arresting Petrus but then he considered his situation. He'd been sworn to secrecy by Titus, and he'd come alone – otherwise the interview would never have taken place. He was out of town and no one apart from the Christians knew where he was. He wasn't in the strongest of positions. In any case, what good would arresting this tough old man do? Petrus had an aura of sadness, even of regret, but to judge from the words he spoke he was no diplomat, and sooner or later he'd meet his nemesis. Julius knew from Titus that Petrus had lived in Rome for twenty years or more, but Nero's predecessors had been tolerant of Christians, compared with the present emperor. Nero's persecution, especially after the Fire, had triggered the enmity which existed now, which had created terrorists within the Christians' ranks.

The Christians had no power, and, as Julius had just had confirmed from the lips of the great Christian master, their teaching forbade violence. But there'd been talk that Petrus sometimes tended to forget this. There was an admiring rumour that he'd chopped off the ear of an official with the local forces who'd been sent to arrest his Master just outside Jerusalem thirty years earlier.

Julius decided to do nothing. He'd have Titus shadowed from now on, though. Titus would be seeing Petrus again sooner or later, and he wouldn't be able to shake off a tail forever.

'Thank you for your time, Petrus.' Julius stood up.

Petrus did the same. Julius wondered how the old man felt. The impression he gave was of a man troubled by his conscience, but unable to do anything about it.

Julius made for the door.

'Titus will let you know if we hear anything that can help you.' Petrus' voice interrupted his departure.

'Thank you.'

'And may God protect you; for I believe that Satan controls the killing.'

Julius looked at him.

Petrus' eyes were shaded. 'Perhaps he has always controlled it. Not one of us ordinary mortals can always be strong against him. We have to accept defeats and learn from them; what we must never do is give up the fight. But I do promise you one thing, Julius Marcellus.'

'What?'

'You do not believe, but I do, and my belief is strong. As long as I live I will strive to contain the evil that has fallen on Rome through my prayers.'

Julius thought, fat lot of good that'll do, but despite himself he was moved by the power of the man's conviction. And what in Hades did Rome owe Petrus, that he should pray for the city?

Outside, the afternoon sun was fiercer than it should have been this late in the year. Titus, looking better, was sitting in the shade of a small olive grove with a handful of people, humbly dressed. They were deep in conversation and didn't notice Julius' approach. As he came within earshot he trod more carefully, and stood in the shadow of a tree to listen.

The people – two men and two women – were speaking not Latin, but Aramaic, and Julius saw that their style of dress placed them beyond the eastern shores of the Central Sea – he guessed Syria or Judaea.

Julius could speak Aramaic and Greek well, and listened carefully. These people must have developed a habit of caution, for they spoke quietly and fast; but they spoke with passion. Their conversation was about the situation of the Christians in Rome, how to better it, or whether to quit the city altogether. Julius didn't think they'd do that. However dangerous Rome was for them, it remained the power base of the world.

It was surprising how much you could pick up just eavesdropping for two minutes. There was frequent use of the number 666 in a context Julius knew must relate to the emperor. He had no means of taking notes, and prayed he'd remember enough of it. But he could not eavesdrop forever, so he moved slowly forwards, as if in thought, and deliberately trod on a dry branch, breaking it with his weight as he came into view. He guessed Titus had been teaching the strangers some kind of code.

They stood immediately, and turned to face him, Titus coming forward, unable to disguise successfully the thought that showed itself on his face: how long had his friend been within earshot? Julius looked innocent. Titus didn't know how much Aramaic he understood.

'Worth your while?'

Julius looked at the others. 'Friends of yours?'

'They are my brothers in Christ. I'd introduce you, but they are simply visiting, and they speak very little Latin.'

'Pity.'

'They wouldn't have anything to tell you. They only arrived yesterday, to see Petrus.'

Julius let that go. 'I'm going back to the city.'

'We'll go together. Do you have time for lunch? Time for *cena* anyway, by the time we get back.'

'I didn't know you spoke – Aramaic, was it?'

'Yes. I learned it when I was with the Legion in Syria.'

'Of course,' Julius said.

15

If he'd hoped to get any more out of Titus at the late lunch they had on the terrace of a little taverna shaded by an old vine, where Titus insisted on buying another Greek wine, one from Kos this time, Julius was to be disappointed. He told Titus some of what his conversation with Petrus had been, at the same time wondering if his friend would report to the Christian elder afterwards.

It was an awkward lunch, Julius thought. Two old friends reduced to pumping each other for information while trying to appear not to. Neither would leave the table entirely satisfied, though the food was good, lentils from France followed by pike and then an expensive dish of jugged hare served with leeks, and the usual nuts and grapes to end with.

He made his way back to headquarters, thinking his time

had been wasted. There wasn't anything to pin on Petrus, and dragging him in for interrogation, tempting as the thought was, would inflame the Christians more.

He hadn't asked Titus what the meaning of 666 was, but once behind his desk, sweating in the late afternoon heat and longing to get down to the Baths, he did some research.

He was still sitting there, surrounded by half-a-dozen Aramaic scrolls and an Aramaic grammar, an hour later, when Mercurius came in.

His assistant was surprised to see him, and Julius, equally surprised, had no time to gather up the scrolls which littered his desk.

'Working late?' said Mercurius.

'What does it look like?' said Julius irritably. 'Got anything?'

Mercurius sat down wearily. 'No. I followed up a couple of leads from the *Augustiniani* bosses, but they're not involved. And Vatinius sent a messenger round to deliver a reprimand for bothering them at all.'

'Well, we mustn't bug Nero.'

'Has he sent for you?' asked Mercurius

'He will.'

'We'll have to wait for another death.'

'Jupiter help us.' Julius sighed. He had a headache from the sun. He wanted to drop the whole thing. 'Whoever's doing it has vanished. It's a sod about that girl. Justina. She must have seen something.'

'The extra police are deployed. We'll flush them out.'

'Yeah, right,' growled Julius.

Mercurius turned his attention to the scrolls. 'What's the sudden interest in Aramaic?'

'Can you read it?'

'I get by. What is it?'

Julius told him.

Mercurius pounced like a dog on a bone. 'I can do this.'

He unrolled the Grammar, and turned to the section on Numerals. He pored over it. 'The Jews have a system of some kind, I found out about it when I was with VII Cohort.' He fell silent, reading. Julius watched him carefully.

'Got it,' said Mercurius, looking up. 'This is what they do: they give the value of numbers to the letters of an alphabet. I'll show you.'

He grabbed a stylus, wrote the numbers out on a wax tablet.

'If we find the total numeric value of 666 in terms of letters of the alphabet, we get –'

He wrote some more, not much, passed the tablet across.

Julius read the word *Nero*, in Aramaic. He'd never have got it. It wouldn't work using the Roman alphabet.

'666 means Nero,' Mercurius said.

'So it's a basic code,' Julius replied. 'But what's it about?'

'Whatever it is, it's not flattering,' said Mercurius, gathering some papers and taking his leave. 'More reports on the killings. For all the good they are, I might as well scatter them to the winds.'

'Just do your job.'

Mercurius left in silence. Julius bit his lip.

Left alone as the dusk gathered, he stayed at his desk, looking at the wax tablet as if it would somehow speak to him. Finally, he stood up, put the Aramaic scrolls back, wiped the writing off the tablet. One of Mercurius' papers had fallen unnoticed to the floor. He picked it up, cursing, for he'd reached the stage when the slightest thing irritated him, and something freshly written there caught his eye.

666 is the sign of the Dark One.

Julius made his way to the Baths. He knew he had to force himself to relax, give himself time to think. Maybe then he'd feel less out of his depth.

But he didn't have much time. Soon, the mob would start looking for scapegoats.

16

After the Baths, Julius went home through the emptying streets to his two-room apartment, knowing that it would feel silent and lonely that night. But when he arrived at his block, he found a litter waiting outside with a five-man guard and one of Titus' senior house-slaves in attendance. The man came up to him immediately.

'Quintus Julius.'

'Hello, Geta.'

'We've been waiting for you. The master's giving a late supper and wants you to join him.'

That sounded better than an evening brooding alone; and maybe, Julius thought, Titus has more to tell me than he cared to – or dared to – in the countryside.

He'd had his body oiled and scraped at the Baths, so all he had to do was change into a dinner tunic in his flat, and climb into the litter to be carried to Titus' house on the Quirinal.

Geta preceded him into the airy, well-lit atrium, at its centre a pool, and in the centre of that a fountain which played gently, cooling the air. An Egyptian slave came up with water for him to wash his hands. The stars were lively in the deep blue sky. Nice to have money, thought Julius.

He felt scruffy and, as always when he visited Titus, he found it hard to suppress envy. But it was good to have company, and, fresh from his bath, his head had cleared. He ate a peacock-egg-and-tuna canapé and looked around.

It was an informal gathering. There were only half-a-dozen guests including Titus and himself, all standing or sitting round the pool and chatting as they drank *mulsum* and nibbled titbits dipped in *garum*. The other guests, as you'd expect at Titus', were prosperous friends; one married couple, and two single women, neither of whom Julius knew; one sophisticated and expensively dressed, the other quieter, with dark-blonde hair and deep-green eyes.

Julius was the last to arrive, and after he'd been introduced to the single women, Portia and Calpurnia – he already knew the couple – slaves better dressed than Julius was himself ushered them through to the couches arranged round the table in the smaller of Titus' dining-rooms, where the light was softened by heavy yellow hangings, and where a lyre-player strummed light music discreetly in a corner.

Titus showed his guests to their places, apologising that

there was an even number of them, though none of the people present cared about such old-fashioned superstitions. He clapped his hands for the first course to be served: silver cups for the wine and the beautifully cold water, and Samian pottery for the dishes.

It was a light meal, but, as it was taken late and exquisitely cooked, no one complained. Lettuce, olives and seafood formed the *gustatio*, washed down with a lighter blend of *mulsum* than they'd been drinking in the atrium; and the *fecula* which followed was equally simple: two suckling pigs arranged side by side on a bed of coriander leaves and stuffed with pastry, figs and honey, with fine white bread and a light, twelve-year-old Mamertine to drink.

Julius wished he could enjoy it. He looked at the others. Everyone was subdued.

He was placed between Calpurnia and Portia; the lyre-player strummed on, light classical pieces, Roman, nothing Greek and nothing by Nero. The conversation, polite and neutral at first, circled around the one subject everyone wanted to discuss but would have to leave to their host to open. Luckily for Julius, only Titus knew what he did for a living, and Titus didn't know everything. The couple, who remembered him from other parties at Titus' place, thought he was a scribe.

Julius, troubled, drank little, but as the Mamertine warmed the others, talk became more relaxed. The husband had recently returned from a business trip to Pompeii and was talking about the new erotic frescoes he'd seen there. He wasn't the only one at the party to have seen them; Julius knew that Titus had.

'Are they really *erotic*?' asked Portia, a tall, cool woman in her late twenties, perhaps, with pale skin, dark-brown, ironic eyes, and a cascade of bronze hair which looked natural, but could have been dyed to fall in with the fashion.

'What do you mean?' asked the husband.

'I mean, are they pornographic, or erotic?'

'Is there a difference?'

'Portia means, did they make you want to masturbate, or did they make you want to make love?' said his wife.

'I hadn't thought of it. They are exciting, and the painting's good.'

'And are the women enjoying themselves as much as the men?'

The husband hesitated. 'I think so,' he said.

'Because it seems to me that over the last few years a kind of art has appeared which is more violent than sexy, and that the violence is directed at women. Not many women enjoy being whipped, or tied up and buggered.'

'I don't remember seeing anything like that at Pompeii.'

'Good. Because that is what I think pornography is; and it is created for and by men whom women aren't really interested in, and who want to take revenge.' Portia smiled. She turned to Julius. 'What do you think?'

Julius shrugged. It had always amused him that in the

114

pornographic frescoes he'd seen in Rome the men were paunchy and two decades older than the girls.

'Pompeii is safer than Rome,' said Titus, looking at Julius.

The room fell silent. Everyone knew what he was talking about. He had broached the subject of the killings.

'Is anybody doing anything about these murders?' Portia asked the room.

'It's shameful,' said the wife. 'No one can go out. I'm terrified for my kids. We only came tonight because we have good guards, Dacians, and let me tell you, even they don't like it.' She looked at Julius. 'You work in government, do you know what's being done?'

'Everything possible,' he replied.

'Typical official answer.'

'They're dealing with people who are impossible to nail down.'

'There are more *Vigiles* around at night,' said the husband. 'Though, knowing them, they'd turn and run at the slightest sign of danger.'

'*Everybody's* terrified,' said Portia. She looked across at Titus. 'Are they blaming your people for this?'

'Some are.'

'As if you hadn't been treated badly enough.' Portia was clearly powerful enough not to care what she said among people she didn't know, thought Julius. Or was a seat at Titus' table assurance enough of discretion? He looked at her. No. She was powerful, pure and simple.

'This'll bring the city to its knees if it goes on,' said the husband. 'I've heard descriptions of what the victims' bodies look like.'

'Is there any guarantee they won't start attacking in daylight? No one seems to be able to get near them.'

'There'll be work going on in secret,' said Julius, cautiously.

'Do you know that for sure?'

'No one knows anything.'

'It's a curse, a curse from the gods, for what we've allowed to happen to the Christians,' the wife gulped out.

Her husband gaped at her, then lowered his head. 'Be quiet,' he muttered.

'Or a punishment for allowing a demon to rule us.'

'Quiet, I said.' He smiled at the table. 'A little too much wine. Let's draw a veil over it.'

'Certainly,' Titus said. The wife was sobbing quietly now. Calpurnia left her couch, went and put an arm round her. Julius noticed that she walked with a slight limp.

'It's my children. It's not for me, it's for my children that I worry.'

'I'm sure they'll come to no harm,' said Calpurnia. Julius watched her, noticing the softness of her arms, the rich depth of her hair.

'How do you know?' the wife said. 'How can you possibly know?'

Calpurnia stroked her cheek, calming her, though she had no answer to the question.

'Let's talk about something else,' said Portia, but she looked at Julius. 'Your people should pull their fingers out. It won't be long before even those of us who can afford guards won't go out at night.'

'If we've finished,' said Titus, and nodded to his steward.

The table-slaves cleared the dishes away, replaced the cups, brought water for the guests to wash their hands, and exchanged the wine for a sweet Chian, which the women mixed with water.

'That was good, Titus,' Julius said.

'You're changing the subject,' said Portia.

'You suggested it.'

'It wasn't good, it was brilliant,' the husband pitched in, relieved that talk of the killings had stopped. Calpurnia returned to her couch, the wife had composed herself, though he'd have to take her home as soon as he decently could. 'By Edesia, I'd like to know what you paid for your chef!'

He was a little drunk, and Julius saw his wife, who wasn't, flash her eyes at him. Julius himself knew that Titus' chef, a Gaul, had set him back the price of three chariot horses. No wonder the food was good. It had better be. But then, Julius also knew that Titus, on a special occasion, wouldn't jib at giving the price of *nine* horses for one really spectacular turbot.

Titus smiled and said diplomatically, 'More than I should have.'

The slaves brought in grapes and pears and chestnuts, baked oysters and snails – Titus always liked to finish with a flourish and his *mensae secundae* were legendary.

Calpurnia had said very little. Julius had talked to her earlier about the usual small things, and she'd been happy to make conversation, but they'd both found themselves turning back to the others' general chat whenever their own petered out, and that happened a lot.

He looked at her again. She was too dark to be really fashionable. She had tanned skin and her hair was too rebellious to be kept in order; but she was luxuriously dressed in a white *stola,* which, though it covered all but her golden-brown forearms, shaped itself to a figure which Julius tried to stop staring at. She wore few jewels, a simple pearl necklace, only two rings, one on each hand, and no make-up. Her sublime eyes were set a little wide apart. Her neck was long and graceful, her chin delicate, and her nose small and attractively tilted. When they were talking she looked at him directly and smiled easily.

But he knew she was preoccupied. When he made the obvious joke about his being called Julius and she Calpurnia, she laughed politely enough but he felt like a fool.

How old was she? Twenty-two-ish? Where was she from?

This was the worst possible time to get involved with a woman again.

'They're trying to keep it dark,' the husband was saying to Titus, going back to the subject none of them could ignore. 'But of course they can't. They can keep it out of the *Acts*, but not from people's tongues.'

'Nobody knows anything,' said Titus.

'They must catch them soon,' said the wife. 'We're going to leave town until it's over.' She gave her husband a hard look.

'They'll have to catch them,' said Titus, casting a glance in Julius' direction.

'They will,' said Portia. 'We have the best police force in the world.'

Everybody laughed at that. But Julius felt angry. He'd noticed that Portia had begun to cast glances at the water-clock on a sideboard which stood against one wall of the room, and at the velvet night, loud with cricket-song, beyond the windows.

He, too, looked out at the night. What menace did it hold? What might be happening out there now, as he lay here? And how real was the safety and comfort which surrounded him?

Everyone had fallen silent, thinking of the night beyond the brightly lit room, and what it held.

The other guests started to talk about going, but for all his own anxiety, Julius needed to stay. He had to talk to Titus alone.

The thought had crossed his mind that he'd offer to escort Calpurnia home, but he'd hesitated. He'd counted two litters outside, apart from the one Titus had sent for him, each with a complement of bodyguards, and one belonged to the married couple. The other had to be Portia's – had she brought Calpurnia with her? For all he knew, the girl, or both of them, might be staying the night with Titus.

His loneliness was getting the better of him.

'Titus,' Portia was saying, 'you must forgive me, but –'

Titus raised a hand, swung his legs off the couch. 'Of course. Too late to sit about now anyway.' Usually Titus' Reader, a slave who cost even more than his chef, would appear about now and recite. Virgil, if the mood was serious; Ovid, if it was lighter; but it was now close to the twelfth hour.

'Geta,' said Titus. 'Organise the litters. I'll send you home in one of mine, Calpurnia.'

Julius was relieved. He joined his host at the door, tried to catch Calpurnia's eye as she left, failed, and was disappointed.

He watched as the litter-bearers roused themselves and marched off with their burdens into the night, the red-cloaked bodyguards, six to each litter, flanking them.

'It's been a long day,' said Titus. 'I'll call your litter.'

'I'll stay a few minutes.'

'Good! You owe me your company. Not everyone gets to meet Petrus. He doesn't want too many people to know what he looks like.'

Julius nodded. Nothing had come of his surveillance of

Titus and he had called the operation off. But there were still things he needed to know. They made their way back through the atrium, but as the night was soft and warm, instead of returning to the dining room, they walked through to the garden beyond, and sat at a low table.

'How about a couple of games of Twelve Lines? I've got a good board here. Take your mind off –'

'There's nothing I'd like less,' Julius said.

They sat in silence. Geta brought them wine.

'You can go now,' Titus told him. 'Just tell the night staff where we are.'

The crickets had fallen silent; the only sound was the plashing of the fountain in the atrium.

'You don't think we are responsible, do you?'

'No.'

Titus drank, stretched his limbs. 'I'm leaving for the country tomorrow. It's time to shut the farms down after the harvest, and I've been here too long. Sabina's missing me, and so are the children.'

'When are you leaving?'

'Dawn.' Titus looked at him. 'Is there something you want to ask me?'

'Who is she?'

'Portia?'

'Calpurnia.'

Did Titus look troubled? No, it was dark, the torches cast shadows, it was hard to read his expression.

'Calpurnia's a nice girl, but if you've decided you've had enough of your own company, why not think Portia? She's lovely, intelligent, and she's divorced. No children; and she's inherited a big estate near Capua.'

'Tell me about Calpurnia.'

'There's not much I can say. She's a neighbour. From Dacia originally, I believe. Portia introduced her to us. Charming. Shy.' He paused. 'In any case, I've just told you to go after Portia, if you go after anyone.' Titus gave him the ghost of a smile. 'You look all-in. Stay the night! You can leave when I do.'

Julius shook his head. 'Work to do. By the gods, I shouldn't be thinking of anything else.'

'She must have made an impression. But for the sake of heaven, you will nail these people – whoever they are?'

'I wish I could be sure.'

'Why aren't you?'

'Most of the victims owed Nero money.' Julius paused. 'Does he owe you money?'

'Nothing I'm not prepared to write off,' said Titus.

'Are you leaving because you're afraid?'

'No.'

'Do you think it's the work of a demon? A dark god?'

'We've both seen enough to know that the only thing we need fear is other people,' Titus said.

'Do you *believe* in demons?'

'I believe people can be demons.'

'Do you know what is meant by the numbers 666?'

Titus looked blank, but not quickly enough. 'Where did you get that from?'

'But do you know?'

'I have no idea.'

Julius drained his cup. 'I must go.'

'Send me word soon.' They gave each other an embrace.

'Before you go,' Titus said, leading the way back to the door. 'Come into the study.'

It was a small, dark room, containing a desk and chair and little else, though the walls were crowded with scrolls – Titus' library. Titus went over to the desk, produced a slip of wax, took a stylus, and wrote a couple of lines.

He handed Julius the slip. 'Her address.'

'No. I won't take it. You were right.'

'I know what I'm doing. Now let me get your litter.' Titus clapped his hands.

Once home, in his solitary apartment, Julius felt the peril of the night close in on him once more, and nothing in his rational soul could defend him from his own fear.

17

Publius Sergius Rufus was a happy man. Around him, the new Rome was rising triumphantly.

To Sergius' regret, some of the alleyways of wooden tenements still existed, for the poor had to live somewhere; but, increasingly, massive edifices of pale stone rose like decorated cakes from the shanty towns of the workers' billets, and these were laid out along broad, confident boulevards lined with olive and pine trees. The artisans were busy sculpting and placing a host of new statues, most of which commemorated the deeds of Nero and his henchmen. The empire spiralled into debt, but the gaudy new capital might have been at the centre of a booming economy, and the brightly painted sculptures and façades seemed to mock any possibility of ruin. It was like make-up, inch-thick on the face of a sick old woman.

Sergius' salvage business had thriven since the Fire. The pieces in his warehouse near the Circus of Caligula and Nero, carefully catalogued and wrapped on their shelves, even if they were just fragments of columns and statues, rescued frescoes or lumps of buckled bronze, were being recycled either as souvenirs or as material for the rebuilding. Architects and developers' assistants came and went in so steady a stream that his only worry was that he could collect stuff faster than he could sell it. But he hadn't borrowed much, his only serious debtor was the emperor himself, and that stood him in good stead. The debt was investment – he'd never see the money again.

What he hated most was being obliged to leave a large slice of his cake to the emperor in his will. Still, thought Sergius, this emperor couldn't last forever. Patience with him was running out.

But people who owed Sergius money couldn't expect mercy. During a squeeze like the present one Sergius charged ten per cent compound and it amused him to come down hard on the truly desperate and vulnerable. A deprived childhood had hardened in him a deep loathing of poverty and weakness. So his not-strictly-business victims included an elderly couple on their uppers after their investments had gone west, and a young widow who owed him rent, with four young children. The one he'd been to see that afternoon. Marina.

He thought about the events of the last few hours. His

litter-men had let him down at the house; he'd clambered out, sweating under his own weight, and short of breath even at the slight effort of descending. He knew he should do something about his body. Livia was always on at him about it, fat shrew that she was. She should lose weight, the old bitch. Thank Priapus she wouldn't be back from Capua for another week.

Now, he snapped his fingers at his wine-slave and took a deep draught from the proffered bottle, dug from its ice-sack. Melting fast despite the mild autumn weather, thought Sergius. Fucking expensive, ice. He was working himself, enjoyably, into a rage.

He'd had fun that afternoon.

He took four slaves with him, used to this kind of work; but he dealt with the woman personally. One of his men hammered on the door with an iron cudgel. Then they stood back to let him pass. He hadn't seriously expected to be paid, but the woman was attractive, and her two older daughters no less so. He was there to teach them a lesson. How they'd screamed. Scratched him too. Nice. But one of the daughters got wet, so she enjoyed herself, he guessed. Maybe she was into that kind of thing. He'd make a note for next time.

Back home, fresh from his bath, with the blood and dust washed off, he watched night fall. He was tired.

'I'm going to rest,' he told his chamber-slave. 'Don't disturb me. I'll call when I want to eat.'

The man bowed his way out of the room. Sergius hadn't moved house far from his miserable roots, way out on the Viminal, but he'd built himself a place there which was part-mansion, part-fortress. He'd made plenty of enemies, but here he felt safe. Apart from his body-slaves, he'd got three big mastiffs. He let them loose in the grounds every night. They'd proved their worth already.

Sergius awoke from a dream: in it, he'd been a kid again, hawking kindling round the back doors of the big houses.

It was dark.

He got up, put on a linen robe, and made his way into the atrium beyond it. The lamps were burning as usual — only a few, Sergius was careful with his money — but no one was about.

That wasn't right. For a moment he listened. Then he called for his chamber-slave. There was no answer. In a light breeze, the flickering flames of the lamps cast odd shadows on the walls. He wanted to move out into the centre of the atrium, where the pool was, but something made him hug the walls.

It was dark in the centre of the atrium. There was no sound, so it was too late for the cicadas. Only the rustling of leaves in the breeze. There was somebody out there. But where were the dogs?

His throat was dry. He swallowed to moisten it. He called out again, his voice less confident now.

The door of one of the bedrooms opposite opened. Livia's room. In the rectangle of bright yellow light it revealed, a woman stood silhouetted. Had Livia come back unexpectedly? It'd be just like her. But it wasn't Livia. It couldn't be.

Sergius peered across the atrium, trying to make out more detail but reluctant to move forward. He didn't like mysteries. Then, slowly, the woman crossed the open space between them. A young woman, wearing a veil which partially obscured her face, but not her athletic, tanned shoulders.

'Who are you?' he said, surprised at how weak his voice was. He should call Varro again; Varro would get the dogs.

'I am Marina's sister.' The voice was a blade of ice on his spine. 'You invited me here.'

He couldn't remember. 'Come to pay me, have you?'

'Yes.'

The woman looked nothing like Marina. Sergius passed over this when he noticed that another girl had appeared in the doorway opposite.

He shook off his initial fear. Maybe his luck was in. If the girls did as they were told, he'd waive a month of Marina's rent. And if there were any male intruders here with noble ideas, Sergius' boys would sort them out. One yell from him would bring them in. He was on home ground. But he should call Varro. What had happened to his chamber-slave?

128

'What's your name?' he asked, placing a meaty hand on the woman's naked shoulder. And, getting his courage back, stroking it. Only a woman, after all. Nice, copper-gold skin, fine blonde hair, hardly visible, skimming it. Strange eyes, so pale a blue, like the shell of a duck's egg.

'Justina,' she said. She motioned behind her towards the doorway, where the other figure hovered. 'And that is my other sister, Apuleia. She is shy. Forgive her.'

Apuleia came forward timidly into enough light to show Sergius that she was a delightful, slim-hipped girl, with small, full breasts. Her delicate, oval face and slender, columnar neck were framed by a shower of dark-gold hair.

She was naked.

Apuleia's eyes were dark, an iris of such a deep green that it might as well have been black. Sergius looked into them, tried to stare them down, but he had already entered a dream.

Justina took his arm – gently, caressingly – and led him through the atrium and into the room. Apuleia stood aside to let them pass, then followed.

Justina's hand on his arm was cool, reassuring.

He felt like a little boy again.

The room seemed bigger than Sergius knew it to be. And it was dimly lit – some of the lamps must have gone out. He didn't recognise the murals on the walls, which depicted a number of shadowy people in fancy-dress. There had to be a trick of the light, for they seemed to move.

He felt humble, no longer the rich bully, but the beaten-up kid forced to do the rounds selling firewood. He looked back through the open door at his atrium, but was it *his* atrium? He saw a high-walled, colonnaded garden, in which sombre plants grew to a great height, and along whose pathways flightless birds the size of dwarves stalked restlessly.

Apuleia closed the door, and Justina led him to the bed, where she began to caress him. Her head rested against his chest, but when she looked up, her eyes seemed to suck his being into them, and if the exquisite pleasure she was giving his nether parts hadn't been so great, he might have been frightened. As it was, though he knew he was awake, he felt as if he had passed back into the dream again.

The bed, whose frame was of gilded wood, was big enough for three or four, and the sensual pleasure of the soft mattress which engulfed him was like nothing he had ever experienced before. When Justina drew close and brought her lips to his, her mouth and tongue tasted like the delicious grapes of Lesbos. He caught the scent of honey and roses, and his head swam.

He raised his head from the cushions which, though soft and voluptuous, threatened to suffocate him, to see Apuleia cross the room to join her sister on the bed.

Soon he found himself transported to an Olympus of ecstasy, as Justina's tongue penetrated, gently licking and caressing, his ear, and Apuleia took his penis into her mouth, rolling her tongue voluptuously round it. *Her tongue was as rough as a cat's.* He couldn't cry out. He had never felt such pleasure. At last Apuleia released him from her mouth, and mounted him, as Justina greedily seemed to devour his ear.

When the pleasure turned to pain, he could not at first distinguish which was which. The tongue in his ear suddenly thrust down it with the force of a bony needle, snaking past his brain, and down through his throat beneath, while his attempts to struggle free were frustrated by the hard grip of Apuleia's thighs. What was left of his consciousness was screaming. And the hideous sudden *weight* of the woman on top of him, who held him so hard between her thighs that her vagina might as well have been a beak, and the stench – no longer honey and roses, but rotten meat and stale urine – of the scaly creatures clawing his body as they sucked his life out through his ear and through his penis, were the last sensations left to him.

18

Julius faced the fact that he would make no progress without another victim. Now, gazing down on the mangled remains of Publius Sergius, he had his wish. It was three days since the last attacks. Was that the time it took the beasts to become hungry? They had to be *real*, he told himself repeatedly. They had to be physical beings, who'd conform to some pattern, who'd make a mistake, leave a clue. Something.

Calpurnia hadn't left his thoughts before now. He had walked past her door twice, a letter ready for delivery tucked into his belt, only to turn away. At his age, he thought, what a damned fool. But on his third visit he'd delivered his scroll, which contained the blandest invitation to dine he could concoct.

He'd had no reply.

And this – love, of all fucking things – was something he could have done without. He'd be lucky to last another week in his job if he didn't come up with something now. And the mystery was as deep as ever.

She was nowhere in his mind at this moment, as he looked at the purple, scum-encrusted, bloated wreck of an animal – possibly a dog – they'd found in the courtyard of the house out on the Viminal. The principal victim, a member of the emperor's outer entourage, lay in a modest bedroom off the atrium. The whole body was sucked dry, legs, arms and torso; even the bones had had the marrow pumped out of them. Julius was confronted by what looked like a badly-tanned cowskin. Only the head was recognisably a head, but the eyes had been eaten.

There was a dry, shrivelled hole where the man's genitalia had been.

Scattered about the house and grounds lay the corpses of what looked like other dogs, and half-a-dozen other men, slaves or freedmen by the look of their dress, dismembered, their eyes gone, noses and ears half-torn, balls and nipples (by the look of things) bitten or chewed off, the filth of their fear evident in the flux of their bodies. He kept a cloth pressed close to his nose, but still his stomach lurched.

What in Hades to do now? This wasn't the work of humans. It wasn't possible.

And yet Julius had seen the spectacles served up in the Arena. *Anything* was possible. Anything was within the scope of human depravity. There were no demons. There was no need of any supernatural horror: Mankind provided enough.

And yet . . .

19

The imperial summons came the day after III Cohort had
reported their discovery of Sergius' corpse. Julius made his
way to Nero's temporary quarters, where he lived while
his new palace rose massively from the ruined town centre,
a quarter-of-a-mile east of the Forum.

He felt less fear than he might have if he hadn't begun
to see a thread linking the killings.

It wasn't a watertight idea, but it was good enough to
run with, and he had to have something to throw to Nero.

He was met in the antechamber by Petronius Arbiter,
which surprised him, since he'd scarcely ever seen the man
conscious between dawn and dusk. Petronius was grey-faced
and ill. In daylight, even with make-up on, his skin looked
like a plucked quail's.

'He's not in a good mood,' warned Petronius. 'Hasn't

been for days. And he's giving a concert tonight – he's ordered five hundred *Augustiniani* to be there. I'm supposed to be directing him.'

That explains why you're up in daylight, thought Julius, looking at the man and wondering at his preoccupations, compared with his own.

The god-on-earth was picking at food when Julius arrived. An early lunch and a light one. Nero was wearing a blonde wing and a lilac *chiton*. He'd had his body hair shaved, and he glistened from his late-morning oiling. His eyes looked shifty and tired, but he went into his usual act.

'Quintus Julius. I've forgotten your *cognomen*. No!' squealed the emperor. '*Don't* tell me! I'll get it – it's the same as that handsome Syrian, that big bloke with the moustache – Wait! – Aha! Marcus? No – Marcellus! Am I right?'

'How gracious of you to remember.'

'Of course I remember,' replied the emperor beadily. 'I remember very well. You are the policeman who is failing to nail the scum who are making mincemeat of my friends!'

Julius looked round the room. This didn't look like a formal interview. Poppaea lounged on one of the other dining couches, swallowing oysters. Petronius, after bringing Julius in, went to a third couch but sat upright on it, and sipped water, occasionally running a hand over his brow. The only other guest was Nero's old tutor and adviser, Lucius Annaeus Seneca. Seneca sat in a chair beside an untouched bowl of fruit. The gaunt old man didn't look at him, and Julius was surprised to see him there at all. His relations with Nero had been strained over the past few years, but the emperor still called on him *in extremis*. What could have brought him back to Rome from the Campania now? Someone else was conspicuous by his absence. Tigellinus. Unusual, Julius thought. Tigellinus liked to be in at these meetings.

'I'd expected better of you, my dear,' Nero said, giving Julius a treacly smile.

'I have found a link between the killings, Lord.'

'What you mean is that I owed the buggers money,' said Nero drily, biting the tip off a gherkin and belching lightly. 'But I'm told they were all enemies of the Christians. Or had you forgotten that?'

For Titus' sake, Julius didn't want to involve the Christians in the emperor's plans any further.

'This isn't the work of the Christians. They are strange, they have an extremist element within their sect which we must extirpate, but they haven't the organisation or power to mount a campaign of killing like this.'

Nero shrugged. 'That sounds reasonable. And surely we've whipped those bastards into submission by now. Not that I've the slightest intention of lessening the pressure on them.' He looked at Julius. 'But effectively, you have *nothing* to report.'

'Lord, we are up against forces which –'

'I've got to have something to show the Senate. But I am convinced you'll have exposed this menace and destroyed it by the end of this month, when I'll summon you again. If you don't have anything to show for yourself by then, may the gods help you.'

Julius bowed. What else could he do?

'For myself, I have absolute faith, but there are others who don't share it.'

You don't know what we're up against, thought Julius. But he saw the emperor was troubled. Hesitant.

'Follow me,' said Nero, rising and leading the way out of the room while motioning the other people – even his bodyguard – to remain behind.

'I didn't want to sound so threatening just now,' the emperor continued, his mood swinging again once they were alone and making their way down a short corridor. 'I'm working on a rather wicked role, and I needed to try something out on you. Got you going, I'll bet!' The emperor swung his hips a little, and giggled, but his act lacked conviction. Something was wrong. Something was really bothering him. He looked like a man – and Murcellus' words came back to Julius – who'd lost something which he badly needed to find.

They arrived at a door which opened into a small, plain room, of a kind Julius would never have associated with the emperor. Its walls were whitewashed and undecorated. It was simply furnished: a plain table, two hard chairs, and a bookshelf crowded with scrolls. It gave onto a pleasant balcony almost as big as the room itself, festooned with a mass of nasturtiums. The sound of birdsong came from the gardens beyond.

'This is my retreat,' said Nero, closing the door behind them. 'From all of them. No one comes here but me.'

'I am honoured.'

'Oh be quiet,' said Nero, shutting him up with a wave of his hand. 'Do you know why I chose you for this job? Because you have almost as many enemies as I have. Because I know you're good at your job, but you're *too* good, just like me, and so there are always people waiting in the shadows to trip you up.' Nero paused, and for once the eyes showed something like candour. 'There are very few people I can trust,' he said. In the emperor's voice Julius thought he recognised that of the man who'd managed Rome, in the first years of his rule, fairly and justly, instead of the voice of the man he'd become: the dangerous playboy who'd had his stepbrother, his mother, and his first wife murdered just because they'd got in his way.

But the voice was worried. 'I said no one comes in here but me. Not quite true. But you're the only person apart from Seneca ever to have been here,' continued the emperor. He looked at Julius hard. He hadn't sat down, nor bidden Julius to do so. 'I can trust you?'

'Yes.'

'You will not betray me?'

'No.' Julius thought it was an odd question. He knew exactly what would happen to him if he did. Nero remained silent, brooding. Finally the emperor perched on the arm of one of the chairs, deep in thought. For a moment he looked younger than twenty-eight. If you hadn't known him, you might have thought he was vulnerable. When he spoke, it was slowly.

'Recently – a few weeks ago – I indulged in a little piece of acting. I wanted to shock some people . . . who have been useful to me . . . back into obedience.' Nero looked up and his eyes were frightened. 'I cursed them.' He paused. 'I am supposed to be a god, and I cursed them. I had every right to do so.'

Julius was silent. He would never have underestimated the emperor's intelligence, but the man Nero had become might well be deluded enough to believe in his own divinity.

'Of course I didn't mean actually to curse them,' Nero continued. 'It was just a bit of theatre. I needed to scare them, to keep them under my control. But they . . . must have believed in what I'd done.' But he paused again. 'Unless . . .'

Then there was a long silence. He didn't complete the sentence. Maybe the *idea* of an imperial curse was terrifying enough, Julius thought. He said: 'Are they under your control now?'

'They *have* to be,' said Nero, dully, standing. Then he

added: 'Can I count on you? If . . . matters . . . get out of hand . . . can I count on *you*, at least?'

'May I know their identity?'

But this brought down a curtain. 'They have nothing to do with your enquiry,' said Nero, briskly, his usual self. He was like a man waking from a bad dream he'd believed to be real.

Julius gathered his courage. 'But they may have. Who are they?'

Nero glared. 'If I need to tell you, I will.' He looked round the room as if seeing it for the first time. 'I must return to my guests. I have much to do before nightfall.' He was in a hurry suddenly, bustling to the door, opening it and already scuttling back down the corridor. But then he stopped and turned and looked like a kid. 'Don't disappoint me!'

The voice had less of an order in its tone then, than an appeal.

But Nero hadn't told the policeman everything. Hadn't confided his worst fears – fears which he scarcely dared admit to himself.

He hoped it would never be necessary to do so.

20

Minerva, guide me, thought Julius as he left. There *must* be a lead before there are more deaths. But his mind and his instinct now insisted, against all reason, that he wasn't dealing with *people* at all.

He went home, sending his most-trusted house-slave with orders to tell Mercurius he wouldn't be back that day. Mercurius could make of that what he liked; Julius knew that his own boss, the head of VIII Cohort, was now the least of his worries, since he would be taking orders directly from the palace too. His hope was pinned on Nero's odd dependence on him, if that could be trusted. And Murcellus had been right: the emperor was worried.

It was evening. A gentle warmth filled the city. His flat, even though the windows were open to the north wind, was hot and uncomfortable. How much longer could he afford even the slaves he had? This was the case which would make him or break him. At this moment, the second possibility seemed the stronger. He was living well beyond his means here. He was still hanging on to the big apartment he'd shared with his wife. Stupid. And he had too many slaves for a born-again bachelor. If he hadn't been so scared of losing standing, he'd have cut his staff down to two. At least the chariot, with its driver and horses, came with the job.

He toyed with the idea of running away. He could get as far as Gaul. He still had friends in the army there. Could he lose himself in the north? Start a new life? Wash his hands of all this? And what had Rome to offer him? A hated regime, and a political landscape as fragile as the city of Pompeii had physically, lying under the menace of Vesuvius.

But what would he do then? Could he get enough of his money out to start afresh? And even if he could, what then? Start a farm? What did he know about farming? And how could he manage such a project alone?

He put the notion back. We all struggle against our lives, he thought, when they aren't going well; but we're stuck with them, and choices made years ago still bind us, years into the future.

On his terrace, he poured himself a beaker of Falernian from the decanter that stood on a table, and mixed it with a little water – he didn't want to drink but he needed a boost. He was finishing it when his body-slave came in to announce that he had a visitor.

'Who is it, Dio?'

'A woman, sir.'

'A woman?'

Dio spread his hands. 'She's young. Kind of dark-golden hair, green eyes. You know – classy.'

'Did she say anything?'

'She says she knows you. Didn't say why she's here.' Dio, a young Neapolitan, kept his face expressionless.

Julius felt his stomach tighten.

'Show her into the study – no, the living-room. Is it tidy? I'll be there right away, tell her. And organise some decent wine and some cakes. *Chilled* wine, for the sake of Silenus – this stuff's warm. And keep your opinions to yourself.'

'Sir.' The slave, the most expensive he owned, but also the one he'd least like to let go, left. Julius, needing a moment to think, waited, drank what was left in his beaker, and followed.

She had her back to him, looking out of the window onto the jumble of red rooftops and dark green pine trees which stretched down to the yellow Tiber below. Julius' home was a flat he couldn't afford in a block he couldn't afford, but as long as he had some savings and a handful of investments and the prospects, however remote, of hanging on to his job, he wouldn't give up this symbol of his

144

achievement. It was true that the paintwork wasn't as fresh as it might have been, and that some of the furniture was worn, but people – women especially – might charitably put that down to his bachelorhood. Some of his slaves might not like it, but they wouldn't complain as long as their food and drink took precedence over redecoration, and as long as their lodgings at the back of the block were secure. And they all knew that Julius would give them their freedom after ten years' service. He was a fair master. He hardly ever beat them, and had never killed or raped any of them.

He knew who she was immediately, without needing to see her face, but instead of greeting her by name he announced his presence and asked formally what he could do for her.

Then she turned and looked at him and Julius needed all the will-power in the world not to fall under her spell then and there. The impression she had made on him at Titus' supper-party wasn't just confirmed; it was reinforced, and who could withstand the hail of arrows from the army of Cupids which assailed him?

She looked confused. He hoped nothing showed on his face.

'I got your letter. I know I should have replied to it, but I thought I would come in person. I am lazy about letters.'

. . . And you wouldn't want me to have anything as compromising as a letter in my hands before you knew me better, Julius thought. A woman's position could be delicate,

145

and she knew nothing of him. She would, however, recognise a bachelor household when she saw one.

'I am honoured by your visit. I am sorry I'm not better prepared for it.' But he clapped his hands and right on cue Dio appeared with a junior slave who carried a tray bearing a silver-gilt decanter and two of Julius' best glasses; and there was water, ice, and a basket of fresh cinnamon-and-honey cakes. Dio was a miracle-worker. He'd give him a bonus.

The junior placed the tray carefully on a low mahogany table inlaid with ivory which an African businessman had presented to Julius in exchange for turning a blind eye to some dubious bills of lading a few years before, and which his ex-wife had never liked.

'You don't look *un*prepared,' said Calpurnia, as the junior withdrew and Dio fussed over the wine. 'But I apologise. I should have sent someone to announce me.'

'There is nothing to apologise for.'

'I might have come at a bad moment.'

But he was sure Calpurnia would have *chosen* her moment. Had she had the place watched? He put that thought aside, and tried to enjoy the company he had longed for.

Dio proffered a chair, wine, cakes, saw that his master was similarly seated and served, and then stood back.

The room had a large window. It was light and airy, simply decorated with one or two sculptures, campaign memorabilia from Julius' soldiering days, and a couple of large palms in pots which flanked the wide couch that lay along the wall opposite the window.

'You may go, Dio,' Julius said.

Dio bowed reluctantly and left, neglecting to close the door behind him.

They drank the first glass of wine in the kind of silence that always hangs over a couple who know why they're together, and skirt the point.

'I'd more or less given up,' Julius finally said, having wondered ludicrously at first whether he shouldn't somehow pretend that this was a business visit. But his letter, though polite, had had an un-businesslike content. The fact that she'd answered it by arriving in person caught him completely off-guard.

But she wasn't a Roman. Maybe they did things differently where she came from. He looked at her again, wondering. She did not lower her eyes. He would ask her. Stupid not to. She was obviously integrated; her Latin was perfect, with just a trace of an attractive but unidentifiable accent.

'I meant to ask you when we first met,' he said. 'Where are you from? Originally, that is.' To his regret, he stumbled over the words. He was being a policeman again. *Where are you from?*

This was no time to be falling for a woman anyway.

'Gaul. Lutetia.'

'Nice city. I was there once.'

'When?' She seemed nervous. He picked that up like a dog picks up a scent. Titus had thought she was from Dacia.

'When I was a soldier.'

'You were in the army?'

'Once upon a time.' Wasn't that obvious from the crap decorating the room?

He'd answered lamely. Now she knew he'd been with the occupation forces. Even after so long, generations, there were plenty of Gauls who begrudged the presence of the Romans in their land. He looked round the room. It looked shabby. Had she noticed? He shrugged it off. What did it matter? This was a stupid time to be giving in to his loneliness anyway. But he needed the comfort of pleasant company more than he had for a long time. And there was something about this girl which drew him to her with the force that can pull iron to iron.

'How long ago?'

'Ten years.'

'But you remember the city well?'

'I wasn't there for more than a month, so – not really, no.'

'Ah.' She relaxed, settled back in her chair. Her pale grey dress moved over her body, caressing it as she moved.

In the silence that followed he poured more wine, awkwardly offered the cakes. She anticipated his next question. 'I was passing. I'd been to see a friend. I didn't think you'd be here. I was going to leave a note.'

'Personally? Then I am fortunate.'

148

She shifted in her seat again. 'I should have replied to your letter.' She paused. 'I was surprised to get it.'

'I thought it would be good to meet again,' he said lamely.

'I agree. Otherwise, I wouldn't be here.' She looked at him directly, and the hopeful lover elbowed the policeman aside.

'I am glad. Will you accept the offer in my letter and dine with me? I know a restaurant which I think you'd like; or my cook isn't bad. He's a fellow-countryman. From Burdigala.'

Calpurnia frowned slightly, but said, 'I would be happy to be your guest here.'

'It won't be quite like it was at Titus' house.'

She smiled. 'I'm sure it will be as good.' She looked at him. 'How long have you known Titus?'

He hesitated fractionally before replying. 'A long time.'

'Since before he became a Christian?'

'You knew he was a Christian?'

'He makes no secret of it.'

'True.'

'Isn't it difficult for someone like you to have a Christian friend?'

'Someone like me?'

'I'm sorry. Aren't you an official of some sort?'

'Yes, but being a Christian isn't illegal.'

'Of course not.' She let her words hang in the air.

'Only criminals have been punished.' Julius hated himself for sounding apologetic.

'Of course.' She paused. 'I am glad to meet a friend of Titus. Titus has been a very good friend to me.'

'How did you meet?'

'We are neighbours.'

'How long have you been in Rome?'

'Three years.'

'And you've known him all that time?'

'Only since I moved to the apartment I have now.'

'Ah.'

'Isn't that long enough to meet with your approval?'

'I am sorry.'

'Perhaps your job makes you suspicious.'

Julius sensed she was uneasy. He was uneasy himself. He hesitated to offer more wine. He didn't want any more himself, and he'd left his second glass virtually untouched. 'No reason why it should,' he said, smiling. 'But I wish you'd tell me more about yourself.'

'I'd rather hear about you.'

He spread his hands. 'I was born here. I went into the army and became an officer, a *praefectus alae*, if that means anything to you. Travelled. Got wounded in action in Mauretania, came home, recovered, more or less, my left foot will never be the same again, went into the civil service, *quaestor* then *praetor*, my father was able to pull a few strings, here I am.' He was talking too much.

'Married?'

'I was.' He paused. 'I think it's your turn.'

She shrugged. 'Nothing to tell.'

'You can't have come here from nowhere.'

'I have some private means.'

'All right,' said Julius. 'I won't pry.' But questions filled his head. Above all, what accident had lamed her? The limp was slight, but he could see how her left foot dragged. Like his own still did, occasionally.

She moved in her chair again, reaching for her glass. He tried not to watch too obviously as her robe once more moved over her body. He felt miserably dressed in his work tunic, and they fell silent again, but both of them were aware of the tension in the air. He wondered if she'd talked to Titus about him.

'I am sorry,' she said at last. 'I know you're an official. I'll have to take what *kind* of official on trust. The fact that you're Titus' friend is enough for me. And I can't let this go any further without telling you one thing.'

She looked at him and he looked in turn into her dark-green eyes. She crossed the room and closed the door, then turned to him.

'I am . . . involved in the Christian movement. If that compromises you in any way I'll go now.' She was suddenly on the verge of tears. 'I couldn't put that in a letter. But you seem a good man. I have to trust my instinct. But if I must go, tell me to go, and promise on your honour as a Roman not to betray me.'

Julius didn't hesitate. 'I have not betrayed Titus.'

'He is known. He is rich. He is protected.'

Julius was silent.

'I have done nothing against Rome,' she said.

'But Titus . . .' Julius had to choose his words carefully '. . . has influenced you?'

'No.'

Julius found his heart taking a decision before his mind could. 'Titus is a friend. He has done no wrong. He has tried to convert me and failed; but that does not mean that I do not respect him, or his belief.'

As soon as the words were out of his mouth, Julius realised what a fool he'd been, but somehow he didn't mind. And then they were standing, and his arms were round her, and hers round him, and their lips sought each others'.

And they heard a knock at the door, and parted quickly, guilty as teenagers.

'Yes?' said Julius, trying to control his hammering heart.

Dio came in hastily. 'Your colleague –' he announced, but he was pushed aside by Mercurius, looking far less than his usual immaculate self.

'Something's happened,' he said. 'Something bad.'

'Tell me.'

'The grave pits – the *puticuli* where they buried the girl –'

'Yes?'

'Something's broken the seal, torn the stones away,' Mercurius swallowed hard. 'There are bodies scattered all round the entrance – it's as if whatever – whoever – did it was looking for something in particular.'

Julius felt the cold rise within him.

'There's no way of knowing if anything's been taken.'

'Or anyone?'

Mercurius was silent. The pits were designed to hold a good thousand bodies each. 'Only the freshest bodies were disturbed,' he said at last.

Coming to himself, Julius looked round in a panic for Calpurnia. She shouldn't be hearing this.

But she had gone.

21

This started only weeks ago, but now it seems as if we have been caught in a web forever.

It already feels like an eternity since the curse was placed on us. The changes have affected the way I think, and my memory. Writing the events down will help me keep my sanity, I pray; help me remain the person I was before this horror fell upon us.

But I must be careful.

The others have gone now. It is safe. We have been talking about the curse. It has affected the others more than me, and I don't know why.

I have been eating animals. I cannot help it. *I must feed* – and the food I once ate, though I can still eat it, and so pass for normal – gives me, gives us all, no nourishment. It is as if we were not eating at all. It is part of the curse. But the others are already growing suspicious, so I was forced to choose a *human* victim to put them off the scent. If I have to do it again, I *must* follow the same path, and select someone who is evil by choice, and not, as I am becoming, by destiny.

But I pray I will not have to. This new life has made us all cunning – our survival depends on it. The night is our domain, and places we never visited before are growing familiar.

It wasn't hard to hunt Sexta. The others were busy elsewhere; but they wanted to be sure that I was obeying the curse as fully as they were. So I brought them a proof of the killing; and the ring on her finger, with her name engraved on it, convinced them.

So for the moment I am safe. Though what would they do to me? We have always been so close, and adversity has drawn us closer.

But I must still be careful.

We were not careful enough before, and that is what has brought this new life – if you can call it a life – on us. The Christians were more astute than we thought. Nero told us to seek out the troublemakers among them and our work increased after the Fire. Perhaps we tried too hard. Perhaps we thought we would bring our freedom nearer if we built up the number of people we delivered to the emperor. We became greedy, and our greed augmented his.

Greed destroys.

I didn't want to send people to the fires and the arena. *I told them*. I am sick of dealing death in order to save my life; but I have been weak too long, and now the choice is no longer mine, unless I can find a way to get my freedom back.

The Christians welcomed us at first. They thought we were slaves, and our disguises served us well. The Christians were eager for converts among the non-Romans in Rome, who have less to lose by joining them, and a lot to gain, since they are a tightly-knit group who look after each other – that is, until the danger we brought them fractured their ranks, and turned some of them to betraying their own people. We did our work well until one night came – perhaps its coming was inevitable.

We were at a secret gathering just south of the Aventine, near the Ostia Gate. It was coming to a close, and most of the members had already left when Petrus and Paulus arrived. It was night and there was no light except for what came from five torches on the walls, and a fire in the middle of the room.

You could see that Petrus was angry. Paulus was more controlled, but he stood at the door with two bodyguards. No one was to pass them.

The two men brought with them into the room a terrible sense of danger. Petrus didn't waste time. The faithful formed a circle round him, cowed even though he had not yet begun to speak. We kept ourselves to the back, in the shadows. We dreaded him.

'We have found the disease,' he announced. 'It is time to root it out.'

It was no good. His eyes found us. He spoke each of our names as if heavy weights were attached to them. The others moved away from us as if we had leprosy.

'You five have spilled our blood,' he continued. His voice was steady and scarcely raised at all, but the power behind it chilled us. 'You have served our enemies. You will do this no longer.'

22

There was a long silence in the room. I don't know how she found the courage but Pompeia managed to speak. She is the eldest and our leader. Perhaps she thought she could brazen it out.

'What have we done? We belong to your flock.'

'Don't pile more lies on those you have already told,' Petrus said, silencing her with his eyes more than with his voice. 'The time has come for you to pay.'

She – Pompeia of all people – flinched as if he had struck her with a lash.

'You have betrayed our people to the Romans. Because of you, many have died. Without your help, the Romans' persecution would never have succeeded. You have all but fractured our movement. If it were not for you, hundreds of us – perhaps a thousand – would still be alive. It was *your* work that drew even some of our own people down into the pit of Acheron, and led them to betray their fellows in a vain attempt to save themselves.'

'Petrus –' But Pompeia's voice was no longer so strong.

'Be silent.' He stared at each of us in turn, and pointed the long index finger of his left hand. The room had fallen so still that you could hear the fire crackling, you could hear the whisper of the torches as they burned.

'You have lived by blood – and you shall continue to do so,' Petrus continued. His voice was calm again, and he let his arm fall to his side. 'I wish it were in my power to make it otherwise, but that power can lie only with you. I came here to curse you, in my anger; but I see that I cannot do that either, because we are taught forgiveness and love, and however hard they may be to grant now, those are what I must offer you. I hope you find a way to peace; but until you do, I tell you that no Christian blood will feed you, ever again, once your victim has made his faith known to you. I do not condemn you to anything and I pray, we will all pray, that you seek a means of redemption within yourselves.'

I am not certain, but I think his eye fell on me for an instant then, as if he knew that I had steered my chariot away deliberately in the arena on that dreadful day. The day on which my poor cousin and secret lover died.

Paulus came forward and whispered something which I could not catch, but Petrus heard him and nodded, saying to him, 'That decision is one which another, greater than I, must take.'

There was a long silence. Then Petrus led the rest of his people out of the room, leaving us alone there. I am glad Titus, who has been kind to me, was not among them. But I dread that he will still find out what has happened. He has said nothing so far.

We looked at one another, not knowing what to think. I saw awe on the face of one of my sisters, anger on another's, and disdain on those of the remaining two.

Then, one by one, the torches on the walls guttered, and went out. Only the fire was left.

As we came to our senses, we felt another kind of fear – the cold dread of facing Nero's agents with the news that we had been discovered. We would be no good to him any more.

We knew the imperial summons would not be long in coming.

23

Nero was practising his lyre when we arrived, but we were ushered into the presence of the Emperor without being made to wait. He wore his hair long – it may have been a wig, it was golden – and he had bronzed his face with dye. I remember he was wearing a sapphire-blue tunic with a golden sash and cloak, golden sandals. He doesn't sing badly.

He stopped his song as we entered, and glared at us. We all thought that spelt the end. Then he dismissed his attendants, excepting his guards, Tigellinus, and one or two others close to him whose names I did not know, but whose faces I recognised from his entourage at the arena.

He smiled craftily.

'I know what has happened,' he said. We were scared,

but he continued: 'Don't worry. It couldn't have gone on forever and you have done good work. My little guard-dogs in the Secret Police have so much to go on now that they have no time to chase their whores at night!'

He giggled and we relaxed slightly; but none of us, not even Pompeia, dared ask whether we would be granted our freedom now. The emperor read our thoughts, for he said then, 'Of course you deserve your freedom, but you see you did make the teensiest of mistakes.' He paused, as he always does, for effect, and you could see him cocking his ear for applause at his great comic timing, but all he got was a look of nervous approbation from Tigellinus, who doesn't understand Nero, I think, in the way some of the others do. 'You were too good!' Nero giggled lightly again and even strummed a chord or two. I could see Pompeia's brow darken but she had the sense to rein in her rage.

'Just a few months more,' Nero continued, trying to be placatory, sensing the anger ranged against him. 'Then I'll let you go, my pretties.'

'Back to the arena?' Pompeia dared ask.

We all held our breath but Nero remained mild, even playful. 'No, never there. I'll send you home when you've discharged your debt to me. In the meantime' – and now his voice hardened – 'in the meantime, I have another job for you, one which you already know to perfection. It shouldn't be difficult for you to learn new techniques to suit altered circumstances.'

'What is it, Lord?'

'Oh,' said Nero idly, blowing on his nails as if trying to dry varnish. 'Killing.'

We hadn't been so close to the emperor for so long without having heard the rumours: who had abetted him, who'd lent him money, and which of them were now beginning to think Rome would be a better place without him. Only rumours, but all together they showed a Rome as volatile as Mount Vesuvius.

'No,' said Pompeia firmly. 'Not that. We have had our fill.'

The rest of us looked at her in surprise, but there was determination on all our faces. She had spoken our thought. Nero's own face darkened. 'You dare defy me?'

'We have done enough.'

'You must obey my commands, and willingly!'

'Never again!'

'I am a god!'

'You are a god we do not believe in.'

'Believe in me or not, you shall never leave my control!' The emperor's mood had changed as quickly as the weather on an April day. He drew himself up and thrust his mantle aside, freeing his arm. With his left hand he gripped Pompeia's wrist and pulled her to him so that their faces were almost touching. He spat in her face and threw her aside with such force that she fell. I could see fury flare in her eyes as her hand instinctively went for the dagger she was used to wearing at her side. It was as well for Nero that she was not wearing it then, for the fastest bodyguard could not have prevented her from killing him. Nero saw the movement and laughed callously. 'You have gone too far.'

'Then kill us.'

Nero seemed to have reached a final decision. A little smile came to his lips, and his eyes became dark, unreachable. 'Oh no. You are far too useful to me . . .' He raised both hands above his head and the room seemed to darken. His entourage shrank back. His voice thundered as he pronounced his curse:

'By the power I receive from my great father Jupiter, I condemn you to eternal life – but not life in heaven or hell. Life *here*. Food shall not sustain you, nor water quench your thirst. Only blood and entrails will feed you, and there shall be no escape from the hunger which henceforth shall gnaw you. Your debt shall never be cleared. You will live for as long as it pleases me in the desert of your agony, for you have committed a crime which robs you of any other right: you have questioned my will. But you are my creatures still.'

Later, alone with his thoughts, Nero was elated. He had put the fear of the gods into them. His performance had been perfection! He had almost believed it himself. But that was the sticking-point. When he had scripted the words of his curse he had taken great care, fuelled by anger and a desire to punish those who had let him down. He wanted to cow these creatures – these creatures who only lived by virtue of his own good nature – into total submission. But there was a fear in him too. He was a god. A god on earth. Up until now, he felt, he had never unleashed his true power. Now that he had tried to, would it be effective? Would he dare to use it? Or was he afraid of it? Was he afraid of what he might discover if he put it to the test?

Could he control it? Did he even really believe in it?

His mind weaved unsteadily, unused to coping with doubt and fear, but now he confronted both, and he did not know what to do.

Until his father Jupiter spoke to him, he thought, he would watch and wait. What he needed now was distraction. Revelry. The theatre. That was what he did best. That would distract him.

He summoned a body-servant. 'Send for Petronius,' he told him.

24

Much has happened since then. But it is ironic that within a day a man who had every reason to curse us stayed his hand; and another, whose evil we had served loyally, placed us in torment.

At first none of us believed in what Nero had done. His gods were not ours. How could they have power over us? And we had never taken seriously the absurd Roman conceit that a man, just because he was a king, should become a god himself.

I don't know if what has happened to us was the work of Nero or of some other dark power of evil into whose hands our own deeds had placed us. But the changes began after the attack, and the attack followed soon after our audience with the blood-soaked emperor.

At first – *nothing* happened. We were allowed to keep

our apartments, and, although we were sure we were under surveillance, we were left alone. Why the emperor has not acted on the new power he believes he has over us, I do not know. But I know what has happened to us. What god has visited this on us is a mystery. Nero? I do not believe he has this kind of power. Time will tell. But in the meantime, we must suffer, and bear, the cruel fate which has befallen us.

It happened on the night of the *Kalends* of the month which followed our fateful interview with the emperor.

We were walking home after sunset together, and we were close to the square where our paths separated. We had no desire to part, but that evening we did not know whether we were being watched or not, and the plans we were making for our escape had not yet reached fruition.

The streets were deserted, and although it was late, the heat still rose from the pavements. The alley we were in was narrow and dark, but we could see the torchlight in the square, only 100 paces away. The square looked comforting after the darkness, and we quickened our pace – because we suddenly sensed that something was approaching from the shadows we had left behind.

Then we heard the whirring – a brittle sound, like a trapped bird makes with its wings. We are trained to fight and kill, but our instincts were thrown into panic.

'Run!' cried Pompeia. But it was already too late. Seconds later, we were caught in a swarm of creatures which we at first thought were locusts – but what would locusts be doing in the middle of a city? And it was no swarm, there were only a few of them, though they seemed to be everywhere, diving and plunging among us, and the noise they made filled my head. They tangled in our hair and when we flailed at them, we found our fingers were bleeding, bitten by their teeth. One landed on my arm, and my sisters' cries, and all the rest of the world, faded as I focused on it. It was neither insect nor bat. It was dark, scaly. It had four legs ending in talons which dug fiercely into me, sending pain howling through my arm, into my brain. Then it drew back its head and looked at me, and in what light there was I could see a pale face which filled me with more horror than I had thought possible before that instant. It was my *own face*, or a repulsive caricature of it, and the mouth as it opened twisted into a rictus of mockery as – and I can scarcely bear to describe it – there uncoiled from it a muscular grey tube which ended in a grey beak.

I felt a pain then beside which all the other pain and suffering of my life melted to nothing. I felt it stab and gnaw first my skin, then my flesh, as it shoved its vile tongue into my body, and thick mucus foamed around the point where it had entered. I looked round wildly and caught an impression, no more than that, of my sisters, dancing, as I must have been, in torment, unable to control their limbs, their mouths open to scream, but unable to utter a sound.

Then something took control of me beyond my own power and I did something none of my sisters did. Summoning up all my strength, I gripped the thing on my arm. Immediately it retracted its tube and beak and tried to rear its head back to bite me, at the same time releasing its claws in order to turn. Freed of it, I flung it away with all the force I could muster and heard it smash against a wall somewhere in the gloom. From where I heard it fall there came a thin, furious yell. It did not return to the attack, but flew off. I saw that I had wounded it, one of its legs hung limp.

My flesh was torn and bleeding, and bubbling pus ran down my arm, but I felt a kind of relief. I watched without being able to move or go to their aid as the other four creatures – I could see no more of them – burrowed savagely into my sisters' arms before wrenching away and rattling off into the night.

They were gone, leaving behind them darkness and silence.

We looked at each other, trembling. We made our way to the lights which burned in the empty square. We did not leave one another. We made our way to Pompeia's apartment and spent the rest of the night there.

It was a long time before we started to talk, and our talk was hesitant, terrified, disbelieving; and achieved nothing. We knew that we had been infected by some god or demon with the most terrible disease, and condemned to the most horrible punishment. I kept the fact of my small victory from my sisters. If they had noticed, they did not mention it.

Soon afterwards, we realised that however much we ate or drank, we were always hungry, always thirsty.

Then the Changes began.

25

We had parted company by that time, keeping our heads down, not knowing what to do, locked in a nightmare.

On the fifth night after the attack, I awoke from a troubled dream, thinking I heard my sisters' voices whispering in the room, but there was no sound.

I was so tired I could hardly think. The lack of sustenance, and the fear which obsessed all of us now, meant that sleep only came when I had gone beyond exhaustion, and then only in snatches.

It started with a burning sensation in my stomach and bowels, which I thought was a reaction to my fierce hunger and thirst. Then the burning spread through my body, from the inside to the skin, the roots of my hair. It was as if I had been staked out in the sun. But the worst was yet to come. I saw my skin begin to ripple and crawl, as if it had an independent life; it darkened and hardened, and as it did so, I felt my body change. I watched as my arms and legs twisted and writhed, as if they were no longer part of me, and turn into something other than arms and legs; but my hands and feet were the worst of all. I will not describe, I cannot describe, the change to my hands and feet. One talon – which had been my left foot – was maimed. Was that because of the harm I'd done to the creature I'd hurled away?

When the Changing was complete, I felt no more pain. I crouched on the bed, listening to a raucous breathing that seemed to come from somewhere else. I scuttled to the window, feeling an irritation as leathery wings on my back extracted themselves from their carapace. I crouched on the sill, watching. No one about. I was ravenously hungry still, but with this difference: I now knew it was in my power to satisfy my hunger.

All I could feel in that part of my mind which I could still control was that whatever I killed it would not be a fellow human being. And I nurtured that feeling against all the other instincts which now raged through me, as I would have tried to keep a dying fire alive, to keep out the cold and the night.

I flew out to the farmlands.

That was the first time.

$$\star \quad \star \quad \star$$

Later, my sisters and I gathered and spoke of it, fearfully. I cannot say what their sensations were, but I know that as the transformations recurred, and they came whenever hunger and thirst became unbearable, I began to feel unassailable, and it was then the practice started in earnest. It wasn't long before some of my sisters began to delight in our new power, despite the hideous pain the Changing caused us.

The sense of power was as exhilarating as it was – to me at least – horrible.

I stay close to myself. I whisper my own real name in the dark, I think that I will not kill unless hunger drives me to it, and then I will only kill domestic animals and only when I have to. If I must kill humans, let me be given the strength to choose my victims for myself. If I must kill humans, let them be people like Sexta, though my gorge rises at the thought when I am myself.

The Changing casts its shadow across our human life. We hunt separately – as I always try to – or in pairs. Some of us are developing our own taste: at the gymnasia or at the Baths, you can find men rich in muscle or fat; at banquets, we watch for who is eating what – for a man who eats chocolate dormice will taste very sweet three hours later when trapped and sucked dry – so the others tell me. Drunkards are no good – wine sours fast in the stomach.

I pretend to agree when they talk. Sexta I know tasted

foul – I think there was a lot of garlic in her diet. I know the others are wary of me, despite my killing Sexta. Justina especially has taken to our new task with a relish I would not have believed possible, and she is more beautiful than any of the rest of us. Her first big killing was in the brothel. Then the man she took with Apuleia. Now she roams free.

But are we free? I look at my sisters and I am sure something is controlling us – even our choice of victims – but what it is I do not know. I cannot believe in Nero's curse. Though where it comes from – the emperor or Petrus – I do not know. Petrus has the greater power, but would he be so unforgiving? But I feel – I know – that as we grow stronger, the control over us will weaken. And I am frightened of the sense of triumph which that idea brings.

We will be free to plunder as *we* choose.

Her hand could no longer hold the stylus she wrote with. The fingers twisted it away as they began to turn into claws.

26

It was a large, ornate hall, overly decorated in blue, silver and gold for a party. Night had fallen two hours ago.

Poppaea's feasts were well known by repute all over Rome, though they were never reported in the *Daily Acts* or anywhere else. The empress surveyed the scene, well pleased that her guests, having drunk enough wine to loosen up, were starting to enjoy themselves, really get into the swing of things. She lay back on the double couch she occupied on a daïs slightly raised in the centre of the room, and surrendered to the caresses of the young Nubian, a new slave, barely sixteen years old, at her side. The girl was already well skilled in the arts of love. She had left off caressing the empress' feet with her mouth and tongue, and now her hands were sliding craftily upwards, not hurrying, but becoming more urgent, more hungry, as they reached

Poppaea's marble thighs and began to edge towards the dark cleft of pleasure, teasing the shaved skin of her mistress' pubis but deliciously refraining from delving further – yet.

Poppaea arched her back and sighed, easing the silk robe which still clung to her, further from her smooth body. But she could not yet abandon herself entirely to the pleasure – and the escape – she sought.

She knew the emperor was worried. It was a long time since Poppaea had cared about her husband and longer still since she had sought – or expected – any kind of gratification from him. The man had caused her little more than pain ever since he had stolen her from her first husband, Otho, now a none-too-complacent member of the Court. But she was still doomed to be close to Nero, and she knew him well enough to see that he had begun to start at shadows, and that this time, for once, it wasn't an act.

She raised herself on one elbow, interrupting the progress of her partner, and looked around the room. There were one hundred women in the vast room, writhing against each other in couples or larger groups, on couches or on the silk cushions scattered over much of the floor. Tables along the walls and in the centre groaned with bowls of oysters and cold meats, chicken and fish; and oranges and grapes overflowed golden vessels in the shape of conches. Eunuchs imported from the east, their splendid bodies belying their lack of manhood, stood ready to serve Falernian to those taking a rest from their amours for long enough to slake their thirst. Fountains played, and on the gallery halfway up the west wall, female slaves strummed gentle music on lyres, the soft chords blending with the moans of pleasure and – sometimes – pain. The columns supporting the roof were draped with heavy golden ribbons held by plaster cherubs flying at head-height and brandishing enormous penises, which could be detached at will and used as dildoes. Some had been deprived of theirs already, and several detached members, oiled and discarded, lay messily flung on the cushions on the gilded couches.

The air was perfumed, but the incense was gradually overpowered by something headier – the odour of sex and women. The lights in the room, at a sign from Poppaea's mistress of ceremonies, who moved discreetly among the revellers, carefully orchestrating the party, were turned lower. Pale bodies turned golden in the warm lamplight. The atmosphere was thick and rich.

The Nubian girl, her mouth poised above her mistress' mound of Venus, looked up questioningly, actress enough to give her expression an air of supplication, daring to catch Poppaea's eye.

'May I, now, please?' she asked.

Smiling lazily, Poppaea nodded, and the girl's head went down slowly, her tongue thrusting, exploring, aided by fingers which penetrated further, inside the empress' body, and, tantalisingly, up and to the front, where the tongue could not reach but where the throne of pleasure lay.

Poppaea tried again to surrender, to be the slave of Venus

she so desired to become, but something still held her back, prevented her from diving into the soft warmth of total acquiescence to the goddess.

Still, it was delicious, and she fought off her dark, shapeless, thoughts. She stretched and curved as the irresistible pleasure – the kind of pleasure no man she'd known had ever been able to deliver – thrilled through her body, through every vein. The Nubian burrowed deeper and became more insistent, more urgent, her movements harder, even brutal, until Poppaea gasped and moaned and at last, shaking her body free, drew the girl to her and rubbed their enlaced bodies together, lubricated by their sweat, devouring her face, already drenched by Poppaea, with open-mouthed, ravenous kisses, licking her and biting her, squeezing her shoulders hard enough to bruise them, to make the girl cry out in pain.

Sated at last, the empress lay back, dismissing the girl and signalling an attendant to dry her and bring her wine. She lounged on her cushions, her mind clearer now, already planning whom she'd have next, perhaps two or three of them this time, and light-skinned, for a change, and she would have one of them held down, and cane her until the buttocks bled . . .

Poppaea's breath came faster. The dark thoughts had fled at last before the anticipation of such pleasure. She could have anything. Do anything. No one would ever blame her, censure her. She looked around the hall again, at the glistening golden bodies entwined and sliding and bucking in the deep glow of the oil-lamps, and listened greedily to the cries and whispers, the moans, the squeals of delight . . .

As her eye fell on a group lying near her, she saw that her daydream had been anticipated, and settled back to enjoy the impromptu cabaret.

Two naked girls, one surprisingly young and innocent-looking, the other long-limbed and lithe, but with the hard face of a gladiator, had grappled a third, a slim blonde whom Poppaea recognised as belonging to the household of Petronius, and forced her to lie supine across a couch. The innocent one held her wrists in a fierce grip, the other, her ankles. The victim whimpered with pleasure, turning her head from side to side until a third girl, olive-skinned and athletic, with startlingly pale-blue eyes and a mane of bronze hair, bent over and tied a scarf over her eyes. With another scarf the girl holding her wrists now tied them together hard, so that the material bit into the flesh, above the victim's head to the couch, then joined her companion and took one of the blonde's ankles. They spread her legs wide.

Poppaea watched the naked Amazon with a mixture of curiosity and desire. The girl was clad in nothing but a broad leather belt which she now unbuckled and, doubling it up and holding it in her right hand, began to stroke the victim's body with it. The whimpering continued but changed into a cry when the Amazon brought the belt up suddenly and smacked it hard across the girl's belly, once, twice, three times.

Poppaea knew all about pain, and started to enjoy herself, fondling herself and smiling, waiting impatiently for what would happen next. The Amazon stroked the victim's body with the belt, drawing it tenderly across the neat little breasts, then raised it and hit her victim again, between the legs, hard enough to raise an ugly red weal, as the blonde bucked and struggled to free herself. Poppaea gasped with pleasure – she would have to find out who these entertainers were – already women nearby were neglecting their own activities to watch.

The Amazon struck again, mercilessly, you could see her arm muscles strain, and this time, on the third blow, blood trickled from between the victim's legs. Had this gone too far? This was not the arena. But Poppaea noticed the pleasure on the faces of her guests as they drank in the spectacle, and raised a hand to stop her mistress of ceremonies from intervening. There was a new smell in the room. The smell of honey and roses.

Then, from the shadows at the far end of the hall, where the lamplight barely penetrated, where couples and groups who preferred darkness were gorging themselves on each other, came a shriek so mind-numbing as seemed not to be of this earth. The sound tore a fibre from Poppaea's brain and in the wake of it the gentle ripple of sounds made up of the lyre-playing and the oily noises of lovemaking gave way abruptly to silence. Only the plashing of the fountains could be heard for a minute. Then there were more screams, as women emerged from the dark far end of the hall, running, yelling, stumbling over and overturning the couches and the food-laden tables, pushing each other out of the way, trampling on each other in desperation as they sought the light.

For an instant, time stood still for Poppaea. She saw the eunuchs looking at each other uncertainly, their hands hovering above the hilts of their curved swords, and caught the scared eye of her mistress of ceremonies. The empress' throat was dry.

Then there was another sound, a dry, busy rustling which resolved itself into an ever-growing rattle, and from the far darkness something emerged, beating its wings, its bloated brown body covered with dark, coarse fur, its face a mockery of a woman's, with the eyes of a mad dog. The mouth dripped blood as the beast hovered just above the heads of the women fleeing before it, and from the claw of one of its four scaly legs dangled what looked at first sight like a large piece of wet cloth or leather, though from its extremities hung hands and feet, and, near the centre, what seemed to be a collapsed ball, except that it had eye-sockets, and the remains of a mouth, and from it hung wet, dark hair.

The mouth of the thing opened and from it emerged a scream as much of pain as of rage. And the sound was joined by another scream. Poppaea tore her eyes away from

181

the monster as beyond her and far away voices yelled for the guards to come, and the eunuchs drew their swords but remained rooted to the spot. Poppaea had turned her attention to the source of the second scream.

The blonde was still stretched across the couch not far away, but now her tormentors had fastened on her. The Amazon had her mouth firmly planted between the girl's legs, gripping her thighs and keeping them forced apart. Her two companions had shifted position, ripped the scarf from the girl's head, and now each had her mouth clamped to one of the blonde's eyes.

All three of the tormentors were concentrated on a task which at first wasn't clear to Poppaea, but when she recognised it her head swam, and for a moment her soul left her body.

They were *feeding*, and as they did, they changed. They were not women any more. As the girl's body was sucked empty, so did those of the creatures bloat, for the Amazon and her companions had changed into harpies – dark scales rapidly replaced smooth skin, hands biting into flesh became brown, horny talons, and the rapidly fattening bodies crouching over what was left of Petronius' concubine – now no more than a bloody, ivory-white sheet – bristled with the kind of coarse black hairs which cover the body of a blowfly.

And there was a stench. Urine and rotten meat.

All Poppaea remembered then was that someone, one of

the eunuchs, swept her up and carried her out of the hall, elbowing his way through a sea of women beyond panic, a sea which threatened to devour itself. Once they were outside, the doors were thrust shut and bolted behind them. They were thick cedarwood doors. You could scarcely hear the sounds the other side of them.

27

There might have been seventy corpses, but it was hard to tell how many exactly, as only two were intact – the others had been so thoroughly ripped apart that it would take a while to connect limbs to torsos and make a final count. Julius, looking at the mess in the unforgiving light of dawn, didn't envy the slaves who'd have to do that, though he'd have to be there himself to supervise.

He was not getting hardened to sights like this. What worried him now was the increased savagery of the attacks. Something which looked like frenzy.

Everything in the great hall was smashed, as if a vengeful fury had been unleashed, as if some god had lost control and lashed out in blind rage at everything his fists could reach. Marble tables had been overturned and shattered, broken bowls and buckled vessels of silver and gold lay strewn among the slimy wreckage of food, wine and bodies which littered the floor from edge to edge.

Nero had already given orders that not only the room, but the whole wing of the palace where it was, should be sealed. The few surviving eunuchs and attendants at the party had been rounded up by the Praetorian Guard and taken the gods knew where, but Julius didn't want to dwell on what their fate might be. The palace had given orders that total secrecy should blanket the event. Nothing was to get out, not even to the Senate, though Julius doubted if that would be successful. The Senate had a thousand ears at its disposal. The only hope for Nero was that those who found out would be too frightened to talk of it.

'What about the guests?' Mercurius asked, as the two men stood in the doorway, looking at the chaos and the carnage. The sight was too much for any simple reaction, like nausea, though both men looked livid, and both felt as if they carried anvils in their stomachs. Mercurius' athletic body was slack, and his face sagged.

'The survivors?'

'How many of them?'

'About thirty.' Julius' eyes were dead. 'I know that five of them have gone mad. Two have committed suicide.'

'What?'

'In the space of seven hours. But Nero doesn't have to worry about them. They won't blab.'

'And the others?'

'They'll be too scared to. If they ever get over what they went through. Nero's packed them off to Capri.'

'What about their families? I don't mean the families of the concubines. The principal guests.'

Poppaea's parties were always orchestrated to include a number of principal guests, usually twenty or so. The rest of the crowd was made up of concubines and sex-slaves, only accountable to their owners.

'They'll have found a way to shut the ordinary girls up – one way or another,' Julius said. 'And whoever owned them will have been compensated. Most of them belonged to the royal household anyway. As for Poppaea's friends, the ones they've sent to Capri, Tigellinus and Vatinius have been sending messengers to the families to tell them one of the attendants had the plague. They've sent the women to Capri to quarantine them – they'll get the best medical attention and the hope is that any epidemic will be nipped in the bud. That's the line they're putting in the *Daily Acts* as well.'

'And the families will buy that?'

'They'd better.'

'Will the women come back?'

Julius considered. 'In a couple of months, I guess. And none of them will talk. I doubt if any of them will ever leave their villas again.' He paused. 'I wonder who'd believe them if they *did* talk.'

'And the empress?'

'Nero's sent her to Antium. With a close guard. And doctors. Plenty of doctors.'

'Can we get out of here?'

Julius shrugged, turned, and Mercurius followed him back through the doors and across a white-columned ante-chamber to a broad window overlooking the building site which was Rome.

Neither man spoke. Each knew what the other was thinking.

'You knew about 666,' Julius said at last.

Mercurius lowered his eyes. 'Yes. I dropped the note in your office, didn't I?'

'You wanted to take over.'

Mercurius looked at him. 'I wanted to verify. And whom could I have gone to? To Tigellinus? To tell him the Christians see Nero as the incarnation of Satan?'

'Who is Satan?' said Julius.

'You know. The god the Christians see as the embodi-ment of evil.'

'There is good and evil in all gods.'

'Their view is simpler.' Mercurius paused. 'They believe in good and evil, unmixed and opposed. We know things are more complicated than that, with us as with the gods. All right. I thought I could overtake you. Get your job. But now –'

'Now you don't think you could handle this on your own.'

'If we fail to crack this, they will nail us to crosses.'

'If we fail to crack this, crucifixion would look like a merciful end, compared with what they'll do to us.'

'What do you think it is?' Mercurius said cautiously, after a long pause.

Julius was thinking of Petrus, of his talk with the old Christian in the farmhouse what seemed like a hundred years ago. 'I think it's Satan,' he said.

28

Their talk was interrupted by the arrival of a captain of the Praetorian Guard, with a summons for Julius to attend the emperor immediately.

He turned to Mercurius. 'You'll have to manage the clear-up here.'

Mercurius didn't look happy, but nodded.

'See what you can find,' Julius continued.

'We've been through everything.'

'We might have missed something.' But Julius didn't hold out much hope. There had to be another way of approaching this problem. It was just that he didn't know what it was. There were some problems in life which you just had to leave to time to sort out – but they were usually personal problems, not ones where you had other people breathing down your neck to fix. Time wasn't going to be his friend.

He wasn't looking forward to his meeting with Nero any more than Mercurius was looking forward to overseeing the mess he faced.

'I'll tell you if I do.'

'Make sure of it.' Perhaps they had cleared the air between them, Julius thought – and perhaps not. But he couldn't handle this on his own.

At the back of his mind throughout it all was something else, something which shouldn't be there, and which he fought against powerlessly.

Calpurnia's kiss. Sweet as honey, and her soft tongue seeking his had been so hungry. Hungrier, if possible, than his had been for hers.

Where was she now? What was she doing? Hard to believe that another life, which days earlier had meant nothing to him, now stood at the centre of his world. Anticipation and pain mingled with apprehension within him; but he felt stronger with them than without them.

Nero was waiting for him in the plain room he used as his retreat. The god-on-earth was dressed in a plain white tunic and white sandals, like a consul's. He wore no wig, and his brown curly hair, thinning already at the crown, looked better. Unadorned and without make-up, he looked better and healthier than Julius had ever seen him. His eyes were angry, which Julius had expected, but behind the anger was a hunted look.

Julius bowed as Nero dismissed the Praetorian captain with an irritable gesture.

'You know this entirely wrecked my evening,' said Nero. 'You should have seen my performance. I was magnificent. I hardly needed the *Augustiniani* at all. They loved me for myself. I was modest though – only did it in a small theatre – the seven-thousand seater near the Capitol. Do you know it? Wish I chosen a bigger one. I wish I'd done a public performance now.' He cast a glance at Julius to measure his reaction. 'Had them in the palm of my hand. Standing ovation. And it was really me that did it.' He paused, bitterly. 'And now this!'

Julius waited, only noting that the emperor was talking too much. That he was talking about himself came as no surprise.

'There were some pretty important people among the victims,' Nero went on. 'How am I supposed to account for it? They're talking about angry gods, about the fire, they're wondering if we'll be struck by another outbreak of plague! And whom do you think they're blaming? Behind my back of course . . .' He paused again, now scarcely bothering to hide his disquiet. 'One of the girls was a favourite concubine of Petronius! Cost him half a million sesterces, a virgin from the Dolomites! Perfect woman, by all accounts, seventeen years old.' The emperor had moved to the window, looking out through the tangle of nasturtiums across the city, but now he turned to face the policeman and spat at him, 'Fuck it, Julius Marcellus, what are we going to *do*?'

'My first concern is for the empress,' Julius began.

'Fuck her!' yelled Nero. 'If she hadn't decided to throw one of her disgusting little orgies this wouldn't have happened. How did those creatures get past security? What are we dealing with?' There was real fear in his eyes now.

'You have removed all the survivors.'

'I have. And fast!'

'I wish you might have considered allowing me to speak to some of them at least before doing that.'

The emperor looked crafty. 'A lot of good your speaking to witnesses has done so far. I had to place these people under my protection. I have a reputation to protect.'

'Without hearing from someone who was there and saw what happened . . .'

'There was hysteria. Everyone was drunk or packed full of aphrodisiacs. They might have thought they'd seen anything.'

'But, Lord, this was a massacre –'

'I know, Julius! I know it was a massacre. In my own palace. In a hall surrounded by my own guards. I might easily have been one of the victims myself!' He became thoughtful. 'It's a revolution isn't it? Is it Galba? Otho? One of those bastards is after my throne!'

Julius had thoughts of his own. 'Lord – you said *creatures*?'

192

The sly look came back, but behind it there was still fear.

'You mentioned the power of your own curse,' Julius went on, not knowing how far he dared go, and clinging to what he hoped was a diplomatic approach. 'That – in your own imagining – you might have gone too far.'

'That is nonsense. Between these four walls,' Nero said in a flat voice, 'and the two of us, you know I cannot have that power.' But then his eyes became distant again, as he added, with a hint of pride, 'Or can I?'

'There has been a pattern,' Julius went on. 'The attacks have been on individuals so far, wealthy and prominent citizens, most of them –'

'My creditors, I know!'

'Your friends and supporters, Lord.'

Nero looked at him. 'But now?'

'This was a mass attack. Tens of people killed, indiscriminately –'

'There were plenty of prominent women there who met an end beyond imagination, let me tell you!'

'And many others –'

'They might have been killed to mask the true victims!'

'Why?' flashed Julius before he had time to rein his words in. In the silence that followed, he lowered his eyes, awaiting Nero's reaction to his outspokenness. All he could think of was not the kind of fate which might now be in store for him, but that he might never see Calpurnia again. What was she doing now? Was he in her thoughts at all?

The silence lasted forever, the breeze outside stirred the stalks of the flowers surrounding the window in silence, tiny motes of dust danced in the sunbeams which entered the room, in silence; the air stirred silently in the room. Beyond it, life went on. Not a hundred paces away, people went about their business oblivious to what was going on behind that plain closed door in the palace.

It didn't seem possible.

But the intelligent being who still inhabited the emperor's skull alongside the madman, the being which was responsible for his survival so far, had not yet lost its grip.

'Go on,' Nero said, his eyes calm and pensive.

'There have been attacks about every three days,' Julius proceeded cautiously. 'I don't know why, but I wonder if it takes the attackers that long to . . . digest.'

'To get hungry again?'

'Yes.'

'May Atargatis protect me!'

'May she always do that, Lord.'

'I know you have my best interest at heart, Julius Marcellus.'

'Be assured of that.' Julius' breath was coming more easily now. But it had been a bad moment.

'There is no conspiracy,' Nero said. 'We are fighting demons.'

Julius thought of the farm animals which had been killed, of the blonde harridan Sexta. If only he did have a pattern, he thought. Something he could follow.

Nero whispered something to himself, his face troubled again.

'What, Lord?'

But Julius had heard him. He had said: 'They are out of control.'

29

'He's keeping something from me,' Julius reluctantly told Mercurius later, back at VIII Cohort. A slave stood in one corner, fanning the air, but that didn't make it any cooler, the heat just moved about, and here, down in the city centre, away from the hills, it was sweltering. It would soon be evening though; maybe the cooler air would let him think more clearly.

Mercurius spread his hands. 'What?'

'Something, I think, which he won't admit, even to himself. Perhaps something he's frightened of. Something he hopes will go away of its own accord. You know what he's like. Besides, if you find a wasps' nest, the last thing you do if you want to get rid of it is give it a kick.' Julius shook his head. 'But he's letting me talk to one witness.'

'Who?'

'The eunuch who rescued Poppaea. He's from Bithynia, must have a cool head on his shoulders because he did something other than panic.' Julius paused. 'Which means I might just get something out of him.'

'The hall's clean now. You wouldn't have thought anything had happened there. But it's being sealed up. It's never to be used again,' said Mercurius.

'How did the killers get out, afterwards?'

'The balconies? Does it matter? You can't lock ghosts up.'

'Or demons.'

'Is that what we're dealing with?'

Mercurius shook himself. 'You tell me.'

'What have you done with the bodies?'

Mercurius shrugged. 'We sorted them out. The slaves complained a lot.'

'How many dead?'

'Seventy-five. As close as anyone could get. Four guests are unaccounted for.'

'Names?'

'None. There was a fixed number of people attending, but that was as far as Palace Security got. If they can be trusted. But the guards might have been bribed.'

'Or, the murderers might have been invited. Does the number of people who attended include sex-slaves and concubines?'

'Yes,' said Mercurius

'Four anonymous girls who've disappeared?'

197

'Looks like it.'

'We can be sure that we are looking for women now. Unless these killings had nothing to do with the others.'

'I think that's impossible.'

'Any way of finding them?'

'You tell me,' said Mercurius again.

Was that insolence? Julius couldn't be sure. 'See what you can do,' he said. But Mercurius' repeated expression brought back his unwelcome thoughts. He looked at his subordinate. 'What do you think is going on?'

Mercurius hesitated before replying. 'We don't believe in demons,' he said. 'The only demons are people who are capable of destroying the happiness and hopes of others without a thought, if that destruction is in the interest of their own gratification.'

Julius nodded. 'There's a legend,' he said, and paused. When he went on he was speaking from experience, something he'd gone through long ago, but which had threatened to damage him for good. 'About a demon called succubus. They can appear in dreams. They have the form of a beautiful woman whom the victim cannot get out of his mind when he wakes. If the victim falls in love with this demon she will batten on him and suck the energy from his spirit until he dies of exhaustion. She takes over his soul, and she gives nothing.'

'A kind of harpy.'

'Yes. Harpies suck the life out of you too.'

'But they don't exist.'

'Love exists. Betrayal exists,' Julius said.

'They are not supernatural and they do not always go hand-in-hand.'

'True.'

'But love always risks betrayal.'

'Who'd rather not take the risk? In any case, you can't choose. You are chosen.'

'Or manipulated.'

Julius looked at his colleague, whose eyes were shadowed. Had he had a similar experience of betrayal? But then, who hadn't? 'What we are dealing with has nothing to do with love,' he said.

'Do you believe in the succubus?'

Julius' own eyes darkened. 'I have never encountered one who wasn't human. Incomplete, damaged, but human. There are no Minotaurs, there are no Furies. The monsters on this earth are people who are sick in spirit.'

30

'I have told you what I saw,' repeated the tall, broad-shouldered man. Only the slight softness of his muscles and skin indicated that he had been emasculated. Twenty years ago, he'd told Julius, at the age of nine.

'But you don't remember how many there were?'

'No. There was confusion. Many. Like a swarm.'

'Not people wearing masks? Costumes? It was dark in there. Could you see clearly?'

'I have never seen such costumes.' The man shuddered. 'I saw the empress was in danger and I saved her. It was all I could do.'

'And they closed the doors after you had got out? Immediately?'

'Yes. Those who had already escaped were the lucky ones.'

'There was no thought of saving the others? No one sent in the guards?'

The man looked at him impassively, as if the question didn't merit an answer.

Julius glanced briefly across at his scribe, who put down his stylus and stretched the hand that had been writing hard for the past half-hour. The scribe's eyes were blank. He knew no more than Julius did what to think of what the eunuch had described. But the eunuch was a strong, uncomplicated man, certainly neither emotional nor imaginative enough to have made his statement up. He hadn't been harassed or ruffled by Julius' interrogation. Instead, it was Julius himself who felt shattered, largely because he now had to face what he had already begun to believe, but couldn't accept.

They were dealing with something beyond reason.

Nero's reaction was simple. 'You find what's responsible and stop it. Leave the rest to me. I'll keep Tigellinus off your back as long as you come up with something.'

It was almost as if the emperor was relieved. Could he possibly, in part of that complicated, warped mind, be pleased at the thought that he had a real power to curse?

'No one must know, Lord,' he said.

Nero smiled. 'You can leave that to me, too, Julius Marcellus.'

As he left, Julius knew that his anxiety about secrecy, vital as it was, had signed the eunuch's death warrant, and probably those of the other survivors as well. Only the empress would escape death – though for how long was anybody's guess.

How many was he dealing with, and how could he track them down? The only place to start was the defiled grave-pit.

'It's impossible to know whether any bodies were taken from there,' Mercurius told him. 'We made a thorough search. Nothing conclusive.'

'But why else would it have been opened? You said only the freshest bodies had been disturbed.'

'Yes.'

'Did you find the body of the girl from the brothel? Justina?'

'The bodies are covered with quicklime – even the freshest . . .'

'Remember how she looked when we found her? As if she were not dead at all?'

'She had only just died –'

'Think, man!' Julius said, knowing that he himself should have thought.

'The place has been sealed again.'

'Then we must reopen it.'

Mercurius was about to object, then saw the look in Julius' eye, and nodded.

'Now,' said Julius. 'Organise it. I'll meet you there in an hour.'

★   ★   ★

It was dusk by the time they'd finished. Sweating and stinking, their nostrils filled with the stench of death, Julius and Mercurius watched as their men shovelled the last corpses back into the pit, and closed the cave-like opening with blocks of stone, finally sealing it again. The crew, specially deployed from VIII Cohort, scarcely bothered to hide their resentment of what they thought was their legate's crazy plan. But they had no idea of its importance.

Fighting down a sense of foreboding, Julius nevertheless felt that he had made progress, though where it would lead him he hardly dared think.

Justina's body was not there.

31

All thoughts of Calpurnia had been driven from his mind, but when he returned late to his flat, Dio greeted him with a letter.

'Who brought it?'

'A courier,' said Dio, looking at his master uncomfortably.

'What is it?'

'You haven't been to the Baths.'

'It's been a long day, and I doubt if they'd have let me in, in this state.'

'I'll prepare one for you here.'

'Thank you.'

'Straight away.'

'Letter first. A courier?'

'Just a city courier.'

'Did he say who sent it?'

'It was delivered to the depot by a house-slave, so he didn't know.'

Julius knew who it was from before he'd opened it. Despite everything that was on his mind, his heart raced.

It was a feminine hand, confident and mature.

Calpurnia set his mind at rest first by excusing her sudden departure, explaining that as she'd seen that she might be intruding on confidential business, she thought it best to make a discreet exit. She went on to suggest that he might like to come as her guest to a banquet friends of hers were giving two days later. The tone of the letter was friendly, though Calpurnia did not hint at any remembered intimacy. He could not divine anything of what she might be thinking from it. Julius noticed that towards the end her writing became less firm, more agitated, and wondered briefly about the cause of this, though he attached no special importance to it.

He bathed and dined quickly and absent-mindedly, debating with himself how best to reply. But he set these thoughts aside. He had more important things to think about than dinner invitations.

32

Calpurnia turned her *cochlear* – her little spoon – round to use its thin, pointed grip to twist a snail from its shell, but Julius had already noticed that she was only going through the motions of eating. The delicious and copious offerings at the banquet held little interest for her, and though she talked animatedly enough, he had the impression that her thoughts were elsewhere. When he caught her face in repose, she looked preoccupied, even haunted.

'Something wrong with it?' he asked her, seeing that she'd spat the morsel out.

'A little over-seasoned for me.'

'You can't taste snails without garlic.'

'I know. I just thought I'd try. But I should have stayed with the crevettes.'

It was a big gathering, maybe fifty guests lying in groups

of five to thirteen around low tables placed by their couches, which house-slaves busied themselves over, constantly replacing dishes with fresh ones, and ensuring that no one's goblet was ever empty. The large circular room had a domed roof and its colonnade gave straight onto a garden so fecund it might have been a miniature jungle, in which hidden fountains splashed and caged birds sang.

The guests circulated from group to group as the main part of the *cena* wound up, and Julius watched them idly. There was a handful of celebrities whom Julius knew by sight, and a half-dozen minor senators and their wives, or boyfriends, or mistresses. He noticed Petronius and nodded to him, and Vatinius, whose eye he avoided. One small group had half-caught Julius' attention earlier, three young women and a young man, because they'd scarcely eaten, and had been among the first to abandon their places to roam around the room, exchanging pleasantries here and there, but never staying anywhere long. Sometimes they separated, only to come together again later, as if to confer. But as the throng grew greater, they were lost to view.

Calpurnia became more animated as they themselves rose from their couches to mingle.

'Good party,' Julius said, but hoping at last to cut through the small talk. 'With friends like these, I'm surprised you don't mind slumming it with me.'

'I've only tried that once, don't forget. I might not like it a second time.'

'Then why did you invite me here? I've done my best to meet you halfway. These are the best clothes I possess.'

'And you look terrific,' she said mockingly.

So do you, thought Julius. The pearl necklace and earrings she wore lent an added burnish to her dark skin. Her hair was gathered in a chignon which left her neck exposed above the low scoop of the white dress she wore, and he longed to kiss the nape of her neck, to bury his face in her hair. As it was, he wondered if he'd get as far as a second kiss, for despite her friendliness, there was a distance he didn't like. But he concentrated on the pleasure of just being with her again, and tried to enjoy the moment.

They'd arrived separately, Julius a few minutes after her, but as soon as she saw him, she'd greeted him like an old friend, introducing him to their hosts – a senator and his wife, both well-known *bons-viveurs* – as if they were already an established couple, and ensuring he took a place by her, and did not leave her side. If it hadn't been for her anxiety, Julius might, for a few hours, almost have been able to keep his own at bay.

'You still haven't said why you've favoured me with this invitation.'

'Do I need a reason?'

'Things broke off so suddenly when we last met.'

The troubled look again – or had Julius just imagined it?

'There are some people I'd like you to meet.'

'Good.'

'Friends.' She paused. 'I hope you find them interesting.'

She guided him through the crowd, weaving her way through the maze of tables, towards a gilded statue of Mercury which stood near the centre of the room. She held his hand as she led him and he noticed that her palms were sweating. There, speaking to two plump members of the *eques* class – knights – were the three young women and the young man whom Julius had noticed earlier.

The young women were tall and athletic, one of them – the oldest – strikingly so. They had copper-blonde hair worn in chignons and were dressed, two of them in grey dresses with white shawls, the other in a white dress with a brown shawl. They wore only sparing make-up, compared with most of the other women in the room, whose overuse of chalk-powder, charcoal and saffron was only too apparent. Their jewellery was equally discreet, though the emeralds and rubies round their necks and dangling from their earlobes were expensive.

The oldest, whom Calpurnia introduced as Pompeia, was a handsome, proud woman with a trace of defiance in her eyes, her hand strong and dry as Julius took it. Apuleia, possibly the youngest of the three, was paler, with an innocent look, lighter hair, and dark eyes which might have been enigmatic, though Julius could read no real expression in them. Flavia, the third, might have been a classic Roman beauty, but for her olive skin – she wore a little more make-up than the others, especially around the mouth, perhaps, Julius thought, trying not to allow the policeman to look too closely, to cover some slight scaliness, some small skin complaint. And there was something else which was distinctly un-Roman – something untameable in her eyes.

But it was the young man to whom the two knights were paying the most attention. Julius greeted them courteously, and they returned his *salve* with just enough reserve for him to know that they were appraising him, wondering who he was, how to fit him in with the other guests.

The young man – Marcus Severus – was broad-shouldered and narrow hipped, and wore a dazzlingly white tunic gathered at the waist with a soft brown belt which matched the expensive sandals whose straps reached halfway up the tanned skin of his sleek calves. It was easy to see why he had caught the knights' attention. He looked too old to have no trace of a beard, but there was none, and the hair on his arms was fine, soft and golden. But the most striking thing about him was his eyes – they were an insanely pale shade of turquoise, vivid, as if such a colour could contain flames. These he turned on Calpurnia as she introduced Julius with an expression which was unreadable.

33

'Are you hurt?' Julius had taken Calpurnia's arm as he led her to her litter, glad she had not simply said goodnight to him when the banquet broke up. She was limping more heavily than usual, he thought. But what did he know? This was only the third time he'd seen her.

'No. I've just been standing for too long. And that senator, Rufulus, trod on my foot when we were dancing.'

'At least I didn't do that.'

'You are a surprisingly good dancer.'

'Did you think I wouldn't be?'

'I wouldn't have bet on it.'

'Thank you.'

She looked at him. 'But you are limping too.'

'I've been standing for too long as well.'

For a long time after their somewhat strained

conversation with the two knights and her four friends, Calpurnia had been distracted, but now she looked at him once more, this time cheerfully. 'Two bad left feet. Something we have in common.'

'I hope there's more.'

'What day were you born on?'

'A Saturday.'

'So was I.'

'You see!'

But she had a dark look again.

'Is that significant?' he asked.

But she didn't reply. They reached her litter, and her six bearers and two attendants stood ready.

'Are these all your people?'

'Yes,' she replied.

He hesitated. 'No bodyguard?'

'It's not far, and I don't pass through any quiet part of town.' She paused, and added archly, 'Why? Are you offering your services?'

He looked around at the other litters waiting to pick up their passengers. All had at least five heavily-armed men standing by them. 'Yes,' he said.

He handed her in, and she kept the curtain raised as her bearers lifted her, steadied themselves, and began to march. Julius walked alongside, glad that these streets were well lit by ordinary torches, large bundles of pitch-soaked reeds in heavy iron sconces every twenty paces on either side of the road. There was traffic too, and the light sound of voices. You might almost have thought that nothing out of the ordinary was happening in Rome at all.

Nevertheless Calpurnia's two attendants were glad of his company, and stayed close to him.

'Have you owned these slaves long?' he asked.

'Titus hired them for me.'

Julius felt a pang of jealousy.

'I shouldn't have made you come with me. Made you walk.'

'Why?'

'Your limp.'

'It's not so bad now.' But the hard lump on his left foot had swollen, and chafed his sandal.

'Let me bathe it for you when we get to my flat.'

Julius' heartbeat went up a notch. 'I'd better –'

'It isn't late.' Her voice was light, with a hint of mockery in it. There was nothing flirtatious, though. Maybe she just wanted to talk to him?

But he couldn't forget that kiss.

It wasn't a large apartment but it was luxurious. The marble hall gave onto a living-room, one side of which opened onto a broad balcony festooned with climbing plants heavy with dark red and pink flowers. Beyond its white balustrade, the city stretched below, dark now except where a few lights glimmered. Most of the light spread over Rome came from the full moon, which rode – Diana's chariot – over the city amid a sea of stars. He saw no house-slaves but wine and *mulsum* and ice had been left with sweetbreads for them recently for the ice had not melted at all and she poured silver goblets to the brim but neglected hers, though he drank deeply from the one she gave him.

The living-room contained two couches opposite one another across a low table, in a sunken central area approached by two shallow steps. The walls were painted with delicate rural scenes evoking Arcadia, three or four chairs and console tables ranged around them completing the furniture. Two broad doors, one in each of two opposing walls, led off the room to a small bath-house on one side; and through the other Julius glimpsed the corner of a crimson silk coverlet draped across the corner of a bed.

Calpurnia motioned him to a seat on one of the couches, and went to the bathing area, re-emerging moments later carrying a silver bowl full of water and a heavy linen towel.

She knelt at his feet, undid his sandals, and gently placed his left foot in the cool water, which caressed his foot like a balm. He hadn't realised how badly it had been hurting until relief came, and he could see that where the sandal had cut into his injury, there was blood, which dissipated wispily in the water.

'I can't work in this dress,' she said. 'Wait.'

Once more she disappeared, this time into the bedroom. When she came out, her hair was down, and she wore only a short white tunic which revealed legs so slim, so long and brown that Julius felt his prick release itself from his control, and stir and rise. He shifted his position so that his own tunic would not betray his erection, but if Calpurnia had noticed, she gave no sign. She knelt again, and placing her hands in the water, took his foot between them and began to massage it, gently, firmly, and completely. His foot ached and tingled as the pain began to leave it. Without wanting to, Julius closed his eyes and lay back, not caring or not thinking that now she would scarcely be able to ignore his tumescence. He groaned involuntarily as her hands worked their magic. Her voice when she spoke came from far away as he lowered what guard he had left and the exhaustion of his mind found relief in this pleasure.

'Better?'

He opened his eyes to catch hers and smiled. 'I've died and gone to heaven.'

'And your watchman is at his post.'

'I am sorry.'

'Why?'

That made Priapus surge harder. He'd been asleep so long, Julius thought. Three years. Was it really possible that now . . .?

'Relax,' her voice was saying. An odd tone, half commanding, half imploring. But he had no choice. He had already yielded. He was in her power.

215

Her hands slowly left off their caressing massage and began to explore his ankles, his calves, his knees, travelling upwards unhurriedly, gently, tantalisingly. He kept his eyes closed, feeling her shift from her knees to sit beside him, on his right, her left arm round him now, her right hand caressing his inner thigh a palm's breadth from the loincloth against which Priapus was straining to escape. He felt her lips close to his and turned to her, opening his eyes now and seeing hers startlingly close, deep green like he imagined the bottom of the sea, bright light in them, devouring him as she pulled him close and his arms encircled her and their lips met ravenously and they melted into one another as she loosened his loincloth at last and freed Priapus, who all but leapt into her cool, waiting grasp.

They didn't know what happened to their tunics but busy, eager hands made no work at all of them and they were gone, and their bodies pressed together urgently, rubbing and sliding against each other, oiled by their perspiration and their warmth. Their lips were barely able to keep apart from one another's, their tongues seeking one another's so furiously that they could scarcely take the time to breathe as he pulled her under him and her right hand guided him into her. There was no time for foreplay, their need and impatience was too great. Her long legs rose high and bent round his waist as he plunged deliciously and hard into the soft firm warmth of her cave of Venus as the muscles there gripped and encouraged him, Calpurnia moaning softly, *yes, oh yes*, softly, *oh my love, my love,* and it didn't seem real, and yet it was, though everything was so far away because he was up there among the stars which shone cold in the dark-blue sky far away beyond the white balustrade and the sleeping city and everything else was forgotten and her arms were tight around him and her legs gripped him so hard that he could hardly move but he forced his back free enough and flexed his buttocks and thrust and thrust, steel in a warm sheath of flesh, and her moans became rougher and turned into cries and sobs as she turned her face away to breathe more freely, lost in her own rapture until she shrieked with uncontrollable pleasure and the stars came down to join her and her cries were joined by his deeper ones and he exploded into her and they whirled together in a vortex of ecstasy up to the skies and down to the depths and nothing else existed then except the wonderful soft cover of darkness.

They lay draped around each other on the couch for a long time after that, not speaking and perhaps not thinking, until at last she shifted her position and released herself from his arms which were reluctant to let her go, hungry for her again, which she sensed, and smiled, reaching down and cupping his balls in her palm.

'Your watchman is alert. Let's take him somewhere more comfortable.'

'I want to caress your feet. Your foot. The one that's wounded like mine.'

217

Only the faintest shadow crossed her face and he didn't notice it. 'It's fine.'

'Later?'

'Later. Come.'

She rose and took his hand and took him to the bedroom. As they walked the short distance across the moonlit room he noticed her left foot drag a little, saw that it was twisted slightly inwards and that its skin was – what? – rougher? – a trick of the light perhaps. What did he care? He drank in the sight of her naked back and her compact, rounded buttocks as she led him, and the dark golden tresses of her hair which cascaded down to them from her head like a waterfall in Olympus. That was enough for him.

'Some wine?' she asked him before they approached the bed. She had touched nothing herself.

'I have no need of it.'

She smiled and knelt on the bed, pulling him with her, but this time he wanted to savour her, to give her what pleasure he could before surrendering himself to her once more. Gently he placed her on her back and kissed her, but restrained her arching eagerness and moved his lips to her neck, dwelling there before kissing her more roughly and more deeply at its base and along her shoulders, under her armpits, taking time, while her body moved luxuriously beneath him, moving to her breasts and savouring each one, caressing the right with his mouth, biting the nipple gently, and rubbing it with his tongue as he held it gently with his teeth, while fondling the left with his hand until she gasped, *stop, stop, stop*, and he relaxed, changing his position to the left breast now, while never neglecting the other with his hand, but gently, letting her get her breath, guided by her, her hands distractedly caressing his hair. Then, always slowly, gently, but firmly keeping control of her, he moved downwards and downwards, tracing the line of her stomach to her navel with his tongue, and on to the soft bronze-coloured copse which grew on the summit of the mound of Venus, then further, caressing the hollows at the tops of her thighs on either side of the cave, itself close to his eyes now, warm, dark-red, welcoming, smelling of musk and Calpurnia's own smell, like jasmine smells at dusk, the cave with a life of its own at the mouth, moist, moving like a rose opening, and now, gently, gently exploring it with his tongue, thrusting upwards where her own little Priapus stood eager to welcome him, gentle soft cries coming from far away as Calpurnia eased her body on the bed, flicking the little erect god with his tongue, kissing and sucking at the fleshy sides of the cave and then exploring its entrance and as far as he could reach with his tongue, strongly but not violently, gauging his actions against her pleasure, his hands around her tender buttocks, squeezing harder as his own passion rose higher and higher until he had to fight to control it.

Her hands caught his shoulders at last and he looked up at her.

'My turn now.'

And he was as trusting as a baby as she turned him onto his back with strong arms. From somewhere she had got essence of walnut oil and she caressed him with it, massaging his body with her long-fingered brown hands, first, then with her own body, sliding and slithering over his, rubbing her nipples against his, kissing his battle-scars, running her tongue over them, her legs wrapped firmly round his, working harder now as he sensed her excitement rise with her concentration, hurting him as she wrenched his nipples in her fingers, rising above him to look at him, the look in her eyes somehow voracious, and then down again, her lips hungry all over his body, her tongue in his navel, then, too impatient to linger, her mouth closing over his achingly hard prick, her teeth holding it gently, but as if she were forcing herself to be gentle, as her tongue roved over it, her tongue less soft, the memory came momentarily of a pet cat he had once when it licked his hand, gazing up at him adoringly without losing the egotism cats retain. And he remembered how you should not excite a cat too much with caresses for with the excitement comes violence and they will claw you.

But then she shook herself and became gentle again, releasing his massively swollen Priapus just before he burst in her mouth, leaving him just able to hold his balance on the edge of the precipice, smiling, shifting her body upwards, mounting him, her legs and arms round him now, pinioning him, her mouth on his . . .

He ran his hands over her back, tracing a line insistently up and down her spine with his fingers. Half-detached from reality, half in a blissful dream, he only just sensed a change in her, a roughness in her skin as if someone – he himself? – had scratched her, leaving grazes there. And her own fingers and – somehow – her toes were digging into him, her arms and legs holding him so that he was unable to move as she rode him now, he was inside her without knowing how, the muscles of her cave holding him tightly there, squeezing and relaxing as she caught her breath as it came roughly and raucously, close to his ear, her face next to his, buried in the pillow beside him and hidden from view.

He hadn't imagined her to be this strong. But her mouth was on his again, and her tongue . . .

Then she shuddered violently and arched away from him, relaxing her hold and shaking her body and her head furiously, while from her mouth came a howl like he'd only heard before on a battlefield.

A howl of delight, of triumph, of victory.

And she came to him again. Her body felt smooth and lithe, and her hands were soft as they stroked him, and her lips sought his, and her tongue's caress was velvet and tender.

34

'We need a bone to throw to the mob,' Tigellinus said urgently. 'And it isn't just them. It's the Senate. Otherwise your position –'

'My position?'

'Lord, it is only your safety I have at heart.'

'I am a god! I have no need of your protection!' But the emperor sounded nervous, unsure of himself. Julius Marcellus was working on the case, he knew that, he trusted him, he knew the policeman would get to the bottom of it somehow, but it was taking too long. News of the orgy-killings had got out despite the precautions, despite Vatinius and his cronies threatening the victims' families, despite the extinction of any witnesses unimportant enough for anyone to care about, and the removal of the rest to a safe distance. Now Rome was in turmoil, and his grand building programme was grinding to a halt because of it. Only work on the Golden House, his vast new palace, still went on, under the eyes of a vast contingent of Praetorian Guards, which was costing him a fortune and whose services he might well need elsewhere soon – to protect him if the anger of the city focused on him.

Which was exactly what this horrible, slippery functionary was suggesting. He'd given the man too much power. Unwise. Nero looked at Tigellinus through hooded eyes. This man would only be his friend as long as it was profitable for him. Like so many of them.

'What do you suggest?'

'Arrest Petrus,' said Tigellinus decisively. 'Arrest the ringleader and make an example of him. Show them how strong you can be.'

'Make an example of him?'

'You know what I mean.'

'There'd have to be a trial.'

'Of course! Make it as public as possible.' Tigellinus leaned forward, unpleasantly close to the emperor. Nero could smell the odour of stale wine and garlic coming through the man's pores. 'He's been a thorn in our side for too long.'

But what if the killings go on after we've disposed of him? Nero thought; and then another wild thought flashed through his mind – what if they didn't? What if the Christians were at the bottom of this – a primitive sect, believing in all sorts of mumbo-jumbo – wasn't it possible

223

that they, and not he, had unleashed this horror on the capital?

Nero didn't know. He convinced himself now that he had not believed, in his heart of hearts, that he had the power to curse. There was no real sense of divinity in him, and he had to admit that to himself. But what was happening was frightening and it was certainly not controlled by him, much as he would have liked to be sure it was otherwise. But there was a consolation. If the girls *were* responsible, and he wasn't even sure of that, some of the victims were convenient losses for him, so they were as good as doing his bidding; and if he could blame the Christians, well, that would be another nail in their coffin.

He could turn all this to his advantage, if he threw the dice carefully. For the moment, he would take no action against the girls. He would leave them alone. If, later, the need arose, he would have them killed. It would be a small matter.

But why, an inner voice whispered, do you not kill them now?

And the same voice answered for him, in the same insistent whisper: *because you fear them*. He realised in an instant that that was why he had not used the girls in the way he had intended to. It was because he had not really believed in his own power to do so. He had simply wanted to cow them, to make them feel afraid. He wondered whether they still feared him, and he did not dare find out.

These thoughts were too dark for Nero to contemplate for long. Time would sort this out, he told himself, and in the meantime, let things take their course.

He would allow the arrest of Petrus. And he would do nothing, say nothing. He would go on keeping his secret fears to himself. For as long as possible. Let Julius Marcellus find his own way to the truth – whatever it turned out to be. It was vital that he – the emperor – should never be associated with this curse. If, in the depths of his tangled mind, he believed anything could bring him down, this was it. The thought that he might never see the completion of his cherished Golden House, never live in it, in the splendour which was his due, was too much for him to bear.

He looked petulantly at the documents Tigellinus had prepared for him. He pushed them away.

'You don't need my signature,' he said. 'Do it on your own authority.'

35

Petrus had elected to remain at the isolated farmhouse alone, despite the protests of his followers. For some time he had known that his time was borrowed now, but he felt no despair, only that he had done his work as well as he could, and that the only end there could be would be a joyful one – that he would be reunited with his Lord. So he had sent Paulus away, and refused all the aid and protection Titus was willing to offer him, insistent though Titus, begging him with tears in his eyes, had been. Titus had returned from the country to stand by him. Petrus' instinct was to send him back to his family.

'Why risk your own necks?' he had said. 'We must spare as many as we can for the struggle.'

Now, as the sun's light broke cover over the eastern hills, and Petrus watched it through the window of his simple room, he was unsurprised at the noises outside, of horses' hooves and the creaking wheels of an ox-cart. He was already dressed and waiting, drinking a beaker of goat's milk. Only his taut shoulders belied his state of mind, for he kept his face tranquil. He would not show fear to these people, but courage. It was only human to falter. Hadn't the Lord himself faltered, for a moment, when his own hour came? The thing was to withstand the frailty.

He moved to the door to open it just as they started hammering on it with the pommels of their swords. Through the window he's already glimpsed the red cloaks. A twenty-man unit, he guessed. They could have saved their money and sent two. But that wouldn't have been showy enough for them.

They were surprised when the door opened, perhaps even disappointed that they didn't have to smash it down, that, by the look of things, there wasn't even going to be a fight. Just this burly old man dressed in faded blue and scuffed sandals standing there, a wooden beaker of milk in his hand, looking at them calmly.

One of the sergeants dashed the beaker to the ground as if Petrus might have used it as a weapon. The beaker bounced on the stony ground and what remained of the milk spilt, darkening the dust as it sank in. Then there was a moment during which Petrus, allowing himself a moment's amusement, recognised the embarrassment on the sergeant's face and the self-consciousness on those of his men. He wasn't

227

playing their game. He wasn't frightened and he wasn't putting up a fight.

The young officer in charge of the unit was different. He was plump and beefy, his sparse hair cropped close to his skull, his expression smug and his manner officious. A man to whom imagination, humour and pity would always be strangers.

Out came the official scroll, and out came the expected words.

'Petrus Nazarenus?'

The old man nodded.

'You are under arrest.'

Petrus said, 'What are my crimes?'

'Crimes against the State.'

Petrus nodded. Three soldiers came forwards with manacles which they attached to his wrists and ankles, and he was bundled roughly into the ox-cart, where two warders in brown uniforms waited for him, chaining him to a crossbar, looking at him with dead eyes, keeping their ugly short swords unsheathed and ready, as if at any moment he might cast off his fetters and tear at their throats with his teeth.

The soldiers formed up round the cart. Petrus steadied himself on the crossbar as the oxen lurched into motion and set off with their escort down the rough unmade road which led back down to the city, now shining below him in the first light of the risen sun.

He squinted against the light and looked at the city, but his mind went back thirty-five years, to the sparkling water of the Sea of Galilee, and he could hear the creak of the boat and hear the slapping of the waves as it sailed, and smell the tangy smell of fresh fish, as he remembered a time, so soon to end, had he known it, when his thoughts had been of nothing but those fish, and catching them.

36

The trial was short and held in public. The prosecutor declaimed; the defence, a man in Vatinius' pay, mumbled. Petrus said nothing, but held his head high, and met every eye that sought his with a clear, untroubled look. He had panicked once, resorted to violence once, but he had never done so again, he had learned his lesson at Mount Olivet. He knew what would happen, and he tried to concentrate, to discipline his mind against the pain he knew his body would soon have to bear.

When the inevitable verdict was pronounced by a judge who hid his embarrassment better than the soldiers had, there was silence, and some looked up at the tempest clouds which had been rolling up over Rome during the day. No one dared say they thought the clouds were ominous, except the Christians, in the privacy of their houses, keeping their heads down, some of them, many of them, also thinking that now was the time to renounce their new religion.

The storm broke over the city with violent force that night, a monsoon rain and a wind which smashed down the scaffolding clustered around the Golden House and the Temple of Jupiter. A storm which lasted three days, delaying the execution.

But the fourth day dawned bright and the air was clear. They came for him early, and he was ready for them. He had grown paler since his arrest and his skin was slack, but his expression was firm and strong. His eyes gave nothing away.

The chief warder struck off his manacles, and offered him wine and bread. He took both, eating and drinking with appetite. They watched him silently as he did so, and when he had finished, he stood. Two guards flanked him.

'Anything to say?'

Petrus was surprised to see that the man addressing him was no ordinary captain-of-the guard, but a florid creature dressed in the resplendent uniform of the commander of the Praetorian Guard. Tigellinus himself. Blinking in the white sunlight, Petrus could see the hill in the distance, and the huge crowd. Others were making their way to join them, little figures in white and brown, green and blue, following the path through the scrubby landscape towards its top.

'I have already said that to die as my Lord died is too great an honour for me.'

Tigellinus said, 'I have arranged to save you any embarrassment on that score. You are a proud man, Petrus, but your example will not be an inspiration to anyone.'

Petrus pondered that, as they handed him up onto another cart and roped his wrists to its crossbar.

His last journey.

When he reached its end, he barely listened to the short exhortation Tigellinus delivered about this, the final exorcism of demons from our beloved city, and how by this act the evil running through the veins of Rome would be washed away. He was looking at the cross they had prepared for him. There was something unusual about its construction. He was a practical man and had soon worked out the reason for its design, and he felt glad, for he knew he was about to experience pain such as he had never felt before, and few ever would; pain beyond imagination and endurance. Yet he would endure it; he would endure it when they nailed his wrists and ankles through the tough tendons to the crosspiece so they would hold, and placed the slats of wood under his shoulders so his arms would not hang down.

Tigellinus had taken him at his word. Petrus was to be crucified upside-down.

It was a novelty. No wonder the crowd was so large.

The executioners came towards the cart and untied him, pulling him down and throwing him on the ground. He just had time to glimpse the anguished faces of Paulus and

Titus in the crowd, before one of the executioners kicked him in the stomach, robbing his body of breath and all resistance. Then they manhandled him onto the frame of the cross and the blacksmith came forward, with his knife, his nails, and his hammer.

37

'The official line is that the head of the monster has been cut off,' said Titus. 'The *Daily Acts* reports that the authorities are confident that the limbs will die of their own accord, without any further action.'

'This has nothing to do with me.'

'Hasn't it? As I see it, you want nothing more than a quick end to all this.'

'Calm yourself,' Julius said, shocked at his friend's anger. 'Think. Do you seriously imagine I believe that condemning your leader to death by crucifixion is going to solve all this?'

'The emperor believes the Christians are at the root of it.'

'He hopes so. He needed a scapegoat. He's buying time, he's buying off the Senate and the mob.'

'There was no need for this.'

'Nero has not raised his hand against the Christians. There has been no purge. Much as Tigellinus would have liked one.'

'Yet still we are sent to the arena in droves. Still they burn our bodies to light the streets.'

'It is done to break your spirit.'

'It is succeeding.'

Julius tried hard to think of something to say. 'If I can bring an end to this, show that your people are not behind it . . .'

'How? How will you do that? There have been no killings since Petrus' death. The people are certain he was behind the curse.'

But both men knew that was not true. Both men knew that it was only a question of time.

'You should return to the country.'

'No! I should stand with my fellow-sufferers.'

'Then you may risk the lives of your family as well as your own. Don't underestimate Tigellinus. If there are more killings, action against the Christians will start again, and harden. The only thing that restrains Tigellinus is Nero.'

'And why does he restrain him?'

'Because he does not want more unrest in the city. He wants to be loved, to be seen as benevolent. He wants Rome rebuilt, not crumbling, falling into uncertainty and riot.' Above all, Julius thought, he does not want

Tigellinus to gain any more power or popularity than he has already.

And because he is scared of something else.

'He wants to stay on the throne,' Titus said.

'He is the only stability we have.'

'Like it or not.' Titus breathed hard. Then, slowly, he began to calm down, pacing the airy room on the upper floor of his house which served as the office for his development businesses. Julius did not mention that his friend's fortunes, as much as anyone else's, depended on the rebuilding of the city.

Titus snapped his fingers at a house-slave and ordered him to fetch wine. He looked hard at his friend. 'When Petrus was killed, I was blind with rage. I wanted you dead.'

Julius gripped the back of a chair. 'You let me see him. I took no action. You know that.' But he was thinking how easily Titus might have had him killed. And Titus knew that there was no love lost between him and Tigellinus. There would have been an investigation – the death of a legate of VIII Cohort would be no small thing – but if it had seemed like an accident, Tigellinus would have made sure that not too much time would be spent looking into it.

'Forgive me.'

Julius steadied himself. 'You did nothing, so there is nothing to forgive.'

'Forgive the thought, then. The intention.'

'What stopped you?'

236

'Calpurnia.'

'You told her?'

'She guessed what was in my mind.' Titus looked at him. 'I know you have grown close. And I know Calpurnia is a Christian at heart. You would not cause her or anyone who shared her belief harm.'

'I would not cause my friends harm. Their belief has nothing to do with it.'

Julius didn't know Calpurnia had seen Titus. But, though he knew he could not stop the flow of his feelings for her, he also knew that he could not understand her. After their night of love, she had distanced herself from him. He had only seen her once since, but there had been no return to their passion. Soon after Petrus' execution, she had told him that she needed time apart, but offered no explanation. He had agreed, but later regretted not being more insistent. He had sent letters, which went unanswered. He went to her apartment, where the one house-slave in residence told him that she had left Rome for a while. 'The mistress has gone to the country.'

'What do you know of her?' he asked Titus.

'I know what I have already told you. I expect you know more than I do now.'

'What makes you say that? What has she told you about us?'

Titus looked at him again. 'Enough to know that I believe she loves you.' The wine arrived and Titus dismissed the slave, pouring it himself and handing a goblet to Julius. 'There is nothing to worry about. She is a good woman, though —' Titus hesitated.

'Yes?'

'I believe Petrus had misgivings. I was not there at the time, but I heard later that he had her and some others expelled from our circle.'

Julius put down his goblet. 'What more do you know?'

'A disagreement.'

'Come clean.'

Titus drank. 'Petrus could be . . . impatient, angry. He was over-protective of our movement, especially when the persecution was stepped up.' He looked at Julius hesitantly. 'I believe he suspected Calpurnia — and others — of being infiltrators — Nero's spies.'

'But what happened? You must know!'

Titus was uncomfortable. 'That is all I know. The truth is that I have myself withdrawn from close contact with the Christians.'

'But that is sensible,' said Julius. 'I am relieved that you have outgrown this belief of yours. I have feared for your safety.'

Titus said nothing for a moment. Then drank again before speaking. 'I wanted you killed because I wanted to do something for Petrus, to avenge him. And I wanted to do that just to convince myself that I had not lost faith. But I have, and I have lost faith because I am a coward. I am ashamed.'

38

'Tigellinus wants your balls,' Nero told him.

It was late afternoon, the long day which had started with his conversation with Titus was edging towards its close. Julius stood by the golden desk at which Nero lounged, eating olives and walnuts. He wanted to go to the Baths, to soak and steam and relax and banish the thoughts which had been crowding him for hours, and which he knew wouldn't go away whatever he did. He longed for Calpurnia to stop being an unwanted tenant in his mind. He longed just to be able to wipe away the sweat which was stinging his left eye, but he just stood there and said. 'Why, Lord?'

'Oh, I think you know why.' Nero looked at him with his intense little eyes and popped another walnut into his mouth, washing it down with a nip of grappa. 'He wants to take over. He's lost all patience. He wants you exiled.'

'Lord.'

'To Tomis. On the Black Sea. But I won't let him do either. He's had his way so far.' Nero straightened in his chair. 'Do you think he's managed to lift the curse by killing Petrus?'

'I cannot say. It is to be hoped.'

'Meanwhile, I have other problems. I am planning a new series of combats at the arena. They must be the most spectacular yet.'

To distract the people, thought Julius. Well, it wouldn't be the first time that ploy had been used. 'With your charioteers again?' he ventured.

Nero spat out an olive stone angrily. He had thought of it. Persuade them back into the arena and arrange to have them killed there. But he knew why he hadn't dared to approach them. He feared them.

The olive stone pinged accurately into the little silver bowl he was aiming at, to join a number of its fellows. Less successfully aimed stones lay scattered near the bowl, but Nero smiled brightly at his little triumph.

'Tomis,' he repeated. 'Bleak place, I hear. Living there would be enough to drive a Roman like you mad. Nothing to do but watch the sea and fuck Dacian girls. Think about it. You can go.'

At the Baths, letting the masseur do his worst with his tired limbs, Julius did think about it. Tomis was in Dacia. Dacia, she had confessed, was where Calpurnia came from. Would she go back there, ever? He wondered what it would be like? A quiet life in the country, far from Rome – maybe he'd never see Rome again.

He could live there with her, be happy, let all of this go. Read, drink, live on . . . Apollo knew what he would live on. He was not a countryman. What would he do in a place like that?

But to go now, and go quietly, would be a better fate than the one which would await him if he couldn't nail down the killers – whatever they were. For he was sure they would strike again. As soon as their hunger returned.

And now his thoughts drifted back from an idyllic fantasy about a country he'd never visited, and a woman he hardly knew, who was at the very least enigmatic, and returned to the dark streets and squares of the huge capital he lived in, with its overblown population and its mad emperor, its pollution and its heartlessness, its vibrancy and its danger.

And he motioned for the masseur to stop, and took a cold shower before having himself towelled down.

Fresher for that, he made his way home. Whatever these bastards of creatures were, he'd send them to Hades before he was done. And fuck everything else before he had.

He got back to his flat in an uncertain temper. Determination was one thing, but if you didn't know where to direct it –

Waiting for him was news which changed that.

39

The shawl and the necklace lay on Julius' desk, the necklace – pearls – neatly coiled and the grey shawl neatly folded, the bloodstains uppermost. The blood had long since dried and had turned the colour of rust. The pearl necklace was expensive, the chain of pure white gold.

'I was finishing a report on them,' Mercurius said, but he would not look Julius in the eye.

'Without informing me.' Julius bridled. 'You told me the place was clean.'

'You had enough to do. I wanted to be sure. Not to make a fool of myself. I thought –'

Julius closed his eyes for a moment. He didn't know whether to believe his subordinate or not. 'When were you planning to tell me?'

'Soon. Tomorrow. Look, the report's almost finished.'

'But you discovered these at the time you cleared the room?'

'Yes.'

'Five days ago.'

'Yes.' Mercurius paused. 'Look, I wouldn't have got Quintus here to write it up if I'd wanted to keep this from you.'

Quintus was Julius' personal scribe. So there might be something in that. 'And how long has Quintus known?'

'I asked him to write my findings up last night.'

'And he came straight to me. I've read it.'

'I had everything ready for you. As I said, it's nearly finished.'

'But you kept all this to yourself. At first. What's the matter? Didn't Tigellinus want to play ball with you?'

Mercurius looked as if Julius had hit him. 'I didn't try to peddle this to Tigellinus or anyone else.'

Julius knew that he had been unreasonable then. Of course if Tigellinus had got wind of this discovery – their first tangible clues – he would have jumped at it. Maybe Mercurius was more of a fool than a knave – but having this over-ambitious sidekick was getting to be a serious pain in the arse. The thing is, the work he'd done was good – and he'd done it while Julius was busy wrapping his legs round Calpurnia. Julius thought hard. He'd better snap to attention fast or he'd find himself overtaken for real.

'I just hope for your sake you were discreet about this,' he said.

'Yes.'

'This is the last time, Mercurius. Try anything like this again and you'll find yourself on crowd control at the Circus Maximus – for good.'

Mercurius looked suitably crestfallen but there was still a glint in his eye, and Julius knew his Number Two didn't really believe he had the clout to carry out his threat. Did he have anyone backing him? Who? If not Tigellinus, who was powerful enough? Seneca? Petronius? Vatinius? But what interest would they have? And Julius had the backing of Nero himself – as long as that remained worth anything.

He put his suspicions to one side and made Mercurius wait while he read the report again. Carefully.

'Following a minute search of the hall following the removal of the bodies and body parts, the enquiry found two distinct artefacts – a blood-stained shawl and a pearl necklace of Thracian design. Enquiries into the ownership of these items indicate that they belonged to none of the known victims or survivors (as far as can be ascertained) and that as they are of high quality and therefore unlikely to have been in the possession of slaves (even highly-paid and skilled sex-slaves) the conclusion reached is that the artefacts belonged to one or more of the perpetrators. As the perpetrators themselves cannot be directly identified through them, the proposal is that – given the quality of the goods – the investigation should make discreet enquiries at high-end retail outlets regarding recent transactions (the shawl is clearly new) involving such artefacts, and through such seek to identify purchasers, who in turn may then be discreetly approached . . .'

The report took up another two wax tablets, in a similarly official style, detailing lines of enquiry which Julius thought more hopeful than focused, but it was progress of a sort and gave him something to show Nero – if the emperor allowed them to continue along the lines Mercurius suggested.

'One last factor may be relevant but must be considered speculative at most . . .' The unfinished report ended in mid-sentence. Julius looked up from the tablets, wondering if he should have them written out properly for the archives or whether he should commit the information to memory and have the tablets rubbed clean. That course would serve two purposes – greater security, and the suppression of any evidence that Mercurius had shown greater initiative than he had himself. Julius decided on the second, telling himself that security was paramount. But he'd instruct Quintus in private about that.

He tapped the tablets with his left forefinger. 'What were you going on to say?'

Mercurius had been watching him attentively. 'I did some background work after our last conversation. About the likelihood of our dealing with something –' he looked for

the right way of expressing himself '– out of the
ordinary.'

'Yes?'

'And I found something in Tarquinius' *Unnatural History*
which has sections on –' he hesitated.

'On?'

'What we were talking about. Succubi, Lamiae, Empusae
– witches and bloodsuckers –'

'No! The title of the book says it all – *Unnatural History*.'

'Malevolent spirits which take the form of women,'
Mercurius continued. 'Tarquinius says their true form may
be like a leech, or a mosquito.'

'What else does Tarquinius say?'

'Two things I noted. These creatures can never enter a
house uninvited, but after the first invitation, they can come
and go as they please.'

'The second?'

'He says that these creatures are most likely to have been
born on a Saturday – and that those best suited to hunt
them down share that birth day.'

Julius thought that this was the kind of help he didn't
really need; but then, he needed all the help he could get;
and something Mercurius had said nudged his memory,
though he couldn't grasp what it was. Then he remembered: he and Calpurnia shared the same birth day – a
Saturday.

He felt cold, though everything rational in him told

him to ignore such nonsensical superstition. He closed his mind to it. He would not accept it. He could not.

'This is a murder investigation, not a witch-hunt,' he said. 'I think we can forget about your book of fairy-tales.'

40

Something was pressing down on him. He knew he'd been dreaming, he even knew what was coming, and tried to wake before it happened, but now he was struggling under a great weight which threatened to crush and smother him. He struggled and his limbs flailed but he was hopelessly pinned down – something like an overfilled sack, except that it was warm and alive. It was covering his face now, his mouth . . .

He awoke suddenly, gasping for breath, drenched in sweat. It must have been close to dawn, for the light from the windows was grey and uncertain, and the objects in the room shimmered and moved, like ghosts.

He saw Calpurnia's silhouette by the window. She seemed thinner than when he'd last seen her. One hand rested on the low sill and she was looking out at the coming day. She hadn't noticed that he was awake and he raised himself on one elbow to look at her. How long had she been there? The sheets beside him felt cold.

She sensed he was awake and turned to him, with a look that seemed relieved, and came and bent over him, kissed him.

He'd found a note from her when he'd got back the previous evening and replied to it immediately. She'd been there an hour later.

'I'm glad you're back.'

'I'm sorry. I had things to do in the country.'

He didn't press it. He was intrigued and a little disturbed that she'd decided on time apart so soon after they'd met, but it didn't preoccupy him. What did preoccupy him, as any possible pattern to the killings was breaking down, was her safety. He wanted to watch over her, and he couldn't if she decided there'd be times when she'd just disappear for a while. He stroked her arm, and looked at her.

'Is this real?' she asked him.

'I hope so.'

But there was still something in her that he'd noticed the evening before – a slight absence, a concern, which he couldn't put his finger on. When he'd asked her about it, as obliquely as he could, in the quiet time after they'd made love, she'd given him vague answers, told him there was nothing to worry about. But now he saw the distant expression in her eyes again. She caught him looking at her and said, 'There's nothing to worry about.'

'But I do.'

'There's really nothing.'

'I won't let anything happen to you.'

She gave him a sad smile.

'Is it because you're a Christian?'

She looked at him. 'I don't think that has anything to do with it.'

'But you are afraid of – whatever it is out there?'

'Aren't you? Isn't everybody?'

'Yes, but –'

'Then I'll take my chances with everyone else. I don't go to orgies and Nero doesn't owe me money. And the emperor can't send every Christian in the city to the arena. And just being one isn't illegal.'

'Are you still one?' Julius asked, thinking of what Titus had said.

'I try to be. But I don't sing out from the rooftops about it.'

That was true of most Christians now. Since Petrus' death, Paulus had taken over the leadership of the sect, and his policy was one, for the moment at least, of discretion.

'I was sad when I heard about Petrus' execution,' she said after a long silence.

'Is that why you are low?'

'I'm not low now. I'm glad to see you!'

She kissed him again, and he took her in his arms as she pressed her body against his, and he stirred, forgetting everything else again as they made love, though even then the slight distance remained and he sensed it. He couldn't have found her, only to be losing her already.

'Let me ask you something,' she said, as they lay side by side on the bed, spent, and his thoughts crowded back to him now that the brief reprieve was past.

He wondered if she knew already, and was disinclined to put her off with vague answers any more. But still he waited for the question, and it came:

'What is it you really do? You're not really just some penpusher for the Senate, are you?'

He told her as much as she needed to know. That he was a Legate, and that he was involved in some supervisory role in the investigation of the killings.

'I knew you were involved somehow.'

'How?'

'I just knew. Closely involved?'

'Closely enough.'

'Can you tell me anything?'

'It'd be better if I didn't.'

'But are you getting anywhere?'

'There's been progress, yes.'

And he found it was a relief to talk to her. Apart from Mercurius, and he didn't know how far to trust him, there was no one. He'd talk to Titus, but Titus was wrestling with his own demons, and their friendship wasn't the kind which admitted any great intimacy. But still he only described a general picture.

'But have you found a track to follow?'

'Perhaps . . .'

And he told her more, finding that talking to her, rehearsing some of his thoughts, was helping him not only refine them but formulate new ones. And he could talk to this semi-stranger whom he instinctively trusted. He didn't reflect on the hard fact that a long loneliness can tempt you to give too much, too soon, once its spell is broken, to the person who breaks it. A lesson he should have learned, but which no one ever really learns.

The talk was bringing his mind squarely back to his work. He needed to get on, his day was already wasting, and he was forgetting his duties as a host. Apologising to her, and taking a last kiss, he rose, and went to give orders to Dio to arrange baths and breakfast.

When he returned to the bedroom, she was gone. A note on the bed, which she must have made – it looked as if it hadn't been slept in at all.

'Soon again – but let me be the one to be in touch.'

41

Three days followed, days in which Julius saw and heard nothing of Calpurnia, days during which he and Mercurius waited impatiently, infuriated, for permission to come for them to pursue their investigation of the shawl and the necklace. Nero was away from the city, planning, it was rumoured, a voyage to Greece, 'to drink at the fountain of Thespis'; in other words, to recharge his artistic soul by visiting what he saw as the birthplace of his first love, the theatre. He either couldn't or wouldn't grant Julius an audience, and Julius suspected that for reasons of his own, Tigellinus was blocking him.

But as the three days gave way to a fourth, still nothing had happened. There were no more attacks. People waited fearfully for the lull to be broken, at the same time hoping against hope that the curse had been lifted with the death of Petrus. And soon it would be ten days since they had crucified him.

Julius, on the rare occasions when work permitted him leisure, resisted all thought of taking the route to Calpurnia's apartment block, though more than once he found his feet taking him in that direction. He forced himself to take another path when that happened, but she was seldom far from his thoughts. And around him, work began again on the rebuilding of the city. The Golden House began to take shape on its vast site in the centre of the city, where the workers tore down hundreds of dwellings and shops which had escaped the flames to make room for its future gardens and avenues. Thousands of people who thought they'd been spared, were now forcibly rehoused in new dwellings and businesses in the less attractive and less profitable suburbs. How long did the emperor think he could run the city and the empire as his private fiefdom? But Julius had to concentrate on more pressing problems than that.

And on the morning of the fourth day . . .

'They've gone!' Mercurius told him. 'They've been taken.'

The iron door to the strong-room was open and the shelf on which the necklace and the shawl had been stored was bare. Nothing else had been touched. The office was its usual untidy self but a quick search revealed that everything else, down to the last stylus and the last wax tablet, was in its place. Not one document was missing, not one other artefact relating to another case. No attempt to cover the purpose of the break-in, and there was no trace of any violence in the break-in itself. The night-guard had seen nothing. No locks had been forced.

'Tigellinus?'

'Why?'

Julius had no answer to that. It could hardly be in Tigellinus' interest to take them, knowing that Julius still enjoyed Nero's protection. Even if he had an agenda of his own, it'd be hard to prove. Tigellinus was unassailable. His power, as everyone else's, lay in Nero's gift; but wasn't the emperor a little afraid of him?

'We must find them!' said Mercurius.

'How?'

Mercurius' shoulders sank. It was true. There was no way to begin to know where to look in a city of hundreds of thousands of people, a city disrupted and confused at the best of times, let alone these.

Who else knew, apart from those who had to?

But his thoughts were distracted by a sudden commotion in the outer office, voices raised, panic in them. Julius opened the communicating door and saw Quintus, standing by his desk, his stool knocked over, talking urgently with a tired and scared-looking commander from II Cohort and another from V. As he watched, two more men, centurions from III and VII, burst in.

He had only to look at their faces to know what had happened.

42

They must have been ravenous. Something uncontrolled and uncontrollable had taken over now – there could be no denying it, nor could its effect be minimised or hushed-up. In a rash of killings overnight, over most of the city, there had been twenty killings. Fourteen men and six women. Most of them from the city's elite – the senators and the knights. But here again the pattern was breaking down. One victim was a visitor to Rome, a Greek philosopher here to teach his theories to a keen group of literary young men and women, and another was a rent-boy who plied his trade near the market close to the west bank of the Tiber where the new temple of Neptune was nearing completion. Three footsoldiers, a Jewish artist, an Egyptian athlete, two courtesans and a popular chariot-racer made up the number of people from outside the city or its upper classes. None of the victims, though, was poor, and none was a Christian.

All had been sucked so dry that what remained of them appeared mummified. In three cases the bodies had been torn apart, though whether this had been done by the killers, or afterwards by dogs, no one could tell. One woman's skull had been cracked open like a walnut and the brains partially consumed.

Nero, returned to Rome, had declared a curfew from dusk to dawn, and the number of guards on the streets at night was trebled. Soldiers from the First and Third Legions were recalled from the north to supplement the troops already in the city. People resented the curfew, but few ventured out after dark now, whether permitted to or not, even to go to the restaurant at the corner of their own street.

Julius and Mercurius bent over a map of the city, pinpointing each attack.

'They all happened in the space of three or four hours, as far as we can tell, well after nightfall, but while there were people in the streets.'

'Witnesses?' asked Julius.

'None. No one who'll come forward, anyway.'

That didn't surprise him. People were scared witless. He looked at the map. The killings looked as if they happened at random, there was no hoped-for pattern or diagram to be seen by connecting the locations together. It was as if a blind force, like a hurricane, had been unleashed.

'Here's where the first one was found,' said Mercurius, pointing to a spot near the old temple of Mars. 'But the others, and in what order, is anyone's guess.'

He waved at the map. Marked on it were locations near the Circus Maximus, near the Capitol, the temple of Jupiter, two of the arenas, three of the theatres, a couple of well-known restaurants, and four of the best of the city's nine hundred-odd Baths, only frequented by the senatorial class.

'Not exactly out-of-the-way places. Well lit and well guarded.'

'This is too big for us to handle,' said Mercurius, and Julius could see the beads of sweat on his forehead.

Julius nodded. It wasn't just a perverted serial killer they were after now – but he had long known that. Some co-ordinated act of terrorism? Something specifically designed to spread panic and fear and, in the wake of them, anarchy, in the city? Something designed to bring it to its knees from within? Something calculated to stab the Empire squarely in the heart? But even as he clung to that belief, so his own heart told him, with increasing insistence, that despite every belief he held dear, there was something abhuman controlling this, and it would take little less than a miracle to track it down and kill it.

He was also well aware of the fact that the deadline Nero had given him was approaching fast. But the emperor was keeping something from him, something which might hold the key to all this. If only he could get the man to open up. But you might as well expect to be able to prise an oyster open with your bare hands.

He was considering his options when the door opened and Quintus came in with a letter from Titus. Julius looked at his scribe. 'When did this arrive?'

'The courier is waiting now for your reply.'

Julius broke the seal and unrolled the paper.

The farmlands are being attacked. Not much, but three killings of cattle and three of sheep on two estates adjoining mine. I was lucky. No people killed. I am taking your advice and returning to the country, but send word if you need me. Forgive me.

'Your reply?' Quintus asked after a moment.

'Just tell the courier to send him my thanks,' Julius said, rolling the letter up again thoughtfully.

43

The truth is that it is becoming more powerful, harder to control. But I rejoice that I have controlled it – can control it, though I pray that my grip may not weaken as it grows in me like a disease which eats from within. So far it has kept us safe and I won a great victory when I was with him. I should not have gone to him, I should keep away from him if I love him, if I want him to live, for one day it may overpower me when we are together.

Why do you not let me die, oh Sabazios? Why do you let me endure this? The pain of the Changing gets worse and the gnawing hunger grows too hard to bear. When I change my body feels ripped apart and when I am become the Thing I loathe the exultant power I feel and must resist. The human being which is in me still *must* resist and assert herself over the beast.

It is bad with my sisters. I talk to them often but they are suspicious. They would not understand why I chose not to join them at Poppaea's feast, but their own savagery saved me then because they were ravening with hunger and that drove all other thoughts out of their minds. Let her feed on sheep and pigs if that is her taste, Pompeia said. But she will eat no real meat, Flavia replied, asking me, How will you grow stronger if you do not? How will you breed when the time comes? She destroyed the woman Sexta, said Apuleia. But she did not eat her, Flavia said. She vomited her up before she could digest her.

I think Justina said something then to calm them. I was the one who pulled Justina from the grave, where she was frightened, while my sisters stood by, allowing me that task, and Justina still has a shred of humanity left in her. I pray so.

I think Apuleia has drawn ahead of her in this race. Apuleia was cruel before. When we were charioteers she enjoyed giving the crowd the spectacle of a slow death. She kills for pleasure, not just to feed, but she has always killed for pleasure.

But Flavia is the worst. Even when we were properly alive, Flavia never gave the slightest thought to anyone else's feelings, but rode roughshod over everything to reach her goals. If we ever breed, and may Bendis in her mercy and chastity never allow that, let her be barren, for her seed is bad, and only evil can ever issue from her womb. She does not know the sensations of sympathy and pity. Tenderness and truth are not in her.

(I know I have had his seed in me. But I smeared my cave with algae that would kill it. I could not resist him and I want him and that pain is greater even than the pain of the Changing but I dare not risk a child while I am accursed and I think I am accursed forever.)

Was I the only one to hope that Petrus' death would take this bitter cup from us? Perhaps Justina still, but the others . . .

We held off for a time after they killed him. We were terrified they would find us. But then we began to starve. We can no longer pretend that ordinary food and drink nutures us. We can eat and drink but we cannot *feed*. At last we needed to gorge ourselves. I went out to the farms, but the others fed, as they say, properly. We can only nourish ourselves through the tubes that our tongues become during the Changing. And how it hurts when the tongue splits open and the beak forms.

Claudia, you were the lucky one. You died in the arena. When we mourned you, we should have rejoiced that you escaped the fate that has befallen us. But how could we know? Luck lies in wait for some, but misery, defeat, illness and pain ambush the rest of us – and always it is unexpected, always we are unprepared, always we have merely to react to and adapt to what the Parcae hand us.

And fight what is bad, even when we know it is a losing battle.

But I will endure. By the grace perhaps of that god of whom Petrus preached? I do not know. I am beyond believing in any god any more.

But I am torn. When I took him to the banquet to meet them, hoping that he would see in them what I saw, I still suggested to Justina as a joke that she should come dressed as a boy. Why? To protect her because I think she might still be saved? I knew there were witnesses at Poppaea's feast and so I hoped when he met them he might see . . . But how could he see if I blinded his eyes? He had seen Justina dead, but not her eyes. If he had seen her eyes, when she was dead, he would have known her in life.

And then the clues he had which I took. Justina's shawl and necklace. But after the banquet they were suspicious again. Flavia and Apuleia especially. Why bring him? Why not just kill him? I replied that it wasn't worth it because he would never find us, corner us, how could he? That I was amusing myself with him, playing with him, as a cat bats a mouse with its paws a while before sinking the unsheathed claws in, breaking the little neck in strong jaws.

But I must protect him.

When Mercurius found the shawl and the necklace, my sisters knew I was in a position to retrieve them, and if I had not they would have turned on me in fury, and though I long for death, I also want to live, because only if I live can I tell myself that I will get through this nightmare and wake in a happy life again, though it is a life I have already half-forgotten.

So I took them. But I fear my hope for Justina is a vain one.

She it is who wants me to kill again. She tells me it is to satisfy the others. But I know it is also so that she can be reassured. She would envy me if she knew I could still harbour hope of being saved, that there is still a small fortress inside me that is able to hold off the enemy which has invaded me.

I say my name to myself. Not my Roman name. My own name. The name they gave me when they took me from inside my mother and cut the cord, laid me on the sheepskin and towelled me. The name inside that fortress.

But Justina is waiting for me to select a victim.

I dare not disappoint her.

I need to find another like Sexta.

Another that deserves to die.

44

The Baths were no longer full these days, especially towards evening. Julius and Titus found themselves all but alone when they moved to the *tepidarium*.

Titus, briefly back in Rome in response to a message from his friend, had not seen him since his arrival. His manner was embarrassed, and their conversation so far had been reserved. Now he had relaxed enough for Julius to talk seriously at last. But Titus forestalled him.

'How is Calpurnia?'

Julius wanted to steer the conversation away from her. There was something more pressing he needed to talk about, but he said, 'Well.'

Titus smiled. 'I know. I saw her yesterday. She looked *radiant*, my friend. And *sleek*.'

'Sleek?' Julius remembered thinking that Calpurnia, before

she'd left for the country, had looked pale, withdrawn. The death of Petrus had affected her badly, and he'd wished that he could take her away somewhere, to the sea, perhaps. Not that there was any hope of his leaving the investigation now. 'I'm glad to hear it.'

'You must be good for her.'

Julius didn't smile. 'Titus, I have to ask you about the deaths of the farm animals.'

'Is that why you asked me to come to Rome? I told you everything I know in my note.'

'I would have come to your estate, but –'

'I know you can't leave Rome now, and I had other business to attend to here anyway.' He spread his hands. 'You know farmers – they panic at the slightest thing. Apart from that recent outbreak of killings, things are quiet again. And this time we are pretty sure it was wolves.'

'But how did the bodies look?'

Titus looked down. 'They had been sucked dry,' he said.

'Then it's the same as before! Have you ever heard of wolves treating their prey like that?'

Titus shook his head.

'This is important.'

'Julius, don't make too much of the deaths of some cattle. You have enough to think about. Anyway, it looks like an isolated case.'

'Any other attacks like this, tell me. Send me word immediately. And make a note of exactly when they occur.'

'*If* they occur.'

Julius didn't say how much he hoped they wouldn't. 'I'm glad you're out of Rome,' he said.

Titus nodded. 'You had better nail this fast,' he replied. 'The panic is spreading.'

Julius didn't need to be told that. There were no private bodyguards left for hire – every last one had been engaged and there were no volunteers coming forward to meet the demand, though tough slaves had been pressed into unwilling service from the farmlands. The price of guard dogs had risen astronomically, and there too the stock was all but exhausted. It took a good year for a good dog to mature from a puppy, and be trained.

He thought of Calpurnia, of how much he needed to protect her.

They left the Baths together and Julius, regretfully refusing Titus' invitation to dinner, made his way back to VIII Cohort. He would much prefer to have spent the evening with his friend, but any kind of conviviality seemed like a distant memory. He would much rather be anywhere than where he was now. Part of him hoped he would wake up to find that he'd been having a nightmare. But this was real and the only thing to do was measure up.

Between sunrise and sunset two days earlier, there'd been four more killings, again in different parts of the city and again at about the same time. If there was any shred of a pattern, this was the one Julius clung to: none of the recent

267

victims belonged to the plebeian class. But even those who believed themselves immune were taking few chances now. The few victims there had been among the poor were enough for the virus of panic to spread there too. The problem was that the dead were no longer closely associated with the emperor. Julius' hope of finding a link there had faded. Whether Nero would be relieved or not remained to be seen, but his feelings played a very small role now. Whatever had been unleashed was without control, without any master at all.

But there were new traces to follow. One of the victims, a young man, a Gaul who'd made a fortune as a wrestler and been granted not only his freedom but citizenship on his retirement from the ring, had put up a fight.

45

The young man's name was Etius. Near his body they found, half-hidden under some builders' rubble, his dagger, easily identifiable from his insignia at the base of the hilt. The blade was encrusted with a rust-brown, dried substance which might have been blood.

'What do you think?' Mercurius said, looking down at the mangled mess which lay on the ground before them.

'They didn't finish the job.'

'Think he wounded one of them?'

'Perhaps only one attacked him.' If they could be wounded, Julius thought, they could also be killed. Couldn't they?

Most of the body, though contorted, either by agony or as a result of the struggle, was intact. Only the stomach had been sucked out; the arms, legs and chest were complete and the head untouched, the handsome features marred by the open, staring eyes and the mouth drawn back in what was either a frozen scream or a ferocious grimace.

Mercurius retrieved the dagger and carefully placed it in the leather pouch at his side. It was possible that Opimius or another doctor could tell if the rust-brown matter on its blade was blood or not.

'Get our men to visit the hospitals. Any recent patients with stab wounds . . .' Julius trailed off. He was going through the motions and he knew it. But the dagger was also a bone to throw to Nero. He wasn't looking forward to his next interview with the emperor.

'They are plotting against me!' were Nero's first words as Julius entered the now-familiar room. 'They do not recognise my talents! And you are the only one who can help me!'

Julius told him about the dagger, and hope replaced fear in Nero's eyes. 'Etius killed one of them?'

'Wounded, perhaps, Lord. But we have found no body.'

Nero slumped in his chair. 'Then I am lost! Lost!'

'We will find them.'

'It is a conspiracy. I will kill all the senators.'

'You cannot do that.'

Nero knew he had made an empty threat, and cursed his own weakness, his own vacillation. 'The Praetorian Guard will protect me. I am a god! I can do whatever I

270

like.' But Nero could not disguise the doubt he felt. Julius had no way of getting any more out of him. If the emperor would only divulge the secret Julius felt sure he guarded within him. But now Nero became aggressive. 'You aren't doing enough. Only my hand stays Tigellinus. And I need him more than I need you. If he deserts me, nothing can save me.'

'Tigellinus will be able to do no more than I have.'

'You have done nothing! I have heard there are murmurs among the mob that my rule is doomed. That a new dawn is breaking. What do they think that will bring them? A better life? I am rebuilding Rome for *them*!'

'They know that. They only see that the victims come from among their rulers. The deaths of ordinary people have been coincidental.'

'That gives them pleasure!'

'Everyone is afraid.'

Nero became calmer. 'I will stem the panic. You – continue the hunt. I will buy time.'

Julius left, his mind dark. He knew what would follow.

The series of arrests and show-trials began two days later. Units from the Praetorian Guard, directed by Tigellinus, swooped on twenty carefully selected households and cleared them. Julius could only watch as those accused of dissent and conspiracy were sentenced to exile or death – including people, he noted, who posed a real or imagined threat to the emperor, even if that only went as far as mild criticism. The official reports enthusiastically described an end to the reign of terror in the city. But Julius noticed that not all those arrested and condemned were dissenters. Nero was taking the opportunity to do a little house-cleaning of his own as he sought to allay public fear.

The curfew was lifted. Celebrations and games were announced. The sun shone on Rome and there were no more killings.

But Etius' dagger had disappeared.

They knew enough about gladiatorial combat to recognise a flesh-wound when they saw one. As soon as they had got Apuleia back to the safety of her apartment, when she was a woman again, they could see that the damage was not mortal. Carefully tended, she would survive. They still had enough control to stay in their human shape for as long as that took, they thought, though they would all go hungry. They fed Apuleia on their own blood.

They kept blinds over the windows. They found they were easily burnt by the sun. Their healthy tans were fading. Only one of them seemed better able to withstand daylight than the rest. But she was one of them. They were sure of that. She would do nothing to harm them. And they had another preoccupation. They had to find somewhere else to go, to hide. They guessed that the only reason they still enjoyed the emperor's protection was that in providing it he was protecting himself. Only now they saw he was buying himself time. But why?

'He is frightened of his own power,' said Justina.

'Over us? He has no power over us,' Pompeia said.

'But he thinks he has. And do we know that we are in control ourselves?'

There was silence then. The sisters looked at each other.

'We can control the Changing,' Flavia said, her eyes exultant.

'We can resist it,' replied Pompeia. 'We can resist it for as long as we choose.'

'No we can't – a moment comes, we all know this, when the Changing will not be denied,' murmured Justina.

'When we are hungry.'

'When we are hungry.'

The shadows of evening crept across the floor in the silence that followed.

'He does not control us,' Flavia said. 'And have you forgotten how it feels? The power? The triumph!'

'But it hurts so much. And what triumph can there be in pain?' said Justina.

'The day will come when there will be no more Changing. The day will come when we are no longer human – like the creatures that attacked us,' Flavia said.

'Where did they come from?'

Silence again.

'We will know when it is our turn,' said Flavia.

'But they were small, like locusts.'

'Then we have an advantage,' Flavia replied.

'To do more harm? And what does it profit us? We are in a prison. Is there no release?' the other sister said quietly.

They turned to look at her. It was the first time she had spoken.

'So you regret it?'

The other sister looked at them. 'Can you not regret the loss of what we are? What we were?'

'You must be *one of us*.'

'I am,' she replied, her voice faltering. 'I have convinced you.'

'You have killed,' Justina said.

'But not often,' added Flavia. 'You must kill again.'

Calpurnia looked at her sisters. Their eyes were becoming the eyes of strangers, as the power ate into them. And she knew it was eating into her too. But why less slowly? Why, where she could see that they felt nothing but the need to survive, did she still cling to her desperate need to remain a human being?

'I have protected you,' she said, wondering for the first time why. Because there had been hope? But was there hope? For any of them?

'Apuleia will be well soon,' Flavia said.

Calpurnia knew the real reason then: because she was afraid. For her sisters. Of her sisters. For herself. Of the creature which now dwelled within her.

274

46

They lay back in the darkness, exhausted. Julius heard her breathing, still ragged, but did not speak. He made to reach out for her hand, but changed his mind and remained still, listening to the vague sounds of the night. He needed to think, if he could. He knew that he was in the grip of something beyond his control, but he was not only unable, but unwilling to resist it. He had at last met someone whom he wanted to protect, to guard, to look after, someone who didn't have the dreary, limited ambitions of every woman he had met before, but also someone who represented the unknown. What was it in him that sought uncertainty, that was uncomfortable with safety? His father had been a professional soldier and his mother a respectable Roman lady, and his life had been mapped out in such a way that he need have done nothing but marry, produce heirs, and move forwards in a career which would progress evenly towards a consulship and ultimately a dignified retirement on estates in the northern hills. Sunshine, a little wine, tending his vines, dabbling perhaps in a little literature and philosophy. Why did he want none of the agreeable things which could so easily have been his? Why had his life been a dangerous obstacle course instead? Why had he not even stayed in Lutetia, where he had been happy, and returned to Rome instead, after only the shortest of stays? He should have made his life there, but he had made another choice.

They had made love for an hour and, as always, her passion had overwhelmed him. But it was passion, he was sure of that. Real passion, not just the desperate fucking that had its roots in loneliness. Neither had said anything about it yet, but he knew he loved her, and hoped she loved him. He didn't yet dare talk about it with her, and yet the way her eyes danced when they conversed, the way she touched his arm lightly when she wanted to make a point, she way she dressed and held herself, called up similar things in him, and he rejoiced in them. Conversation, having things to talk about, was so much harder and so much more important than just sex. They had, it seemed to Julius, both in abundance.

But – as usual with him, he reflected – there were clouds in the sky. He knew her moods of reserve, he didn't like the occasions when she would absent herself from him with no explanation and no communication during them. He had noticed – as now – that she was leaner at some times

276

than others. As now: her cheeks were hollower, her hipbones and the base of her spine more apparent to his touch. At times too, she seemed far more cheerful than at others, though she never explained the reasons for this and he never asked.

Was he afraid of the truth? Of breaking something that was so precious to him? He was intelligent enough to know that he'd fallen under some kind of spell, and wasn't strong enough to break it. But he gave himself an excuse for this: perhaps it wasn't weakness that stayed his hand, but curiosity. Perhaps the policeman still lurked somewhere far away at the back of his consciousness and directed him. And the policeman had not forgotten the missing dagger, necklace and shawl.

She had turned over and her breathing had steadied. She was sleeping. He looked at the white curve of her back, outlined in moonlight which filtered through a crack in the blinds, and wondered at it. That this woman should choose to lie down with him at all was a miracle to him, and her mysteriousness deepened his sense of wonder.

He was determined that nothing should happen to harm her, nothing should happen to take her from him. He wanted to arch his body over her like a protecting sky, to smooth away her cares without ever questioning their cause, and to be with her forever. Nothing else was important. Except that the outside world had to be lived in, and would not leave them alone.

He caressed her shoulder, feeling an intense tenderness; she murmured in her sleep at his touch and stirred without waking. He stroked her hair, softer than her skin, and then withdrew his hand.

But she was awake now, or half awake, and turned to him, murmuring softly, seeking his lips with hers, pressing her body against his, entwining him in her arms. Her hands slid down to his thighs and ran over them, slowly working round to their inner surfaces, then up to embrace his prick, already alert before she encircled it. His own hands, no less busy, caressed her breasts, squeezing them, kneading them gently, then harder as their mouths and tongues sought each other with fierce urgency. Oiled by their perspiration, they rubbed their bodies together and then she slid down his body to take him in her mouth, just the tip of Priapus at first, not allowing him to thrust further, tantalising him with her tongue, digging her hands into his buttocks, but gently, always gently, and slowly, slowly she engulfed him, running her mouth up and down the full length of him, for what seemed like forever and he was nowhere at all and no thought disturbed his mind and his heart swelled and thundered.

And now, without her letting go of him, their bodies pressed urgently against each other in a way that was independent of their volition. His mouth fastened on her engorged lower lips, pink and moist beneath their dark protecting nest of soft fur. He slid his tongue inside her and held on as she bucked and cried, pushing her body towards him.

He felt her lose concentration on him, as she lost herself in her own ecstasy, and he was glad, for to give Calpurnia pleasure was the greatest joy he knew – the only greater one would be to give her happiness.

She writhed uncontrollably but he would not let her go until she shrieked and threw her body upwards, drenching his face in warm liquid, tearing at his hair enough to hurt him, though he did not notice the pain. The root of his tongue ached and she pushed him away, but not far, turning so that her face was level with his again, smiling, eyes bright as emeralds in the light of tapers, their faces close, as she guided him into the warm oil lining her cave. Its muscles tensed on him as he moved inside her, taking his weight on his elbows, then back onto his hands as his body arched, Priapus sliding back and forth within her, rejoicing in his simultaneous sovereignty and service, at the same time emperor and slave. No thought any more; their bodies, he felt, had taken over, and everything was simple and good in the only short-lived heaven humans can create for themselves in this world of endless limitations.

The moonlight shifted over them in the room, over the assaulted bed, over their quiet forms as at last they lay at peace, still free from the thoughts and troubles, which they would not yet allow to occupy their minds again. It may be that the unwanted tenants would not return before the onset of sleep, and would only penetrate again when they woke.

Their noses were touching, their eyes locked on one another's, just looking, marvelling. But at last she smiled at him and turned away again. He stayed awake, listening to her breathing as once more it became soft and low.

He could not see that her eyes were open, and had no idea of the battle that raged within her, and which continued to rage long after he had found refuge in sleep.

47

His name was Gaius Aelius Aculeo. A former captain
in the Praetorian Guard, he'd worked for Tiberius,
Caligula and Claudius before Nero, and under the last
three he had been Head of the Torments. The dungeons
under the prison block not far from the Praetorian
Barracks were supposed to be a secret, but everyone
knew about them. They reached for a long way, thousands of *passi*, spread out along corridors arranged in
a grid system, tiny cells to hold the prisoners, large
halls where the instruments of torment were arranged.

I knew about Gaius from our cousin who died after
the last show we put on in the arena. I knew that he'd
made most of his money working under Caligula, that
then he was at his peak. He favoured the simplest
methods of torture, and had invented many now in the

standard repertoire. His own preference was the Twister. Two wooden handles connected in the centre by a length of wire. The operator wrapped the wire round any part of the human body he chose – an arm, a leg, the torso, a hand – and slowly twisted it tighter and tighter. It would first bite into the flesh, then cut it, and finally, if no satisfactory answers came, sever. Gaius also enjoyed using carpenters' tools, which especially lent themselves to his ingenuity, and of these, long-nosed pliers and the ten *libra* hammer were the ones which came first to hand.

Gaius had retired a rich man and lived alone in a villa overlooking the Tiber from the Aventine. Age had withered his body but not his desire. It was easy to gain access to him, and at night he was ours alone. I say ours, because Justina was with me, to see I did my duty.

I have killed again. Justina stood over me and watched. They allowed me to choose my victim, and I chose according to my sense of justice. If you can call anything a mercy, that was it, but my heart is sour and I feel lost. I think my head will burst if nothing releases me from this. And killing one evil person is like tearing at weeds without destroying the roots. The roots of evil never die, and will always find somewhere to push their life to the surface, and flower, and spread. But I chose Gaius as I had chosen Sexta – and selfishly too, for I know I must kill to live, and when I am hungry it is all I can do – even with *him* – to keep myself in check. It is a good exercise though – it reassures me that my inner fortress is still intact.

Like all such people, people without conscience, Gaius' self-absorption was his weakest point, for he could not know when someone had seen through him. Our first visit was in the guise of collectors for a charity working on behalf of the poor whose houses had been destroyed in the Fire. Because we are young and pretty, he invited us into his house. He gave generously, and invited us back. There was no mistaking the expression in his eyes and his voice.

Once he had invited us back, we knew he was ours.

Delay for me was useless. If I did not do this I would be outcast at best, destroyed at worst. I was beginning to long for death but too afraid to accept it. Where would what was left of my soul go after I left this world? In my state, half-woman, half-monster, what fate would await me? Oblivion? Dreamless sleep? But I did not want that while I could still hope. Even though part of me scarcely believes in it any more, it is hope which keeps me clinging to life, like a shipwrecked mariner clings to a spar in a grey sea.

I wanted to get it finished, and the Changing came over me almost before we had him alone and trusting. Seeing my skin turn into dark scales, and my hands and feet into claws, Gaius tried to escape before I had him properly pinned down, but he was old and the strength of his limbs had left him, and it was not difficult to get him back to the bed and hold him down. I smothered his screams with my mouth, and my tongue, already contorted, pushed out the beak at its tip and plunged down his throat to his bowels. The beak did its work of chopping, I sucked up his disgusting intestines, and felt myself swell under Justina's satisfied eye.

When I'd finished, gorging myself far more than I desired in order to convince my sister, I stood, the mess still dripping from my jaws. Before my tongue coiled back, I couldn't help vomiting some of the vile meal, but Justina didn't look concerned at that. She contented herself with sucking out what was left in Gaius' legs and arms before she picked up her dress with her claws and scrambled onto the balcony, opening her carapace and preparing her wings for flight. I followed suit, ungainly and heavy with my meal, and we flew to a wood higher up the hill, well beyond the last housing. The animals there – the foxes and the stoats, the owls and the buzzards – fled at our approach. We landed in a clearing, grey in the starlight, to await the Changing.

We made our way back home keeping to the alleys and the shadows. But we had nothing to fear except the stray dogs, and they avoided us. We encountered no patrols and were not surprised at that, and no trav-ellers at all were on the streets now. I took my leave of my sister and returned to my apartment alone. I know they permit me to stay there unwatched because they still – just – trust me, and now I think they will trust me more. But I also know that they meet without me and I do not know what they plot then.

My woman's body had already filled out a little, and I hoped he would be pleased. But I will not see him again until the effect of my feeding has become less obvious.

If I ever see him again. Apuleia has recovered and nothing will stop my sisters from hunting again. My only hope of survival, of hoping for a moment when I can do something to stop this, is to assuage them, ensure that they trust me. But to do that, I have to be a traitor to myself, and I do not know if that will weaken me, weaken my resolve. Every day the effort to resist becomes greater. Every day the fight becomes harder.

I wish I could resist him, for his own safety. But I can no more do that than I can resist what has happened to me. I tell myself that my redemption may lie there, with him, and I hope and pray that I am right. So in keeping them away from him, I am protecting myself. But can I also protect him *from* myself?

48

It was a smart town house on a quiet street spared by the fire which wound round the foot of the Palatine. Trees in the street provided shade and the atrium, when they entered it, was calm and well ordered. There was nothing to suggest the turmoil which once again raged in the city outside, or the tension which must have been building now in the household itself – unless you counted the three soldiers stationed at the gate.

The house-slave who'd ushered them in withdrew, leaving them to take seats by the fountain which played gently in the centre of the courtyard. Titus and Julius looked at each other as they waited. Each knew what the other was thinking. Julius had found no trace of the dagger, the shawl or the necklace, but he wondered how they might help him, now that their use as delaying tactics had been spent.

Gaius had been a favourite of Nero's, and following his death there'd been another dozen. Julius knew his own days were numbered. The emperor would withdraw his protection, and Tigellinus would see to it that he was immediately sent to the arena.

The latest killings had made Nero cast around for new victims, and in desperation he had turned with increased severity to the Christians. That is why they were here now.

They rose as their host approached. He was lean, dressed in a plain blue robe, and ran a hand briefly through the thinning hair which covered a high-domed forehead as he extended his hand to them. Behind him, a servant brought wine and *mulsum* and honey-cakes.

The man indicated by a gesture that they should resume their seats, and joined them. He waited while the drinks were served, then raised an inquisitive eyebrow.

'How can I be of help?'

He didn't sound over-friendly and Julius sought immediately to reassure him. 'First of all, Paulus, I am not here officially.'

The man sat back. 'Well, that is a relief. I am expecting them to come for me any day now. Any hour.'

'Julius is my friend,' Titus said. 'No harm will come to you through him.'

'Which is why I agreed to this meeting,' replied the man. 'And I hope we remain friends too, Titus, despite your having left us.'

Titus did not know what to reply.

'Do not upset yourself,' Paulus said. 'It saddens me that you question your faith, but that is your choice. I hope that one day you will change your mind, but I am certain you gave your decision much thought.'

'You must believe that I did.'

'I am encouraged that you have left your estates again – I hope not exclusively on my account.'

'Business calls me often to Rome.'

'But these days you feel more . . .' Paulus sought for the word he needed '. . . *relaxed* on your estates.'

'You can say the word you mean, Paulus: safer.'

'Who would blame anyone for seeking safety? Especially in times like these. If I had a choice, I might well do the same thing.'

Paulus had been under house-arrest for two years. Lenient at first, he was even allowed to leave the confines of his dwelling occasionally. And occasionally he had been able to do so without permission. But restrictions were tighter now. He had not left the house since Nero's first purge.

He turned to Julius. 'Tell me what you want to know.'

'You know I spoke to Petrus.'

'Yes. I can add nothing to what he told you.'

'If there is anything you are holding back, you must let me know now.'

Paulus considered. 'Petrus could be impulsive, but he never lacked mercy. If you are asking – and many have – if we Christians have anything to do with the slaughter, my answer is no.'

'There has been talk of a curse.'

'No curse has been placed by us on anyone.'

'I have heard that Petrus expelled a number of people from your sect.'

'People who did not truly belong to us. People sent to spy on us.'

'And they went?'

'Yes. It is not illegal to be a Christian. Though we are victimised. It is the victimisation that is illegal.'

Titus motioned to him to be careful what he said, but Paulus answered with a sad smile. 'I don't think anything I say to this policeman friend of yours matters much any more. And I cannot do any more damage to our cause than has been done already.' He paused, drank a little. 'We must suffer and bear, until we win through. We expect that.'

'But things can be made very unpleasant for you personally,' Julius said.

'I expect that too.'

'If anything happens to you your people will be left leaderless.'

'My people, as you call them, will never be left leaderless.'

'Your god will not help you.'

'Our god is constantly helping us.'

'I see little to prove that.'

'Proof is not something we expect, either. It is something felt. It is faith.' Paul looked at him. 'I was a little like you once. I was worse. I was a persecutor. But once, on my way to Damascus, I was given something far more important than proof.'

Julius listened to this impatiently. It seemed to him clear that Paulus was holding something back, but what, and why, he didn't know. He knew that it was within his power to have the man taken into stricter custody than this, and to have him tortured, but he knew in his heart that such a path would be taken uselessly. He meshed his hands and twisted his fingers in frustration. 'We can help you – I can help you. I can make things much easier for your companions if you will co-operate.'

'I am co-operating. As far as I can. And I do not need your help.'

'If you do not recognise the law you live under –'

'I recognise it and I obey it. What else should I do?'

They heard the approach of marching soldiers outside the gate then, and the guards there clattering to attention. Each of the three of them was instantly and instinctively alert.

'Sooner than I thought,' said Paulus, looking at Julius.

'This is not my doing.'

'It doesn't matter.' To Titus he said hastily, 'My friend, I do beg one favour. I have made all the arrangements, but your aid would be invaluable.'

'Anything.'

'My librarian has all the details – but help him look after my papers. I would not like to see them lost.'

The gates opened to admit a squad accompanied by an officer, a small pinched man who spoke with a southern, country accent. He read out the arrest warrant with difficulty, concentrating on the words, all but spelling them as he read. Paulus' household had already gathered in the atrium and he calmly murmured some orders to his chief slave, who bowed, tears in his eyes. Then he nodded to his guests and took his place as the soldiers formed up round him. One made to put fetters on him but Paulus stopped him by the simple power of the fire in his eyes.

'I am a Roman citizen. You will not bind me.'

The soldier glanced at his officer, who nodded, and stepped back, shoving the manacles back in his belt. The guard formed up, and Titus and Julius watched as Paulus was marched away.

'This will do no more good than the rest,' Julius said quietly.

'Do not blame yourself for what is happening,' said Titus. 'These things were meant to be. These things would happen with or without the curse. The curse is merely an excuse for them.'

'Let us follow.'

Everything had been arranged in advance, though with obvious haste. Paulus was not taken to any prison, but straight to a courtroom, crowded with the emperor's supporters and heavily fenced in by Praetorians. It was hot in the room, and the press of people made it hotter. Julius and Titus squeezed into places on the raised rear benches and watched as Paulus was led to the centre of the room, to a space cleared in front of the long table where the judges sat. There were no jurors. The principal judge was an experienced man but Paulus was well versed in the law too and conducted his own defence. The judges looked uncomfortable. The arguments their prisoner presented were concise and clear and in any other trial but this . . .

But the judges had their orders and they had their job to do, and this Paulus knew, for Julius and Titus, and the ten or twenty other people in the room quick-witted enough to acknowledge it understood that Paulus was less defending himself than justifying his belief. He was using his trial as a last platform to preach. The pens of the scribes recording his words flew in their hands. Julius wondered how long these records would survive, for this was only the semblance of justice, not justice itself, as every single person in the room knew. But the words would be heard by minds which would commit their gist at least to memory, and that could not be easily expunged.

The trial continued into the next day, and might well have run into a third, except that the judges cut it short. They had run out of arguments. It was time to pronounce sentence.

Paulus was unsurprised when he heard it, but interrupted the official who was passing it.

'You presume too much,' he said, with authority. 'My citizenship of this city gives me privileges which cannot be denied. If I am to be condemned to death, then I claim my right to be executed by the sword.'

The judges looked at one another, conferred. This dignified death was not the one desired for the Christian leader by the emperor. A humiliating, slow death by crucifixion was the only one possible for a dissenting non-believer, and the only one which would show the Romans that the curse was being fought with the utmost force. But to dismiss the rights of one who wore the iron ring of a citizen would look like contempt for the very authority Nero still desperately sought to embody.

Grudgingly, looking foolish, the judges announced that they would defer sentence until the following day.

Paulus allowed himself the faintest smile, a smile just for himself. He would get his way. He had been thrust into a game with nothing to play with, and he had won from it what was important. He had made his trial look meaningless.

Titus watched the scribes gather up their papers as Paulus was led away. 'None of this will get out. There will be no records. History will never know what went on here today.'

Julius was not so sure.

'Will you go back to the country now?' he asked Titus.

'I have business here,' Titus replied. 'I will help you if I can.'

Julius wondered what business could possibly be so pressing as suddenly to detain his friend now, but said nothing.

49

'He's waiting for you,' Mercurius said. Mercurius was a different man these days – less assured, more eager to help, and always curious. His hunt for the missing clues had been diligent and unrelenting. But still Julius couldn't bring himself to trust him. Yet there was nothing he could put his finger on, except Mercurius' ambition. Was the man trying a different tactic?

Julius couldn't allow himself to be distracted by it. He was already compromised enough by Calpurnia, but only Titus knew about them, of that he was sure. But he knew the game he was playing was dangerous, and left him as vulnerable as if they'd thrust him naked into an arena full of lions. What astonished him was that he could not give it up. Could not give her up. Whatever happened, he would not do that. He had not closed his mind to the dark suspicions which lurked in its depths, but something stronger than them, something at the core of his being, told him that, when the time came, a route through the labyrinth he was in lay through her, and that she would show him the way. And though he preferred reason to instinct, he was in no position to turn his back on this conviction.

Days earlier, Calpurnia had announced another of her mysterious absences to him. He had lost his temper, but she would not be moved, and he had to respect her decision. At least this time she had told him it would not be long.

'Who is it?' he demanded of Mercurius now.

'Didn't you know he was coming? Murcellus.'

'The applauder?'

'That's him.'

'What does he want?'

'He wouldn't tell *me*,' replied Mercurius, with a trace of camp reproach, which was unusual in him these days.

Julius went into the room where Murcellus, fatter than ever, slumped on a folding chair which supported his weight by a miracle. He was staring into space, his face vacant, his arms on his knees and his hands folded in front of him. He looked up at Julius and smiled.

'Got something for you. Thought I'd show my gratitude.'

'What for?'

Murcellus shrugged. 'You know – keeping me out of trouble.'

Julius remembered the uncle, and the farm, and hoped Murcellus' news would be worth it.

'There's someone you should have a look at.'

'Yes?'

'Might be more up your mate's street though.'

'You mean Mercurius?'

'Bats for the other side, don't he?'

'Who are you talking about, Murcellus?'

'There's a huge race at the Circus Maximus on *Saturni dies* and you should be there. Look for a bloke called Caeso Fabius Strabo.'

Julius knew the name. He was the brother of the murdered senator, Barbula. Not involved directly in politics himself, he'd made a name for himself as a liberal philosopher, which as far as it went in Strabo's circles meant he was a critic of the Senate and, as far as he dared, of the Throne. But he was popular, and membership of a powerful family protected him. Until recently, his brother's closeness to Nero had ensured his safety. He'd been noticeably quieter since Barbula's death.

And he preferred boys to girls, though that didn't play any role at all. Just a footnote worth remembering in case it ever became significant.

'What about him?'

Murcellus looked crafty. 'Just keep an eye on him.'

'Why the races?'

'See who he talks to.'

'I'll want to talk to you again.'

'Sure,' Murcellus' confidence was bordering on insolence. He rose. '*Lunae dies*, before the sun begins the descent. I've work that afternoon.'

Julius knew well enough that crowds could be the most secure places for private conversations. He was also aware of the rumours of a conspiracy against the emperor. It wasn't too much of a jump to link them to a powerful dissident. And the governor of the Hispania Tarraconensis province was quietly gathering strength in northern Spain. Word was that he had already established a strong link with Julius Vindex in Gaul. But of course nothing was proven, and any plot was only spoken of in whispers.

And Rome was too preoccupied with the terror which held it in its grip to unite behind a conspiracy. In fact, Julius reflected, the terror suited Nero very well. For the moment. All he had to do was get his timing right to be seen as the saviour of the city. And that was where Julius came in. Was the emperor simply waiting for the right moment to throw him the information he needed to crush the terror? Or was the terror wholly out of control?

Nero knew something he wouldn't talk about. It was possible that Caeso Fabius Strabo could be helpful, one way or another, though Julius would have to tread carefully. Nothing could be predicted, and the dark reservation remained in his mind that, comfortable as it'd be to think otherwise, he was dealing with things beyond human control.

'Thank you, Murcellus.'

'I want you to remember this,' the fat young man said. 'If things change in Rome, I'll want insurance.'

Julius grinned at him, reassuringly. It was amusing to think that Murcellus believed that, if things changed, he would ever have any influence at all.

Saturday was hot, and the sun beat down on the Circus Maximus. This was a big occasion, with some of the biggest star charioteers on the bill; and a large crowd had already assembled by the time Julius arrived, even on the sunny side of the course. He made his way to the shady side, where the rich were taking their seats, and the block reserved for Strabo and his party.

The seats were unoccupied, and remained so when the first race was announced. The chariots, representing the Red, White, Blue and Green teams, drew up at the starting line. It was a *quadriga* race, and the drivers wrapped the reins round one wrist, ensuring that the *falx*, the knife they carried to cut through the leather to free their hands in the event of a *naufrigia*, the kind of mass pile-up keenly anticipated by some of the spectators and dreaded by others, was well within reach, and slipped easily from its sheath. The animals were tense, and an *auriga* of chestnuts racing for the Blues reared in their harness when the lead horse, the *funalis*, got irritated by a fly. The driver, a wiry Macedonian whom people were already calling the greatest driver since Eutyches, brought them under control with difficulty. Seeing this, some of the punters rushed to the stands to spread new bets. Maybe the Blues would be unlucky today.

Julius watched idly. Though he liked the races, he seldom bet on them and he didn't have time to take the kind of interest which was rewarded by real pleasure. The freshly raked sand of the course burned in the sun, and from it he raised his eyes, squinting in the light, to the *spina* which ran along the centre of the course, and to the obelisks at each end. As usual there would be seven laps, covering four thousand metres. The crisis points were always the tight turns at each end of the *spina*, and there it was that the pile-ups were most likely to occur, since there were no marked lanes, and each chariot would try to seize the tightest position into the curve.

At last the teams settled down and the starter gave the signal. The chariots roared off, careering perilously close to one another as they turned at the far obelisk and straightened up for the long chase down to the one nearer Julius, but there were no collisions. Only the Reds broke a harness and the driver, a Gaulish slave named Bratonos, one of the up-and-coming drivers favoured by the emperor, was thrown clear as his chariot foundered, just finding time to slice through the reins wrapped round his right wrist with his knife.

He was uninjured and ran to the safety of the sides as attendants rushed out to steady the horses and clear the wrecked chariot from the track before the surviving three teams came round again.

After the eighth turn, the Whites were in front, but the Blue chestnuts were level with the leading chariot's wheels, their heads straining forward as the Macedonian urged them on. Into the straight, he pulled away and a huge roar went up from the crowd, but he couldn't shake off the White team, which dogged his heels, the grey mouths of the horses flecked with foam as their hooves hammered the sand and sent it spraying. The Greens were nowhere, but even Julius could see that the black horses in its team were good strong animals, bred for the track. Was it that their driver wasn't pushing them hard enough? He was a tough-looking man from Cilicia, one of the top five on today's bill, and, at twenty-seven, a lot older than the others. Julius heard muttering among Green supporters near him that the race was fixed.

But there was a strategy. At the end of the sixth lap the Whites and Blues, thinking themselves the only teams in competition, had begun to tire. They'd vied too hard and too soon for the lead, and the Greens had been slowly but surely catching up since lap five. There was huge cheering when, after the penultimate turn, the Cilician let his team rip in the straight. His horses had enough energy left in reserve to charge past the Whites, now in second place, and passed the Blues well on the outside of the last turn. The Macedonian looked over his shoulder at the last moment, and swerved to interrupt the Cilician's progress, but too late. The Greens were past him too and now surged to the finish as the crowd went mad. But passions ran deep. Hardly had the winner been announced after the last lap marker had dipped than a fight broke out on the sunny side of the Circus between Red and Green factions. It took fifteen minutes for the stewards to separate them, clubbing the worst offenders to the ground and dragging them out. When they'd restored order, the line-up for the second race, eight teams of two-horse chariots, was ready on the sand.

But Strabo's block of seats was still empty. One or two people had already sat down in them, only to be moved on. And the seats remained empty for the next three races.

It was a short day – there were only to be fifteen courses run altogether, and after the seventh, Julius began to wonder if he wasn't wasting his time. But then, during a pause between the eighth and the ninth race, when the real stars would begin to compete, Julius noticed movement in the crowd over to his right and saw that about ten people were moving into the vacant places, seating themselves amidst much chatter and laughter. It must have been a good lunch.

Strabo was clearly the host, and Julius was not surprised to see that his immediate entourage consisted of a cluster of shapely, bronzed young men between sixteen and eighteen years old. But there were other guests. Two older lawyers whom Julius recognised by sight and knew to be part of Strabo's intellectual circle – no doubt they shared his political views too – and four others. Julius drew in his breath when he saw them.

Calpurnia was with the three girls and the young man she had introduced him to at the banquet. The young man with eyes like blue flame. Marcus Severus. Julius was barely twenty metres distant from them and, acting on instinct, drew back behind a dividing wall between blocks of seats, so that Calpurnia should not see him.

He watched them discreetly from his vantage point. Calpurnia seemed ill-at-ease, but it was clear that Marcus Severus had made a hit with Strabo. The older man made sure that Severus was seated on his right, and constantly leant over him, touching his shoulder and asking him questions, as if their acquaintance were a new one. Strabo was strongly built, athletic for his age, with a domed bald head fringed with elegantly-cut white hair. His humorous blue eyes sparkled intelligently, but they were never still, as if he were scanning the people immediately around him, and this, Julius noticed, happened especially when he was speaking to the lawyers, one of whom sat on his left, the other immediately behind him. Nothing like a crowd, he thought again, for intrigue, especially when one had as one's cover an attractive young date at one's side. The secret police weren't known for their perspicacity, and if Tigellinus had plants in the crowd, Julius wasn't aware of them.

But what were the girls doing there? And the young man? Were Nero's spies closer to Strabo than he suspected?

The final race had just started, and the sun had moved over the Circus, bringing shade at last to the cheap seats on the opposite side. Julius had shifted his position, wondering whether or not to follow Strabo when he left, but in doing so had moved out from the protective cover of the wall. As soon as he realised his mistake, he took a pace back again, but not before Calpurnia's eyes had fallen him. Their glance met for only a second, but in that moment he recognised fear and defensiveness in hers. He didn't have time to see if any of her companions had noticed, but surely it had all happened too fast for anyone else to see.

But he would have to talk to her about the connection. If he could ever pin her down to a rendezvous. The pang in his heart reminded him of how much he wanted to see her, and for them to be together, with all this behind them.

50

Murcellus didn't keep his appointment. Nor did he turn up with his gang of *Augustiniani* for Nero's performance on Monday afternoon. But it didn't take long to find him. He was in his apartment in the luxury block on the Caelian, overlooking the Via Sacra. In his bath. The water had gone cold and there was no sign of any slaves. The door was open and the dogs, far from challenging Julius and Mercurius as they entered, whined and fawned, distraught and lost.

The water in the bath was red with Murcellus' blood, and his face, resting just above the surface, was drained of any colour. His hands floated just under the surface, but the wrists were not cut. No one had attempted to make this look like a suicide. Instead, Murcellus' throat had been sliced wide open.

'Someone got rid of the attendants, came up behind him

– he probably thought it was a house-slave – and opened him up,' Mercurius suggested.

'Possibly.'

'Good to get back to a plain old-fashioned killing.'

Julius looked at his assistant. For him, this just muddied the water further, though it didn't take genius to suspect where the blame probably fell. It looked as if he hadn't been the only one Murcellus had been talking to. He thought about the lawyers he'd seen with Strabo at the Circus Maximus.

But when he went to talk to them, it turned out that they'd both left town.

'I don't know of any conspiracy against the emperor,' Titus said, when the two of them met by appointment in a noisy restaurant overlooking the Tiber later that day.

'Of course you don't. But you can tell me a bit about Caeso Fabius Strabo.'

'Barbula's brother? You won't find anything to stick on him.'

'I know he has influential friends.'

'It's more than that. He keeps himself apart.'

'Do you really think so?'

'If he doesn't, he's a hell of a lot craftier than I thought.' Titus considered. 'He's a strong supporter of freedom of expression, freedom of speech. But he's neither said or written anything to criticise the emperor.'

'Nero's hardly a supporter of either of those things.'

'Not any more, it's true.'

'Not that he can keep them from bubbling up.'

Titus nodded. 'I've seen the graffiti around town.'

'Plenty to worry Nero there.'

'Are you serious? Slogans and cartoons scribbled on walls?'

'He's frightened of something.'

'He still has plenty of loyal dogs to guard him.'

'But will they catch the scent of a man like Strabo?'

'You said yourself, he has guard-dogs of his own.' Titus glanced round the restaurant. There was a party at the next table – someone had just been made *procurator*, by the sound of things in one of the outer provinces, the island just off the north coast of Gaul, and he was drowning his sorrows with his friends before setting off for that bleak and rainy place. No one paid Titus and Julius the slightest attention. The man's friends were telling him it was only for a while, to look at it as a stepping-stone in his career, and that the time would pass quickly. He'd soon be back on the mainland again, richer in experience and hopefully in money too. He didn't look convinced. He was an oldish man, in his mid-sixties, and Time wasn't doing him favours any more.

'So you think he silenced Murcellus?'

'I've said enough.' Titus toyed with the two dishes in front of him: one contained fried peacock's tongues, the other, baked dormice dipped in honey and rolled in poppy seeds. In the end he took just one of each, and concentrated on the olives and salad which accompanied them, but he didn't do justice to anything. Julius, who'd chosen grilled tuna with shallots, ate well. He was, after all, paying.

'The friends he was with are no longer in Rome.'

'Sensible of them to leave,' Titus replied drily.

'Are you staying?'

'For the time being. As I told you, I have business to settle.'

'Must be complicated stuff.'

'Don't delve where you don't need to.'

Julius spread his hands, but wondered how far outside Rome Nero's tentacles reached. The city was the centre of the empire, but the empire was wide, and the secret service, he knew, wasn't everywhere.

And investigating political conspiracy wasn't in his brief. It was just that it might have a bearing on his own enquiries.

He placed his elbows on the table and placed the tips of his fingers against his lips, thinking.

51

Paulus' death will leave the Christians utterly vulnerable.
But now even the emperor is convinced that they are
not to blame for the killings. How long will it be before
he turns on us at last? We do not believe he has ever
had any control over us, and I think he must fear us,
or he would have had us killed by now. But why does
he let us live? Will his fear of us hold him in check
when it is finally gone, or will he try to destroy us?
Did he ever believe in the power of his curse? Did he
ever believe that the curse came from him?

If it came from him at all, was he just the agent by
which it entered us through those loathsome creatures?
Perhaps our affliction used his malevolence as a
channel through which to reach us, but what controls
us is more powerful than Nero could ever hope to be.

But he is a madman and we cannot look for logic or sense in him. He will turn events in such a way that it seems to him that he controls them, until the day his intelligence – and he is, alas, intelligent – convinces him otherwise. Then and only then may he take action. But as long as he fears us, as long as he is uncertain, he will do nothing. He will be afraid to draw our anger onto him. Perhaps he thinks we plan to kill *him*. But he takes no action against us, and we must be glad of that. We will not attempt to cross him, unless whatever it is which controls us directs us to do so.

I do not know if there is anything controlling us. Perhaps only a blind fate.

And am I only luckier than my sisters because I fought off the beast which attacked me before it could finish its work?

Whatever happens, we are held in its grip forever, and though my sisters think they are free, they are as much prisoners as I am. Worse, for I can still control it, though I do not know for how long. The last time I was with him I was proud because I could keep it in check and it did not manifest itself at all. But what of the next time? I try to keep away from him when I am at my most vulnerable, when the hunger is strongest, but I cannot resist him even though I know that the best way to protect him is to avoid him. But it is not even that simple now, for I am sure that my sisters, and Flavia and Apuleia are the worst, know about him, though they say nothing.

Perhaps a day will come when there is no more Changing, when we become the creatures within us forever, without even the pretence of human form. For my sisters, two of whom are already welcoming the Changing as they would a lover, the transfiguration becomes more frequent, and lasts longer.

It is certain too that my sisters are finding it harder to go out in the sunlight, and keep the blinds in their apartments permanently drawn. This disadvantage I can pretend to share, but as for mirrors . . . Their reflections in polished metal are fading; Flavia's is already reduced to a shadow.

I can still see my face. But I do not look in mirrors when I am with them and they have not noticed yet. I am triumphant about this and at the same time frightened. If I do not check for a few hours, I become scared that the next time I look, I will be gone.

What I share, and share to the full, is the hunger. The food and drink of my fellow humans, if I may still call them that, gives me no nourishment. I must feed as they feed. I do my best. I pick my food with what care I can, though I abhor attacking even animals, seeing the terror in their eyes, transfixing them so that they cannot flee from me. The two people I have killed of necessity, I have chosen, as much as for any other reason, because they were evil – as if I were in any position to judge evil – and the taste of them revolted me, but I had to do it because otherwise my sisters would surely have turned on me, and without me he would be unprotected.

But it is not just for him that I try to survive. My hope of a cure is still greater than my longing for a release through death. He may be able to help me. I pray that he may.

I am terrified, for him and for myself.

If they decide to attack him . . .

52

'He should have left Rome when his friends did.'

'He probably only stayed to get rid of Murcellus.'

'We'll never know.' Julius stood next to Mercurius in the *sudatorium* of the Baths of Agrippa, looking down at the bloody sack which had once been Caeso Fabius Strabo.

'All we know is that he came here with a young man, but that wasn't unusual. A new young man. No one here had ever seen him before.'

Julius didn't reply. He knew who the young man was. He needed to know how Strabo had met him, and what he was doing with Strabo at the Circus Maximus in the company of Calpurnia and her three women companions; and only one person could tell him that. He'd see her later, when he'd shaken Mercurius off. No need to let his assistant have any clue about her, or where she lived. But he dreaded what he might find out.

He turned to the third man in the group, Drusus, the chief masseur. A large man whose muscle was turning to flab with age, but whose skills meant that he still had a long list of clients. He was grey beneath his tan, and looked worried.

'What happened?'

'If a word of this gets out –'

'Just tell me.'

'They could close us down.'

'No one will close you down.'

'It's your job to protect us from things like this.'

'And with your help we will.'

'You're doing nothing. Nothing!'

'Shut up!'

Drusus looked as if Julius had hit him. 'No need for that,' he murmured.

Julius looked at him.

'Fabius Strabo came here often, at least twice a week,' Drusus began, sitting on a marble bench where Julius joined him. 'He was a regular for years.'

'And today?'

'Well, he arrived about the tenth hour, later than usual for him, with a couple of colleagues, and he sat in the atrium with them for a while, you know, talking, watching the boys exercise, before leaving them and going through to the changing rooms. He spent the usual amounts of time in each section but we were worried when he seemed to have been in the *sudatorium* so long. It gets really hot in there and you shouldn't stay for more than a tenth of an hour, but you know that, I can see you bathe regularly yourself. Besides, he was overdue for his massage . . .'

'And the boy?'

Drusus hesitated for a moment. 'We're a respectable place, this is one of the most reputable baths in Rome, and –'

'Yes, yes. Never mind about your reputation. What happened?'

'Well, you know what it's like, there's nothing wrong with some of our clients . . .' Drusus hesitated again before continuing, '. . . for some of our clients to bring along a friend, or sometimes, if they meet someone here. Fabius Strabo was an important man and a regular customer, the place wasn't crowded, business has been falling off a bit, especially later in the day, and it looked as if he wanted a little privacy, so . . .'

'So he was in the hot room alone with this young man?'

'Yes.'

'Get his name?'

'The boy?'

'Yes, the boy!'

'Marcus Severus, I think it was.'

Julius almost wished he hadn't had that confirmation. 'Was he with him from the beginning? Or did they meet in here?'

'Fabius Strabo arrived alone. Maybe they had a rendezvous.'

'What happened to Severus?'

'What?'

'What happened to him afterwards? Did anyone see him leave?'

'When we got worried one of the *tepidarium* attendants went into the hot room and found – and found poor Caeso alone.' Drusus stifled a sob. 'He was a lovely man. Never harsh. Always polite. I always enjoyed looking after him.' He glanced almost shyly at Mercurius, as if they shared an understanding Julius was excluded from. Mercurius only held his eye for an instant.

'Alone.'

'Yes.'

'And no one saw the boy again?'

'I don't think so. You can imagine the state we were in.'

'And of course no one saw or heard anything else?'

'I told you, we knew they wanted to be left alone.'

'How did you know?'

'You get to sense these things.'

'So – what do you think?' Mercurius asked his boss when they were outside the baths, and walking towards the vast network of scaffolding which marked the building site of the emperor's new Golden House. The site was the biggest in Rome, sprawling well over a *centuria* of land on the

316

slopes of the Palatine. Already artisans were applying gold leaf to the concrete and brick walls which had risen with great rapidity from the ruins of the great houses which had once stood there, destroyed in the Fire. Julius looked at it gloomily, wondering if Nero would survive long enough to live in it, a thought he didn't share with his colleague.

'I think we are getting closer,' Julius replied finally. He didn't choose to speak to Mercurius then of the trail which was forming through the chaos that had ensued once the pattern he thought he'd traced broke down. Strabo had suffered the same fate as his brother, and there was the mystery of Justina, the novice whore, and her death, and her disappearance from the common grave.

And then Marcus Severus, the beautiful young man with the striking eyes.

Julius wondered what Justina's eyes had been like. They'd been closed when he'd seen her body.

But someone at the brothel where she'd worked would remember.

He told himself that the hunch he was following was ridiculous, and he certainly wasn't going to share it with Mercurius. He merely ordered his assistant to start a manhunt for Marcus Severus. Someone must know him. He couldn't have disappeared into thin air.

But all the time, ridiculous or not, his own idea held him. And he had nothing to lose by pursuing it.

And another thought had formed in his mind: one which, now that he faced it, he knew had been there a long time.

Leaving Mercurius at VIII Cohort HQ, and telling him that he'd make his way back home to do some thinking, an excuse which he knew Mercurius saw through immediately, Julius ordered one of the *biga* chariots from the pool and had the driver take him halfway home before, having made sure no one was following him, he ordered the charioteer to change direction, and head for the Capitoline. The sun was dipping towards the horizon over Ostia, gilding the city and the hills beyond with a golden light which was intensified in the walls of the Golden House, rising in the midst of Rome like a nuptial cake planted in the midst of a shitpile. The city. The centre of the world. Teeming with life, more than half of it hungry, lonely and desperate, men preying on men, every other person eaten up with his own anxiety and doubt. How did the place function? How did it manage to fool the millions of people under its dominion, the hundred nations it had brought under its heel, into continuous subservience? And how long would it be before it crumbled? The city. A bigger monster than any he was pursuing, it would survive this threat as it had survived plagues and fire and riot, as it had survived republics and emperors and hatred and tears until its own time came, and it would leave scarcely a trace behind, and nothing of its power. And the Golden House, a pompous monument to an unimportant young man's vanity and greed – how appropriate it was to this sad place.

They reached the street the brothel stood in and the driver pulled his two black horses to a halt.

'Shall I wait?' he asked, and Julius could see in his frightened eyes that he hoped the answer would be 'no'. He gratified that hope, and stood for a moment watching the *biga* clatter away over the cobblestones, watching until it reached the corner at the end of the broad avenue and disappear round it.

Julius stood for a moment in the air which already smelt of the night, warm and dusty and curiously calming. He wondered why he felt no fear himself. Perhaps he no longer cared enough to be frightened – at least, not for himself. But one thing redeemed him, the thing that redeems everybody and the only thing that really electrifies life – love. Not many people were given that gift, and even then it was usually not a gift at all, but an illusion, or at best a loan on which harsh interest would be charged when it was spent. He could only hope that his was real, and that it would last long enough to see him through – if not to the end, then to the next stage. But for now he was grateful that it gave him a reason for not dying. For now that contented him, and gave him the strength to carry on. Death would come soon enough, and for now he did not see why he should meet it halfway – though if the need arose, he knew he would not hesitate to take that course.

Better that than an empty life, one whose signposts pointed only towards ruin and despair. Hope, he thought. Hope and love. What sand we build the foundations of our lives on. Even the most dispossessed among us. The ones who ought to know better.

The doors of the brothel were closed and Julius could see no lights in its windows. He walked up the steps and pounded the knocker, listening to its echo in the hall beyond. He waited patiently, sensing that the house was not empty, and at last he was rewarded by the sound of footsteps approaching. The wooden flap to the peephole was opened and through it Julius could see just enough of Drogo's face to recognise it.

Drogo closed the flap and opened the door without saying a word, standing back and ushering Julius inside. Julius followed the servant along the familiar corridor, though it seemed like years since he was last there, to the atrium. It was well lit, but only five girls sat in it, draped on couches. Dorcas looked up at his arrival and stopped dressing the hair of the girl she sat by. She rose and came to meet him.

'I thought you might be a client,' she said, not attempting to keep the disappointment out of her voice.

'I couldn't afford your prices.'

She shrugged. 'The way things are going, I'd give you a discount.'

'Then I'd be tempted.'

She looked at him. 'Not you.'

'Things not so good?'

'They're no good for anyone — at night. We still do a brisk trade in the daytime, better than ever. Better than it was, in fact. People find comfort in sex.'

'I hadn't thought of it like that.'

'Oh yes you had.' She looked around the room, and he followed her gaze. The girls were looking at him curiously. They were all pretty, all young, and all bored to tears. 'Have a drink anyway. You might give in to temptation. The little Galatian's nice. And you'd only be her fifteenth.'

Julius took the beaker of wine Drogo passed him and sat on a folding chair next to the couch on which Dorcas settled again, shooing the girl away to a more comfortable distance. 'Is it all right if they stay? None of them is very bright and three of them barely speak Latin.'

'They can stay. What I have to ask you would mean nothing to any of them, unless any of them were here when —'

'No. They're all new. We've had quite a sharp turnover after poor Fabius Barbula met his end.'

'Of course.'

'We don't talk about it.'

'Naturally.'

'Tighter security, too.'

'I can imagine.'

'Mind you, it all costs.'

321

Julius drank half the contents of the beaker. He hadn't realised how much he needed a drink, but now he was in a hurry. Sensing this, Dorcas said, 'What is it you want to ask?'

'The girl who was with him.'

'Yes?'

'What colour were her eyes?'

53

From the brothel, Julius went straight to Calpurnia's apartment, without sending any message ahead to warn her, but the place was dark and no one answered when he knocked. Perhaps it was as well. He needed to cool off, to consider what his best strategy would be. In that frame of mind, he returned home, but once there, his thoughts refused to leave him alone, and he found it impossible either to relax or to marshal them.

Sleep was equally impossible, and long after night had fallen over the city he was still pacing his rooms liked a caged lion, unable to settle to the simplest task and unable to do anything more than struggle in the net of his own perplexity. He knew that the more he struggled, the more entrapped he would become, but reason was fighting a losing battle within him, and it was almost a relief when

Titus' house-slave Geta arrived, attended by three nervous-looking and heavily armed bodyguards, to beg him to come to his master's house immediately.

But Julius didn't need to see the look on Geta's face to know that this visit was bringing no real relief at all.

'Is he safe?' he asked.

'Yes – but he is severely shaken. I have never seen him like this.'

'Did he send you?'

'No – but I know that he needs you.'

Half-an-hour later, Julius was sitting in a small inner room in Titus' house on the Esquiline. A fire glowed in a brazier, giving a comforting light, which was reinforced by gently burning tapers. The walls themselves were covered in heavy fabrics, and the small window was shuttered. An untouched supper and a flask of wine stood on a low table near the upright chair where Titus sat, still in his street clothes, which he'd clearly refused to shed yet, though Geta had draped a sheepskin cloak round his shoulders. Everything had been done to make the room as safe and secure as possible, and guards had been posted around the outer and inner perimeters of the house, as well as at the entrances and at the door of the room itself.

Julius knew better than to speak yet. Titus sat rigidly, his left hand grasping the arms of the chair, but not tightly.

His right hand rested on his chest, lightly holding an amulet of some kind which the hand masked. His eyes were open but they looked inwards, the reflection of a taper glinting in them as they seemed to watch its flickering flame. Titus' lips were dry. His tunic was torn and there were deep scratches on his legs, his arms, and on his left cheek. These Geta had tended.

'He won't undress, won't let me bathe him,' Geta said quietly.

'Leave him. He feels safer clothed.'

'He is safe here.'

'Yes, I think he is out of danger now.'

'Do you think it was —?'

Julius looked at him. 'I don't know. And I don't know why whoever it was didn't finish the job. But he will tell us that when he is ready — if he can.'

It was another hour before Titus even moved, and then it was only his eyelids that drooped wearily, and his parched lips that moved as if murmuring something to himself. Geta quietly mixed wine and water in a beaker, but Julius took it from him and held the vessel to his friend's lips. Titus inclined his head and Julius put his other hand on it, holding it gently, while he tilted the beaker so Titus could drink.

He sipped a little, moved his lips and ran his tongue over them, then raised his eyes to meet Julius', and traced a smile.

'Thank you,' he said.

Julius smiled in return, but said nothing, only asking a question with his eyes. There was a long pause as Titus turned in on himself again, but then he shook himself, drawing the cloak more closely about him, and sat up straight. 'Geta, attend to our guest. I am drinking and he has nothing.'

Geta poured more wine.

'Thank you. Have some yourself. You look as if you need it.'

'Sir, I couldn't –'

'Go on.'

Geta fetched a third beaker, poured for himself, uneasily, and drank discreetly but gratefully.

Julius watched his friend in silence for a long time. He was patient. He knew Titus would only recover slowly from his experience – if he ever fully recovered at all. Titus drank a little more wine, but refused food, and left off drinking long before the wine took hold of him. Geta fetched another cloak, for Titus shivered despite the sheepskin. At last, Titus fell into a troubled sleep.

He awoke from it after less than an hour had passed, and looked around him in fear and panic, his eyes glittering. He seized Julius' hand.

'It is over, isn't it?' he said.

'Yes.'

'I am safe now?'

'Yes. You slept well. You slept calmly.'

'Apollo has been with me in my dreams.'

'Can you tell me anything yet? Are you ready?'

Titus made a visible effort. 'I will try.'

'Was it them?' Julius asked.

Titus nodded. 'I was returning from my friend Vitulus' house. We'd had a meeting about the new aqueduct to bring a fresh supply of water to the Caelian. If it ever gets built.' He smiled and paused. 'Not that that would have mattered to me at all, if they had –'

He shuddered, and Julius touched his arm. He flinched at the contact, then apologised. 'I am still on edge. I must smell of them. I can smell them on me. I must bathe.' He made a restless gesture, as if he wanted to rise, but made no other movement. The hand grasping the amulet moved away for an instant and Julius saw what it was.

'Time for that.'

'Yes. Right now I cannot bring myself to. And I must tell you all this first. I must get it out.'

'Go on.'

'Vitulus' house is not far away. He offered me an escort home but I refused. Foolish of me, but you never think anything is going to happen. And a walk of so short a duration . . . I have done it a hundred times, and darkness had only just fallen.'

The cloak had fallen open and he drew it round him again, as if it would protect him. Nevertheless, he shuddered. His face was pinched and looked frozen, though the room was warm.

'Geta – bring more lights.'

Geta looked around the room as if wondering where he could place more lights, but bowed, and left, returning soon afterwards with two house-slaves bearing five tapers each which they placed on tables near their master. When the house-slaves had withdrawn, and Geta had taken up a position close behind Titus' chair, Titus relaxed a fraction, and drank some wine.

'I was within a few minutes of here. There's an alley which cuts between two gardens. It's never been well lit, but there's a full moon and I could see my way. Nevertheless I paused and listened before entering it. There was no sound but the wind in the trees.'

'You sensed nothing?'

'Nothing. At the other end of the alley I could see the glow from the lights of my own entrance.'

Julius sat back, giving his friend time. Titus shuddered once more, then braced himself to go on.

'I was halfway down the alley when it happened. Suddenly, I felt that there was – *something* – close behind me. I thought I could feel its breath on my neck. I told myself I was being absurd, but that kind of feeling cannot be denied. I didn't know whether to turn or run. I was terrified of what I might see if I turned. There was still this awful silence. Even the wind had dropped to nothing.'

Julius leant forward, close to his friend, uncertain whether or not to place a reassuring hand on his arm. Titus met his eyes and Julius could see the fear in them still.

'I stopped dead. I listened. Nothing. Ahead, I could see the lights of my house. Another minute and I would be there. But a minute seemed a very long time. The silence was like a mantle. Everything seemed to have stopped with me, even Time. Then I heard the rustling.'

'Rustling?'

'Yes – a dry, brittle noise, like dead leaves stirred by a breeze. But then I knew that it was not rustling I had heard, but scuttling. Something was positioning itself, ready – I sensed it in an instant – ready to pounce.'

Titus paused and gulped wine. It was Geta who reached out and put a hand on his shoulder. Titus reached back and put his own hand over his slave's, withdrew it again, and continued.

'Time unfroze. I looked behind me and saw it, seven paces away, crouching in the shadows. I think there was one, there may have been more, it was hard to tell in that light. My feet took charge and I turned again to flee, but another of the creatures – maybe the same one, though I knew there were still others behind me – had got ahead and lay in my path, looking at me with eyes that were – *somehow* – human, but their stare was bottomless, dead, without pity or humour or a trace of warmth. I recognised a kind of mouth, but hard, more like a beak. It drooled, and something soft and grey lolled within it, like a parrot's tongue . . .

'It stood on four legs, poised to spring. It was covered in soft, dark fur, spread thinly over a scaly body which

329

wasn't hard, like an insect's, but muscled, like an ape's. The legs were muscled too, but ended in claws like a lizard's. It was smaller than a man, but powerful. All this I saw in the moonlight, in a fraction of a second.'

Titus shivered again, and drew the cloak closer. Geta refreshed the beakers of wine, not hesitating to drink again himself.

'You had better get this over with, Master,' he murmured. 'Then we can bathe you and let you rest. We will watch over you.'

Titus smiled, reassured by his house-slave. Julius knew Geta would never let his master go out unaccompanied again.

'I drew my sword, knowing I had little hope of using it effectively. Immediately, the thing behind me made a noise halfway between a croak and a scream, and leapt onto my shoulder. I felt its talons clench in my arms and thighs. Its head craned forward, and its tongue sought my mouth. At the same time, the other one crawled towards me, unhurriedly. I swear, if it had had lips, it would have been licking them.

'I don't know what made me do what I did then, but I had already dropped my sword when the first creature pinioned me. I still had the use of my left arm, though, and with it I managed to pull *this* out from my tunic.'

Titus repeated the gesture now, and revealed a plain silver crucifix, tied round his neck on a leather thong.

330

'When it saw the Cross, the eyes of the first creature, the one in front of me, did not change – those eyes seemed incapable of change – but it hesitated, stopped moving. The one on my back had sensed something too. Its hold slackened.' Titus paused, breathing heavily and deeply. 'Then I heard voices and saw people running towards me from my house. That it all I remember.'

Julius turned his eyes to Geta.

'We heard the Master screaming,' Geta said. 'We ran out. He was in the alley, only a few paces away, on his knees, flailing at something. But we saw nothing except the blood on his tunic, and the wounds. We thought he'd been stabbed.'

'I am certain I owe my life to this,' Titus said, cradling the crucifix.

Julius wasn't so sure, but he remembered that there had been no Christian victims.

'You have rediscovered your Faith,' he said to his friend.

'Perhaps it never truly left me,' Titus replied.

'Leave here. Until this is over.'

'I am tired.'

'Leave here.'

'If you need me –'

'You have done enough.'

It was dawn by the time Julius reached home, but he didn't stay longer than it took him to wash and change, to drive the sleep from his eyes and his mind.

He arrived at VIII Cohort to find Mercurius waiting for him. His assistant looked equally drained. He hadn't slept either. And it didn't surprise Julius at all to learn that there was no sign anywhere of a handsome young man called Marcus Severus.

54

'I want you to wear this.'

'It'll do no good. I do not believe.'

'For me.'

He had not told her everything, but he had told her enough. Some of that was against his better judgement. But he was powerless. He found that he was simply relieved she was back, and unharmed.

He could not protect her during her unexplained absences, but he found himself unable to ask her where she went, and had to be satisfied with her vague explanations. But she knew what was in his mind, he was sure of that.

Once again she held up the little amulet. It was in the shape of a fish very simply outlined in a loop of silver, the intersection of the body and the tail forming an 'X'-shaped cross. He bent his head and allowed her to place it round his neck. It rested, suspended by a silver chain, just above his sternum.

'For me,' she said again, drawing him to her and kissing him. He wished he could believe in that kiss. It seemed real enough. And when he plumbed the depths of his soul, he sensed no danger.

'But you don't wear one.'

She gave him the enigmatic look he had expected and turned, walking across the room to a side-table where a house-slave had left a jug of *mulsum*, a small bowl of precious ice, and two beakers on a tray. Her limp, he noticed, was far less pronounced, and her body was sleek. He watched as she poured their drinks.

'I do not need one. I have you to protect me.'

Julius impatiently started to take the amulet off, but she stopped him. 'Humour me,' she said. 'My nurse always said, *it never hurts to be sure.*'

Julius was not in a mood to be fobbed off by humour, but he let go of the chain and left the amulet where it was.

'The Cross saved Titus,' she reminded him.

'Titus believes.'

He had told her what had happened to their friend, but he had not spoken of the attack in the Baths and the death of Strabo, nor of the disappearance of Marcus Severus. He did not want to put her on her guard against him. Mistrust and love made very, very difficult bedfellows.

'You believed too,' he said.

'Believed. Yes. But now I am not sure.'

'Then why –?'

'Please. For me.'

'If I'm to hedge my bets, why not you?'

'I've told you why. I have faith in you. I want to protect you.'

He sipped the *mulsum* she'd given him and sat down on the couch next to her, but he was silent. He wanted to be with her, but he also needed to be away from her, to think. He'd been relieved to find her returned home when he'd paid another unannounced visit. Her household was in order, as if it had never been closed up, and he listened to the usual story about her having had to go to the country.

His relationship with her was no longer one in which he could simply put questions, especially ones whose answers he half-sought, half-feared. He had gone there to confront her, but he was afraid of what he might uncover, so he resisted; but a lot had come together in his mind. He remembered she'd been troubled by the fact that each of them had been born on a Saturday, and he knew about the significance of that birth day, for both hunted and hunter. Despite the strength of his rational mind, he could not dismiss this from the equation as just an old wives' tale. But it was still superstition. The facts were harder to contend with. Julius had not forgotten Nero's fear of the curse which the emperor had himself placed on persons he refused to identify, nor could he ignore Calpurnia's acquaintance – at the very least – with Marcus Severus. The young man with the striking, pale-blue eyes, who had always struck Julius as distantly, but ungraspably, familiar.

His stomach was a bag of nails. Somehow she had to be taken away from this, somewhere there had to be a place where they could be, with all this behind them, and, if not forgotten, buried forever.

She had drawn closer to him. He felt her breath on his shoulder as she pulled his tunic away to kiss the base of his neck, drinking him in with her passionate mouth.

'I have missed you,' she said. 'You are hard to resist.'

But afterwards, when they lay back, running with sweat and pleasantly exhausted, and he leant to lick the perspiration from her skin, she shuddered, and instead of nestling in to him, drew away, though not forgetting to give him a quick smile of reassurance, running her thumb across his lips and tidying a stray curl of hair behind his ear. 'I have to go.'

'Why?'

'I'll be back before you leave.'

But she didn't return, and he made his way home alone, perplexed. She had made deep scratches down the left side of his back, enough to draw blood. He hadn't noticed them until afterwards.

55

I can write no more here and I must destroy all that I have written. They know, I am sure. If they change so much that they forget our bond of blood, I am lost, and I must provide no fuel for that. But one last time I must exorcise my thoughts by setting them down. The next time I need to confess, I will confess to him, whatever it costs. How close I came to doing so today, but I fought shy of it, again, and sought refuge in love, and that is dangerous, for in slaking my desire I have to control my hunger, and it hurts, how it hurts.

If he destroys me, at least there will be no danger of my destroying him. But how will he destroy me – any of us? How can he?

We were not born to slavery and we were not used to calling anyone Lord. We sought to spare those who were obliged to do so, but we have killed men who grovel before Nero, as well as men who spoke against him, though I myself have never done that. Our malady is ferocious and seeks targets to assuage its hunger without focus. All humans are food to us. Christians we cannot seek, for Petrus' words, spoken against us, prevent that, and they too are among the oppressed. But now something is unleashed within us which is ours to use – until it starts to use *us*, and I fear that day has already dawned. What the creatures were which attacked us, and who or what called them down on us, I do not know, and perhaps will never know, but I believe they were parts of ourselves, brought into being by the blood we shed in the arena and by our readiness to betray the Christians to the emperor. When we failed to complete that work, they were ready to descend. They were Beings born out of our desire to take arms against our sad fate, born out of our degeneration into cruelty by accepting a life as charioteers and gladiators, rather than bowing to an honourable death. In refusing death, we chose a life which depended on taking the lives of others. *A bitter death means fame forever* – we have deprived ourselves of that.

But I saw my cousin in the arena, the day Claudia died on the cruel blades of her own chariot wheels. Even if I had not seen him I would not have been able to kill any more. The two I have killed since, I have killed from choice, and I selected them carefully. Sexta and Gaius.

Though I had, even then, no right to judge them, no right to take from them what was theirs and theirs alone. They should have been free to meet their own deaths – it should not have been my decision. But I cannot regret saving my own life by sending such people to Acheron, if I use that life to destroy the evil which has come into us, and which I am part of. To destroy it before it destroys me, for I fear it has already taken full hold of my sisters. Pompeia was always the strongest, now she is angry and dominant. Justina's sexual energy is warped into ruthlessness. Apuleia, the most innocent of us after Claudia, finds her relief in all the refinements of cruelty. All want to breed, I sense it, the power needs to survive and grow – but that desire is fiercest in Flavia.

It must end and only I can end it. Something in me, the same thing, I believe, which made me turn away my horses in the arena under the pretence of having lost control of them, the same small quality of mercy keeps me from sinking utterly into the pit which has swallowed my sisters. May Kotys and Derzelas guide me.

I do not care to protect them any more. He did not take up the scent when I led him to it, but I know what he suspects and I will make him follow the right path. Even if it leads him into danger. But I am already leading him there myself by refusing – by being incapable of refusing – to deny my love for him. Every time I hold him in my arms it is a battle, though each time I win, I feel stronger. I am playing a dangerous game, for I do not know at what pace the infection may yet be spreading within me. I am always hungry. The Changing still comes at times when I have no control over it. I do know that my will is still strong, and that somehow I can stave off the worst excesses even when I have become the beast within me. I know that to stay human, I must fight every hour for the independence of my mind and spirit.

But can I depend on my strength, and even if I can, for how long? There are sicknesses which the most powerful spirit cannot ward off forever, and if there is a cure for mine, I can only grope towards an understanding of what it might be. Even then I may be confusing that understanding with what is simply, after all, just a vain hope. And isn't hope just a companion that makes life bearable by diverting our eyes from the truth?

I am still enough of a human to believe that this thing isn't as powerful as I am. I am still enough of a human to believe that love might redeem me.

But I do not *know*.

She stopped writing and folded the parchment. Then she took the other scrolls from their hiding place and gathered them together. How long had he been gone? It was dark and the wind through her window stirred the taper she'd been writing by. All was still outside. Would he be home now? Now she wished she had stayed, but she had not seen him for a long time and she hadn't been sure she could trust herself.

She listened to the silence and as she did so a toxic feeling crept into her gut, for the silence contained the ghost of a cry. She went to the window and grasped its ledge, looking out over the city where a few lights still shone. Her hands gripped the marble ledge harder and harder – so hard now that the nails dug into the stone, chipping it. The skin began to tauten and pull back from her mouth.

She crouched on the ledge, in agony as her back hardened and expanded, as her skin grew rough and the scales formed. But her mind remained her own.

He needed her help, and there was only one way she could give it to him.

56

They had stopped burning Christians as torches to light the streets when the seasonal winds changed direction and the stench became too much to bear. What was worse, people had begun to murmur against the emperor again, too many tongues for the Secret Police either to report on, or even keep track of.

Julius was halfway home when he sensed the danger. He was a fool. He should have stayed at Calpurnia's until dawn, for he couldn't summon an escort without revealing that he'd been with her far later than any call of duty would require – policemen's tongues wagged more energetically than fishwives'. But he had his short-sword and his dagger, and he continued on his way. There was nowhere to seek refuge on these empty streets, and the only sound was the sound of his own footsteps.

Until he heard, faintly at first, the whirring.

The noise might have been made by some enormous insect, or a swarm of them. He backed to the wall of a house, pearl-white in the moonlight, where a balcony's shadow gave him partial protection, and stood his ground.

He saw the first one as it flew across the disc of the moon, eclipsing its light for an instant as it hovered, sensing its prey, ready to home in. Then it was gone, a blur too fast to catch.

There was silence again, worse, it seemed to Julius, than the dry wingbeats which had interrupted it. But not as bad as the furtive scuttling in the shadows a few paces to his right and left, which came next.

Then he saw them clearly, and the last traces of a rational explanation for his case crumbled, and fell to pieces.

In a nightmare which was real, the creatures jockeyed for position, manoeuvring in readiness for their attack. The leathery sound of their bodies and the moist chopping of their jaws filled Julius' ears as he feinted, left and right, poising his sword to slice and his dagger to stab. If, by the time they were in range, it was still possible to fight. He thought of the wrestler, Etius. This was how he had felt in his last moments. These things had evolved and grown bolder.

He couldn't see how many there were, they moved fast and there were too many shadows. At first, he had thought there was a swarm of them. Now, he estimated four or five,

343

six at most. But he wasn't sure. He adjusted his hold on the sword, feeling the grip slip against the sweat on his palm. How big were they? Almost as big as a man. From what he could see, their form was as Titus had described – part lizard, part ape, and part mosquito.

Julius' mind seemed to ride high above his head, his body. He was looking down on the scene as if he had already left it; but that moment, in its unreality, brought at the same time an enormous sense of clarity. He braced himself in the on-guard position he had learnt during basic military training all those years ago, when he was a boy of twelve. The soldier took over.

Sensing his aggression and his lack of fear, the creatures in the shadows hesitated, though only for a second. The closest to him opened its beak and from it whirled a long, muscular tongue, grey and moist in the moonlight, which came at him with the force and flexibility of a whip. Its end caught him on the thigh and a white-hot flame of pain seared through his body as it hit him. Looking down, he saw that the tip was snaking up along his leg towards his groin, seeking a soft entry where it could burrow into his flesh. He slashed at it with his sword and although the blade was only able to nick it before it glanced off the tough skin it was sheathed in, the weird organ retracted with lightning speed and there came from its owner what in any other creature might have been a howl of pain, but this was not a noise Julius had ever heard before or would want to hear again. It was a shriek in which rage and agony and surprise and sadness were combined in such a way as to shake his very soul.

Shaken, the small wound in his thigh throbbing out of all proportion to its size, Julius took up his stance again, praying to all the gods he didn't believe in to give strength to his wounded leg. If he could no longer stand, he was finished.

There was a pool of moonlight just in front of where he stood, and just beyond it he could sense, rather than see, that they had gathered in a semicircle round him. His every muscle tensed, he was beyond thought now, even of the thought of his own death. He concentrated on the moment. Something flashed at his neck. It was the amulet Calpurnia had given him. For a moment, hope rose stupidly in him.

They flew at him, reared up, mouths agape, tongues twisting out. But before they could reach him something at their rear baulked one of them and made the others hesitate. One was being drawn back into the darkness by a force as great as its own. The others turned to focus on this attack and Julius was left alone, listening to the fury of the battle which came from the shadows. Once or twice, a dark limb glistened in the moonlight before being drawn back into the night. Then there was quiet. Then the whir-ring again, fierce at first, then dwindling. Then the silence fell once more.

Julius didn't move, knowing that something was still there.

But the sense of danger slowly passed, and finally he convinced himself that only his fear had made him think that. Little sounds of the night crept into the silence, a small beetle waddled into the pool of moonlight and made its way across it until it was stopped by the edge of his sandal. It hesitated, attempted to clamber up, and halfway through its manoeuvre fell on its back, helpless. Julius stooped to right it, and it scurried away. His limbs were stiff and he felt the onset of the cold which is the first hint of dawn.

57

VIII Cohort was hectic when Julius arrived late. Dio had bathed him and he had changed, but he was still shaken, and he felt defiled by his contact with his adversaries. Part of him refused to believe in them still, and only his conviction that he must, at base, be dealing with something which had its origins in humanity gave him the strength to continue. This battle, wherever it led, must be fought to its conclusion. He knew, too, that Nero would be waiting impatiently for a progress report. How to couch such a thing occupied another part of his mind.

Dio also showed him a letter from Titus but he brushed it aside. He would deal with it later. There was nothing more important than his work, now.

Mercurius greeted him, ushering the scribe, Quintus, out of the office, and closing the door behind him. Julius had immediately noticed something furtive in his assistant's eyes, but their talk first was of the activity around them.

'It's about the murder of the *Augustinianus*, Murcellus,' Mercurius said.

'What have we got?'

'It's what our friends in the Secret Police have got. They're treating it as political.'

'The tip-off he gave us?'

'Yes.'

'How did they get wind of that?'

'The gods know. Everything leaks like a sieve. But it would have come out anyway, after the body was discovered.'

Julius was silent. That was true enough. But he was glad of this business because it bought him time – he could be seen to be doing something. He was more than aware how close he was running to the deadline he'd been given.

'They're pinning it on the conspiracy against the emperor they think Galba's involved in. But Galba's out of reach, in Spain, and his legions are loyal to him.'

'Then it'll come to nothing. Besides, what proof have they that there is a conspiracy?'

'You know what the Senate feels about Nero.'

'Some of them.'

'All right.'

'Bottom line?'

'Murcellus was murdered by Strabo's agents when they

discovered he'd been to see us. I've covered us with the Secret Police and thanks to your special understanding with Nero they won't come poking around here, but everyone's twitching.'

'Especially Tigellinus?'

'Got it in one.'

'And who do they think killed Strabo?'

'Nobody's talking.'

'Do they think Marcus Severus did it? Do they think he was working for Nero?'

'We know what happened to Strabo.'

Mercurius still looked uneasy. Julius said, 'A lot has happened since yesterday.'

'Yes.'

Julius watched him, wondering whether to tell him about the attack. Then Mercurius, apparently gathering courage, surprised him by saying, 'Something happened to you.'

'What?'

'I had word about what happened to your friend Titus.'

On his guard, Julius said, 'Who told you?'

'Geta. He thought I ought to know in case anything happened to you. He also told me that his master is closing his house and returning to the country. For a long time. He was to have sent you word.'

'Is he involved in this Strabo business?'

'No suspicion has fallen on him. But last night –'

'Yes?'

'I came to talk to you – confidentially. I was on my way to your house when I saw you.' Mercurius hesitated. 'I saw them, too.' He paused again, and then plunged on. 'I could not intervene. I was terrified. I lost my nerve. Forgive me. I am so glad you are safe.'

'For the moment, at least.' Julius was at a loss what to say. 'I thought someone came to my rescue. But not you.'

'I could not see clearly. I could not see how many there were.'

Perhaps you hoped they'd finish me, clear the decks for you, thought Julius, though he did not say it. Mercurius read his thoughts, however. 'I did not wish your death. Do you think I could finish this investigation on my own? Last night I all but decided to tell you nothing, just to resign. This is not for me.'

'What changed your mind?'

'I didn't run away. I waited. I hoped they could not smell me. There was a kind of fracas. I didn't see what disturbed them but I saw them split up and flee. One of them lingered, not for long. I stayed and watched. It was still there watching you when you left.'

Julius felt a cold hand close on his heart. He said nothing, but listened, nodding for Mercurius to go on. The man could hardly get the words out, but he had started, and knew he had to finish. 'After you'd gone it slunk down an alley where I dared not follow. I stayed where I was. I had decided to leave myself – I'd come without an escort but

I knew dawn wasn't far away. Then I saw it again. It had changed.'

'A woman.'

'Almost completely a woman by then. How did you know?'

'Did you see her? Well enough to know her?'

Mercurius shook his head. 'It was still dark, gloaming rather. Difficult to see clearly in that light, and I kept a good distance.'

Julius didn't want to hear any more, but he had to.

'I knew she had not sensed me. When she was whole, she gave a kind of sigh, there was a world of sadness in it. I was astounded that I could hear it, but the night carries sound in a way that the day does not. She looked around and walked away. I followed.'

Mercurius fell silent again, as if waiting for some cue from Julius, but the Legate gave none. He looked pensive and abstracted. Mercurius wondered if he was still listening, but went on. 'We passed no one in the streets. She was in a hurry, because she was naked. She kept to the shadows. At last she arrived at an apartment block on the Caelian. She went in and I waited. By the time the sun had risen, a group of people had left the building, all house-slaves by the look of them. When they had gone, and the sun was just at the level of the lowest rooftops, one of them returned with a litter and bearers. A woman emerged from the block then. I could not tell if it was the same one but she was in a hurry and the coincidence would have been too great if it had been someone else.'

'And still you didn't see her – to recognise her?'

'She was veiled, and still I kept my distance.'

'And then?'

'The litter took her down the hill, away from me.'

'Did you follow?'

'I stayed to find out which apartment she had left. I'd watched the building and knew which floor from the activity beyond the windows.'

'Why did you not follow?' Julius said.

'I had to make one choice. I couldn't take both courses.'

Julius, whose mind was racing ahead, thanked Apollo for the choice Mercurius had made. So much depended on so little.

'The place had been abandoned. The door wasn't even locked.'

'So you searched it?'

'Yes. But quickly. I didn't know if anyone would come back.'

'Find anything?'

'These.'

Mercurius turned to a wooden box which stood on a table by the window. From it he produced a necklace, a shawl and a dagger. 'We've been missing these.'

Mercurius left off talking and looked at his commander expectantly. When Julius said nothing, he prompted: 'What should we do?'

'Have the place watched,' said Julius. What else could he say? The rediscovered clues were useless now. He was already fastening his cloak.

'Where are you going?' asked Mercurius.

'Someone I have to see,' he said. Before it's too late, he thought. The truth he had not dared to face had exploded in his face. He could no longer deny it, and he felt lost, like a ship with its rudder torn away. He felt guilty, because he knew he had closed his mind to what he hadn't wanted to face; but most of all, he felt relieved. His path was clear now.

58

It was a sullen day, humid and overcast. The sun was hidden by a dark mantle of unbroken low cloud which brooded over the city from dawn to dusk.

In the large apartment on the Esquiline Hill, the blinds were drawn, the mirrors shrouded. What dim light there was, was just enough to see by, but no lamps were lit. Though the atmosphere was stifling, the women wore shawls over their heads, shawls long enough to cover their dresses. They were still beautiful, their bodies beneath the clothes as toned and sleek as when they had been warriors. But their eyes had a dark, haunted look, in which an angry fire glowed. Their movements, for they were all restless, were fidgety and irritable. Apuleia moved more easily even in her human form on all fours; Pompeia's fine mane of hair had thinned. Flavia and Justina had been spared most outward effects of the disease which gnawed them, though Flavia's teeth were several shades darker than they should have been, and Justina's bright eyes had a tarnished look.

But their mood was exultant. Only one thing marred it.

'You came late to the attack,' Pompeia said.

'I am at the Caelian. You four are here.'

'But you heard us call.'

'Yes.'

'The attack was spoiled,' Flavia said. The others looked wordlessly at Calpurnia. Apuleia ran a dark tongue over her lips.

Calpurnia prayed the others did not sense her fear, but it seemed that they didn't know. She'd seen the flash of the amulet she'd given him, and had used that as the cue to make her move. A moment later and she would have been too late. She could not have overpowered them all.

'But our attack was spoiled,' repeated Flavia, looking at Calpurnia. The others also turned their gaze on her. 'And we sense a distance in you.'

'You are my sisters. We share this burden.'

'You call it a burden?'

'It gives us pain.'

'Pain is the price of freedom.'

The silence deepened. The four women had formed a loose circle round their sister, as she stood in the centre of the room, one hand resting lightly on the back of a couch, appearing relaxed, but ready to spring.

But she could not deceive them in that. Apuleia darted up to her, lips drawn back from her teeth. But Pompeia called out to her.

'Think,' she said. 'We are united in this. We all suffer the same fate.'

Doubt crossed the faces of the others.

'Think how it was with Titus.'

Apuleia, after a moment's hesitation, reluctantly drew back, and, using the couch to aid her, clambered into an upright position, stretching. 'The amulet,' she hissed.

'We cannot attack Christians. Petrus' *word* stands against us.'

'The policeman is no Christian,' Justina said.

Calpurnia prayed that one of the others would say what she did not dare say herself. She could not prompt them. That would only deepen their suspicion.

They were silent again, but not for long.

'He had an amulet. I saw it lit up by the moon as we attacked,' Pompeia said. Turning to Justina she added, 'And we recoiled. Just as we did when Titus raised up his Cross.'

'Something came at us from behind,' snarled Flavia.

'Something spread discord among us,' Justina said. 'There are those among the people we cannot take. Titus is one. Julius, another.'

'For now,' growled Apuleia. 'When we grow stronger . . .'

The others murmured assent. 'Yes. When we grow stronger.'

'Then the discord was spread by the power of his amulet?' Calpurnia asked, as if it were not her own idea.

'He does not matter. Titus does not matter. Titus has fled and Julius Marcellus is powerless to stop us,' Pompeia said decisively. Calpurnia looked at her sisters, but there was no reading the thoughts in any of their eyes. Flavia and Apuleia avoided hers, looking down. Apuleia growled softly. Calpurnia fought down her fear, thinking they would smell it. Then she realised that they could not, because she was not, except in the fortress of her innermost mind, different from them. Their horror was her own. She was, despite herself, one of them. And for how much longer could the walls of her fortress withstand the battering of the disease?

And now she saw that the best path towards saving herself from her sisters was to blend with them, with their thoughts. A dangerous path to tread, but there was no choice.

'We are ready to leave Rome,' Pompeia announced. 'That is why I have summoned you all here. Before we go, we will wreak a last vengeance which the city will never forget. We will bring a sorrow to the slavemasters and landtakers which will turn daughter against father, son against mother. We will bring a grief which will crush the bloated little emperor and hurl him from his throne, and in his wake there will be destruction and doubt. The world will be without a centre. And we will go home, and, before all our beauty is taken from us, we will breed.'

357

'We should deal with our enemies here,' Apuleia said stubbornly. 'The ones who have done us harm.'

'Single people are not important. We have a duty to the race we have become. We must find men and use them to beget what we know will grow in our wombs.'

'And the men we use will feed what they have planted in us,' smiled Flavia. 'It is just.'

'Tell us what comes first,' Calpurnia said, and once more all eyes were on her. But this time there was guarded approval.

'We will leave these apartments,' said Pompeia. 'The emperor's fear will not protect us any longer. His fear for himself is greater than his fear of us. We will hide in dark places in the city which I have sought out, and in three days I will summon you. Do not hunt during that time. Starve. Hunger will sharpen us.'

And they listened as Pompeia told them of the task ahead.

59

She lied about coming from Gaul. She lied about being a
Christian. Has she changed, or is it simply that that is what
I want to believe?

As he waited, sure that she would come, but ready to go
and seek her if she did not, seek her anywhere in the
labyrinth of Rome, sure that he would find her, his thoughts
fought each other. He knew that she had saved him. Whether
her sisters would know it too was another question.

He'd sent Dio with a letter to Titus – it'd keep him away
for at least two days. Dio had objected; it wasn't a body-
slave's job, to be a messenger. But Julius had convinced him
that none but he could be trusted with it, and he'd confined
the other slaves to their quarters until he called for them.
He didn't want to be pestered, and above all he didn't want
anyone around if she arrived – when she arrived. He'd also

sent a message to VIII Cohort that he was to be left alone. Mercurius could handle his business there. This wouldn't last long, this waiting, he told himself. All his senses shouted at him that things were coming to a head. They had to be. Logic dictated nothing else.

He paced his living-room, settling to nothing. At last he felt trapped in the room and ranged over the apartment; no part of it held him long, but he would not leave until the belief that she would come died in him. And at last, as the light was dying, she was there.

They threw themselves into each other's arms as if their lives depended on it. He closed the blinds before drawing the heavy veils from her face and kissed her with a passion he hadn't thought himself capable of, such was his relief at seeing her. The face was pale and tense, but she was smiling too. He could feel her ribcage against him. She was thinner.

'Do they know?'

'I would not be here if they did.'

'Is it safe for you – here?'

'This is the last place they would look. But there is very little time. I have been given a place to hide and I must go there or they will suspect.' She drew back and looked at him. 'How long have you known?'

'Since you saved me. Before, I had only questions.'

'And now?'

'Now, I do not care.'

'But can you trust me?'

I have no choice, he thought; but he returned the anxious look with a smile, and nodded.

'Then I must tell you everything.'

She hastened through her story, stumbling over words, hesitating sometimes, crying, and then plunging on. As she told it, a strange thing happened within her – she felt the walls of her fortress grow stronger. She felt warmth, not hunger, for the first time in what seemed like a lifetime. He held her face in his hands and she felt safe. But they were not safe.

Part of what she told, he knew, or had guessed. It didn't surprise him now to hear how Justina had had the power to fake death to confuse her pursuers, how Calpurnia and her other sisters had dug her out of the tomb, how her body had withstood the quicklime the gravediggers had shaken over her as if it had been flour. He understood what she had tried to do when she introduced him to her sisters at the banquet, and her consternation when he had failed to recognise Justina, and when she saw him at the Circus. When she told him of the Changing, she played it down, she didn't want to repel him. She hoped it would never happen again, if her plan succeeded.

Though that meant she would never see him again.

After skimming through her story, she interrupted herself, and stopped his questions by putting a long finger to his lips.

'There is something much more important to tell, and

I have wasted enough time already. But it is vital that you should know all, and believe, fantastic as it is, that it is true, before I give you what you need to act on, to finish this.'

'Then tell me.'

'First, you must swear that when you take action, you will not hesitate. You must finish the job. Whatever happens. You must show no mercy.'

'To finish this, I will do anything.'

'My darling, swear it.'

Her earnestness disquieted him, but he did as she asked.

'You must destroy this, root and branch. If you leave a single hint of life behind, it will grow again.'

'Tell me what I have to do.'

'We are to attack the Senate. In three days' time, they have an evening session. It will be propitious for us. All the senators opposed to Nero, and some of his supporters, will die. Then we will leave Rome.'

'If you do that, you will leave a city in turmoil.'

'Rome will blame the emperor, but there will be confusion because there will be no real clarity in the attack.'

'The emperor will fall. There will be a struggle for power and our weaknesses will be exposed.'

'You Romans have lorded it over the earth for too long. It is time you bent the knee.'

'Do you believe that?'

'I do not believe in chaos, and nothing will grow in barren soil. But the fate of Rome must lie with the gods.

I care about the destruction of a force which, if it is allowed to grow, will cast darkness over the world from Africa to India. It is here, in Rome, a nest of maggots in an apple, and only Rome can destroy it.'

'What must I do?'

'I have told you when the attack will be, and where. You must be ready to stop it. You must not give us a chance to escape, to flee, and to breed.'

Night had long since fallen, and close to the window, in the darkness beyond, an owl hooted mournfully, making Calpurnia start. She did not tell Julius, but she was glad the sound had surprised her. It made her feel more human, less a creature of the night. And if the only cure for her disease was death . . .

She rose to go, drawing her shawl about her. 'And forgive me for stealing your clues. I still thought then, that by protecting my sisters I might save them. Now I know that the only way to redemption is by protecting you – and I am glad I saw that.'

'I thought I was protecting you. I knew the clues would be valueless, that I was up against something that would always defy deduction.'

'We were protecting each other. And we must go on doing so.'

'Yes.'

He stood too, and followed her to the door, where he stopped her.

'You must not go.'

'Yes, I must.' She placed a hand on his arm and her touch almost burned him, he longed for it so much. 'If we are ever to be together, and at peace.'

'I love you.'

'And I love you. And we must do whatever is necessary to prove it to each other, and to ourselves.'

She kissed him, and was gone.

He would never forget the expression in her eyes as she left him. He wondered when he would see those eyes again.

60

'Then we have them!' Nero exclaimed, clapping his hands. 'At last! I knew you wouldn't let me down. Though of course you were running pretty close to your mark. I couldn't have held Tigellinus off forever. I might have been forced to throw you to the dogs! But, thank the good Lord Zeus, if I may call Jupiter by his better, Greek, name, you have had the last laugh.'

Julius thought that it was about time his emperor came clean – if Nero had done so earlier, his own neck wouldn't have been half as close to the block; but Julius had never regarded the plump boy who stood before him as a god anyway. Nero was just a mortal, and a flawed one at that. 'We still have much work before us, Lord,' he said.

'We'll ambush them. They'll be like rats in a trap. And then we'll kill them. And the curse will be lifted, and the theatres will be full, and the city will rise again – not Rome any more, but Neropolis! A golden phoenix, spreading its wings across a Golden Age!'

'And you will be safe.'

Nero's brow darkened. 'Yes. I will be safe. They will see me as their saviour, instead of a tyrant who only wants glory for himself.' He paused. 'I think I know how we must play this. We must let them begin their attack –'

'What?'

'Just long enough for them to rid the Senate of its own vermin. My enemies are growing in number and audacity. And then –'

'If we do not strike first, we will not be able to stop them.'

'Of course we will. I'll get Tigellinus to call out the entire Praetorian Guard.'

'That may not be enough.'

'What?'

'We do not know how to destroy them. We do not know if we can destroy them.'

'Nonsense. I don't know how you have got your information, but you are a genius. When this is over, I am going to put you in charge of the Guard yourself! Your fortune is made. Unless, of course, something wilful in you chooses to disappoint me.'

'We will use strong nets, long spears, barbed points.'

'That's better!' Nero looked around. 'I shall bring Poppaea

back from Antium for this. She will delight in seeing the creatures who destroyed those dear to her meet their nemesis in me!'

'And the curse will be lifted,' suggested Julius.

'Yes, yes, the curse. But you must understand why I had to keep some secrets from you, Julius Marcellus. Secrets privy only to the gods and their children. As you know, even I did not understand it all completely.' Fear crept into the emperor's eyes. 'This will be the end of them?'

'It is what we aim for.'

'It's a simple question now of winning a battle, isn't it?'

I wish it were that simple, thought Julius, but he said, 'Yes.'

Nero's fear and Nero's vanity, and the overweening pride of Rome, had bred this evil. Perhaps it would be better to leave him, and the city, to their fate. But then he would have to abandon Calpurnia to hers. And that he would not do. He could guess what was in her mind, but unless there was no other answer, he would see her spared death.

It was a relief and a blessing that Mercurius had not been able to make out how many creatures had attacked him, and that he hadn't been able to identify the one he'd followed when it had resumed its human form. Julius admired his assistant's unexpected sang-froid. He thought he was going mad himself to believe that such a thing could happen to a fellow being, or that it could be a person with whom he would fall in love. Events around him were

367

unfolding as in a dream, and it was that, perhaps, which best protected his wits and his sanity. If nothing seemed real, then any action he took would make sense.

He hoped what he planned would work, that was all. He fought his doubts about the wisdom of his course, and the risks it entailed. If it went wrong, at least for him there would be the final refuge of death; but his concern was about the inheritance of evil he might leave to the world.

'I am placing you in command,' Nero was saying. 'Tigellinus will hate it, but he will have to act according to your orders. And you will want to discuss this with Mercurius Varro. Do so freely. He has my full confidence.'

'Mercurius?'

'Yes. He has been reporting to me on your progress. I thought you knew.'

Julius swallowed that, as he had to. If that were the case, he had misjudged his assistant. Mercurius had shown him greater loyalty than he'd given him credit for.

'There isn't much time,' he said.

'You are right. You must make your plans immediately. I give you permission to go. And don't worry – all the resources you need will be available to you.'

Julius left the intimate little room where most of his conversations with the emperor had taken place, the room with its garlanded windows and peaceful, contemplative atmosphere, with relief. In there, he had the sense that nothing was wrong at all. Outside, he knew that far more threatened the emperor than the demons he was about to fight. Nero was sick in his soul, and his monstrous self-regard would destroy him.

Julius visited the apothecary and poisoner, Locusta, seeking advice on methods of ensuring death. He found her at her pharmacy on the Caelian Hill, down a secluded street of shuttered houses, all bought by her as a result of her prosperous business, but kept empty – Locusta liked her privacy. He'd intended to tell her as little as possible, but he'd overlooked the fact that the comfortable, motherly-looking woman, whose shrouded eyes were the only thing which gave her away, was another person close to Nero, though far too dangerous, useful and knowledgeable ever to have been in danger from him. She soon had the truth out of him, and that was good, he realised, for she sold him a dozen vials of a thick white liquid, like milk, culled from a euphorbia which grew far to the south in Africa. One drop of this juice, she told him, would kill an elephant. Her price was exorbitant, but she knew the emperor would pay. What she provided him with was never a luxury, only a necessity.

There followed a terse interview with Tigellinus, already primed by Nero's scribes, and meetings with Seneca, Vatinius and Petronius. Seneca, ever practical, thrust a copy of Tarquinius' *Unnatural History* into his hands. 'This may tell you of ways of ensuring they are dead,' he said. 'If you can kill them at all.'

Then it was time to summon Mercurius, and make detailed plans.

No senator was told. No one except Mercurius in VIII Cohort was informed. The Praetorian Guard's senior officers would receive their orders at the last minute.

And out there, in the dark city, other plans were being laid. Out there, somewhere, Calpurnia crouched in her lair.

What form would he see her in, Julius thought, when he saw her next?

How would he save her?

Ridden by his own nightmare, he fought to concentrate on the work Fate had given him.

61

The Senate convened at sunset. No report had reached the senators' ears because of the speed with which the operation had been mounted. There had been no time for any rumour to be born and grow. But the atmosphere was tense and some of the senators had noticed that the strength of their usual guard was far greater than usual. They murmured amongst themselves.

'What are they saying?' Mercurius asked.

'They fear an attack from the emperor.'

Mercurius smiled at the irony, but the relief was slight. The men of the Praetorians were less on edge than their officers, who knew the truth of what they were up against. But no one except Julius and Mercurius had seen the adversary, and though there was fear and awe in the minds of many of the soldiers, there was military scepticism too.

Most dangerous of all was the assumption that there was no foe that could be equal to the might of a trained Roman force, and this Guard was the elite of elites.

The first difficulty was where to conceal the men. The creatures would expect to confront a certain number, but not a whole battalion. For this reason the bulk of the Guard stood at full alert in antechambers and back corridors and rooms normally used by attendant slaves. The main entrances were left free. The problem would be to deploy the hidden men fast.

Julius knew how quickly the creatures could move. The memory of the slaughter at Poppaea's feast was vivid.

This was an emergency debate on a proposal to take the price of corn back to its normal level, now that the worst effects of the Great Fire had been dealt with. The disaffected among the Senate saw this as a way of stirring up opposition, and the minds of most of the politicians were focused on the issue as the first speaker, a young man named Aulus Accius Celer, stood resplendent in a luminously white new senatorial toga to address his peers. He was fond of his own voice and went over his allotted time. An older man rose to speak against him.

And the time passed as the darkness deepened and the soldiers waited.

'Nothing's going to happen,' Tigellinus said, glaring at Julius.

'We must be patient,' replied the Legate, feeling anything

but. His nerves were stretched to breaking-point, he had not slept in the past two days, and he was more than aware of how thin a thread his fate hung on. If they did not come, if Calpurnia had turned against him, or tricked him from the start . . .

But that could not be.

The strain of waiting, at the side of a scowling man whom he knew saw him as a dangerous rival and was hungry for his blood, told on him. He looked sideways at Tigellinus from time to time and always found the man looking at him, so their eyes always locked.

'I'm calling it off,' Tigellinus said, after two hours had passed.

'No.'

'This is a waste of –'

But he broke off, hearing it at the same moment as Julius and Mercurius. He looked at Julius differently now, his hard eyes containing something of interrogation, and something of terror.

The whirring noise of leathery wings came from nowhere and grew fast. There was scarcely time to reckon what direction they came from, and there were several.

'Over there,' cried Mercurius, pointing to the north gate.

'And here,' Tigellinus said, looking east.

'West gate!' a Praetorian captain called.

'South!' said Mercurius. 'We must give the order!'

'Give it now!' said Julius.

'No!' Tigellinus said, locking eyes. Julius thought, by Pallas, he means to let them at the Senate first. Nero wants everything!

'Give the order *now*!' he yelled at Mercurius, who, too fired up to be frightened any more, took off, yelling to the captains of the men in hiding.

And over his voice Julius heard the wingbeat of a fifth creature approaching. So she had come. But why?

There was no time to think about that now. He drew his sword and shouted orders at the running pikemen. The creatures were already in the assembly room, screaming with rage at the ambush, slashing and tearing at whatever man they could seize and throwing bloody lumps of ripped-out meat into the air.

Senators and soldiers ran blindly, in fear, colliding with each other in panic. Julius saw soldiers pierce one another with their lances, kill senators, in the bloody confusion, as the torches in their sconces were snuffed out by the creatures, plunging the hall into semi-darkness. It was an orgy of death, of obscene bewilderment.

But there was still enough light from the few flickering torches which survived for Julius to see the hall gradually clear of screaming politicians. More soldiers flowed in, and the greater numbers calmed those already in action. Roman order took over, and gained courage as one of the beasts became entangled in a net. Instinct had long since overtaken reason in the men, and although they had never seen such a vile object as the rearing, bucking creature they held captive, they understood that it was vulnerable, that they had disabled it, and that they could win. Those nearest it closed in, hacking at its flailing legs with the sharp blades of their spears, while others fought to protect them from the three creatures which had come to its aid.

The more the stricken beast struggled, the worse it became entangled. A pus-like substance began to flow from its sides and neck, and one eye where spears had pierced it, but Julius did not know whether the force and number of spears, or the poison they'd been tipped with, would be enough to bring the monster down forever. It was mewing now, a strangely piteous sound, though almost drowned by the furious shrieks of the other three as they pounced and dipped like harpies over the soldiers, plunging dagger-talons into eyes and groins, lifting men high like puppets and ripping them apart with their beaks, scattering the remains over the men below like bloody hail.

Then another was caught, and the soldiers rallied, spearing it and screaming themselves as the madness of slaughter grew. The hall seemed filled with the creatures, and seemed to choke under their number.

But there were five. Julius had heard five. He knew there were five.

He left the hall and ran through the empty, echoing corridors, looking for her, not knowing where he ran, but knowing he would succeed.

He found her at last by a window in a deserted

antechamber where tables and chairs had been thrown over to make room for the troops concealed there before the attack. She stood in a thin, pearl-white stream of moonlight.

He was not prepared for how she would look.

He had caught her during the Changing, but he'd interrupted it. His sword was still in his hand. His first sensation was revulsion. Then he saw her eyes. *Her* eyes. Pleading with him.

The thing before him had her form, the slender form of a lovely woman, but the skin was dark and encrusted with the traces of scales and hair. The arms and legs were metallic, bony, fleshless, and ended in hooked, cruel claws. The face . . .

'Kill me,' she said.

'No.'

'Kill me, if you love me. Look at me.' The voice was hers, and not hers. It was harsh, as if articulating human speech was agony for her, as if the rough grey tongue which partly blocked her human mouth could not find its way round language. A jagged sigh escaped her. 'I cannot eat as you eat. Daylight scorches my skin. If I look in mirrors, I see my image as faded as my shadow now is.'

'We can fight this.'

'I had to come. But I didn't know if I could resist the slaughter.'

'You did!'

'Yes.'

'Then you can still fight it. We can still fight it.'

Sounds of the battle came to them from far away. She looked towards them, and, seizing the moment, without thinking, he went to her and took her in his arms.

'No!' She struggled fiercely, but he held her close, hard, his cheek pressed to hers, eyes closed, hanging on for life itself, as the reek of her monstrous form lessened and her skin became soft again.

When he released her, cautiously, slowly, she was Calpurnia again.

'Go,' he told her. 'Go now. Do not think. Do not hesitate. Go to my place and wait.'

'No – better that you kill me.'

'I cannot.'

'There is no hope.'

Then they heard it – a stealthy noise, but a hurried one. Something was scurrying along the corridor behind them.

'They saw you go. They blame you.' She looked towards the window. 'It is no drop at all. Run!'

'No.' He lifted her onto the ledge. 'Go to my place. There is hope.'

But her eyes were looking past him now. In the entrance to the room a dark form reared, braying in triumph. It opened its beak and its long tongue lashed out, seeking him, seeking his mouth. 'Apuleia –' she said, though her voice was too low for him to hear.

'*Go!*' He hurled his weight at Calpurnia, dodging the snaking grey thing, which caught her by the thigh. He hacked at it with his sword and it recoiled as Calpurnia fell from the ledge.

The thing was in the room now, blocking the exit. Julius turned to face it. He had hurt the tongue, he knew, for the creature had retracted it, and yellow slime flowed from it, dripping from the beak to the marble floor. There was an overpowering, sickly scent of rotting flowers. Julius felt his mind reel, but he had something to live for, something to fight for, and this thing could not control his mind.

He hefted his sword from hand to hand. He knew what a puny weapon it was against his adversary, but it was all he had and he knew how to use it. He would fight it as he would any other wild animal.

But this thing was fast. It leapt and danced, confusing his eye. Sometimes he thought he saw two of them in the room, or three, or a swarm, but he knew that could not be, and desperately tried to keep focus.

How long it went on he didn't know. He felt his sword glance off the limbs as they fought, but once he felt the blade bite into flesh, and had to pull it out as if out of a mire. It made a sucking, reluctant sound as he withdrew it, and the beast jerked back, screeching, its cry rebounding off the walls. But Julius was tiring, and he knew it, and there was no sign of the creature's weakening.

It crouched before him, close enough for him to smell

its breath, its talons twitching. He backed cautiously, trying to prevent it from forcing him into a corner. Then stumbled over one of the upturned chairs. As he struggled to regain his balance, it gave it little bark of triumph, and sprang on him. He rolled aside just in time to stop it pinioning him, getting behind a table. But now he saw that he was trapped. He had lost his sense of his position in the room, and his back was against the angle of two walls.

The creature was still again, looking at him, cocking its head. The beak opened.

And then a javelin struck it from behind, glancing off its hide, but distracting it enough for him to run the length of a wall, away from his prison. The beast had turned to face the new attacker.

Julius saw Mercurius silhouetted in the doorway. He'd drawn a sword and stooped tensely, waiting. The thing moved crabwise to the left, then ran in.

'Go right!' yelled Julius, for Mercurius had misread the feint. Mercurius raised his head at the sound of Julius' voice but his reaction wasn't quick enough and the creature was on him. Julius froze as he watched the beast thrust his assistant down, straddling him in the obscene parody of a lover, its upper claws pinning his arms to the floor, the lower ones digging through his thighs, while the grey tongue forced open his mouth and drove down his throat. Mercurius' torso arched as his stomach writhed and the creature began to suck ravenously at his guts, pulling them out of him as its own body pumped up and down.

Julius saw at a glance that it was too late to save his rescuer, but he could at least avenge him. For a few moments, the thing would be intent on its new prey. He ran up to it, and just as it became aware of him and flung what remained of Mercurius aside to turn on him, he leapt up, gripping the sparse hair on its head as it reared, and plunged his sword deep into its left eye. He hung on as it bucked and plunged, pulling himself up so that he could thrust the blade ever deeper, up to his wrist, his elbow, the full length of his arm. Avoiding the snapping beak, he turned the sword as best he could in the glutinous mess he'd buried his arm in, twisting it into the core of the creature's brain. At last it wrenched its head back, throwing him off so violently that he felt two ribs crack as he hit the wall. Then it shuddered, uttered a long moan that sounded as lonely as the sea, and lay still.

Not looking at the mess which had once been Mercurius, he hastened back to the hall. No sound of battle now, just the confused barking of orders and the cries of wounded men, calling for their mothers, their wives. How did the song go? *Mothers that were dead, and wives that were unfaithful . . .* Though why it came into his head at that moment he did not know. He did not know if the creature he had left was dead. He only knew from the *Unnatural*

380

History which Seneca had given him that he had to burn its body fast, that was the only way to be halfway sure, and for that he needed help.

The scene of carnage that met his eye as he entered the assembly hall was worse by far than any battleground he had ever seen. Torches had been lit again and cast their light over a tide of wrecked corpses, bodies like dolls torn apart by an angry child. But the killing was over. Hanging in the nets which trapped them were the heavy corpses of two of the creatures.

Tigellinus came up to him, grey-faced and looking, for once, like he needed someone to tell him what to do. But his arrogant smile, when it broke, had not deserted him as he announced, 'We've got them.'

Julius nodded. 'All of them?'

'Two here, anyway. All we could see, and one that ran from the hall. It seemed there were many of them, but they baffled our sight. '

'I can account for one other.'

'What must we do with them?'

'Get your men to have pyres built. Now. Outside. As close as possible. We must waste no time.' And Julius told him of the other body in the antechamber. 'Mercurius is there too,' he said. 'He came to help me. He is worthy of full obsequies.'

'That will be arranged. Will you inform the emperor of this victory?'

381

Julius looked at him. 'I think that honour belongs to you, Tigellinus. Tell him that the curse is lifted.'

Tigellinus looked at him as if he were mad. 'You'd deny that honour to yourself?'

'And tell him how many senators, for and against him, died. I think he'll find the numbers even out.'

Tigellinus looked at him, and Julius knew the man thought he had ulterior motives for all this. But that was how it was in Rome. There was no trust, except as a commodity that's bought and sold. The song again: *The mothers are dead and the wives are faithless, life's a filthy waste of time . . .*

The pyres were ready in the main courtyard of the Senate, walled from any curious onlooker, within an hour. The guards who were not attending to their own dead and wounded, fearfully drawing lots for the duty, hauled out the dark bodies of the creatures, small and diminished now, and heaved them into the flames. Chancing nothing, once the embers of the fires had died down and gone cold, Julius ordered every ash collected, every remaining bone crushed to powder, and all placed in lead-lined coffers, which were then transported by mule to Ostia and transferred to a galley bearing the emperor's emblems. This sailed as far west as to be out of sight of land. There it cast a sea-anchor and the sailors, unaware of the contents, threw the caskets into the sea. The dark water closed over them.

But long before the ship had sailed, Julius was making his way home. Three creatures had been destroyed, may the gods grant. One he had risked saving.

One had escaped.

It was full day when he returned. He found Calpurnia sleeping. She was Calpurnia again and she slept curled up like a child, one hand against her brow, the other thrown over her shoulder. The blinds were tightly drawn against the sun.

He watched over her while she slept.

62

There were six sisters, then five. Apart from Julius, only Nero and Tigellinus knew of the fate of the five, and Tigellinus, as Julius knew he would, faithfully reported to the emperor that the job had been done. Nero was too relieved to double-check, confirmed Tigellinus in his post, and showered honours on him. But he hadn't forgotten Julius, and summoned him. Julius obeyed the summons with trepidation. He knew the killings would go on as long as Calpurnia's surviving sister remained in Rome, for hunger would drive her to kill. But his own hunt for Flavia was focused now. He prayed he would catch her before she left the city. Calpurnia, he might save. He had to, he could not face the alternative; but if Flavia escaped, carrying the disease with her . . .

*   *   *

When he was ushered into Nero's presence, he found the emperor his old cocksure self. The man's eyes glittered with shifty self-confidence, as if he'd narrowly escaped the blade of a sword which had been sweeping towards his neck. And he was full of the reward he had in store for Julius.

'The governorship of Scythia! Think of it! All the land you can till and all the women you can screw! Boys too. Nice tight arses. Put all this behind you – oops! Come back in three years and I'll put you in charge of the whole fucking army.'

'Lord, it is too great an honour.'

'Nothing is too great an honour. And I want you at the theatre tonight – I'm doing *Priam's Lament Over Hector*. I've given it a few tweaks, with Petronius' help – much better. Might still be a bit long though. You must tell me what you think when you come backstage afterwards.'

'Lord, there is still work to be done.'

'What work?'

'In the interests of your security.'

'What? Still?'

'A loose end. Forgive me.'

'I like a tidy mind. Well, do what you have to do. But don't make me anxious again. I've had enough trouble from this fucking city to last a lifetime.'

'Rest easy, Lord.'

63

The summons had come as an unwelcome interruption, but it assured Julius that the Dacian sisters were now out of Nero's mind; and if he had ceased to care about them, so would Tigellinus. That meant that as long as he was discreet, Calpurnia would be safe. From Nero at least.

It had been three days since the battle. In that time, the god Mercury had shown that he might exist. At first, Calpurnia had refused to eat at all. But on the morning of the third day, she told him, 'I have drunk water, and I am not thirsty.'

Julius looked up. 'That is a good sign.'

'I am afraid. But since the deaths of my sisters,' she paused, hardly daring to say it, 'the need has diminished. The old hunger.'

They did not mention the Changing. But she had felt

386

less savage when they'd made love. Still she did not yet have the courage to hope. Still, she felt the need to protect him; and that meant to protect him from herself as well. He did not know she watched over him when he slept. He did not know how close she still was to the Changing. It would be the only way she could combat her last sister, if she could dominate the monster within her.

'Will you eat now?' He thought, and he flinched at it, that he would have to procure raw meat for her. She must not hunt. What would it take for her to be cured? Would her will be enough? After the killing of her sisters, she seemed stronger, more in control, but he could not predict a certain recovery.

'No.'

'You must try. Normal food? Will you *try*? I will call Dio.' Dio was back from his errand, with a note from Titus saying that he would be staying on his estates indefinitely.

'No. Flavia is still alive. She will call to me when she is ready.'

'You cannot be sure that Flavia lives.'

'Pompeia and Justina led the attack. Their bodies were the ones you burned. And Apuleia's, after you killed her.'

He had had to kill, yet it was her sisters he had destroyed, and they had been human once. As Calpurnia had been, and was, he hoped, becoming again. But hope can be a deceitful companion. Hope, he thought, is only there when we will things to be better for ourselves. It is an illusion.

387

Yet still, he hoped. For her forgiveness. For a happy ending.

'I remember when we played as children,' she had said, once. 'I remember when we laughed together, when we laid down our dolls and began to look at boys, when our father first made us take up weapons. When the Romans came.'

'Where is Flavia?'

She shook her head. 'I do not know. She may have fled the city, or –'

'Or?'

'She may still prowl Rome, seeking vengeance. You should have made sure on the night of the battle.'

'After the battle, it was well that the Guard stood down. If Flavia thinks she is safe, she may not harm us.'

'It is true that she must look after her own safety if she wants to –' Calpurnia broke off.

'What?'

'It is nothing.'

'Is there something more important to her than vengeance?'

'Perhaps.' She looked at him, and changed course. 'You have told me of Nero's reward. Will you take the governorship?'

'It is not in my choice. It is not something I can refuse.' Truly, it attracted him. To be away from Rome, far enough away to lead his own life. But not without her. The

388

question formed on his lips – to ask her to come with him, but she read it in his eyes before he spoke, and forestalled him.

'I will take food with you tonight,' she said.

More days passed, and the time was approaching when Julius would have to make arrangements and accede to Nero's wish that he take the governorship. He had yet to persuade Calpurnia to join him; she was distracted by her own thoughts. But there was no Changing, not a flicker, and, to his great relief, the simple food she had finally tried nourished her again, and the water she drank went on slaking her thirst.

On the sixth day he noticed she had left the blinds open, and she showed him her shadow in the sun. On the tenth day, her image looked back at her from mirrors. But still she was withdrawn. Increasingly, and especially when they made love, it seemed she was not with him at all.

Were they paying for one victory with another defeat?

'What is it?' he asked.

'I am waiting,' she said. 'Forgive me.'

On the twelfth day Julius cut short the conclusion of his affairs at VIII Cohort when a message from Dio arrived for him, and returned home fast.

'When?' he asked his body-slave, furious and bereft, unable to believe.

'I do not know. I did not see anything, there was no preparation. I sensed she was gone when the sun was near the hills to the west. I went to your room and found this. I sent you word immediately.'

Dio handed him the letter.

Flavia has gone. I know where she has gone and what she intends to do. I am following her, to stop her, before she can spread the disease. I believe that I am almost free of it now but I am not sure, I cannot be sure, and I do not know if it will ever leave me. It is too dangerous for us to be together, my love, and we must both accept that. I cannot bear the thought that I will never see you again but I cannot bear to think of you in danger any more. If I must die to be free of this curse, I will at least die trying to free the world of it. There is enough evil left in me to counter Flavia's and to prevent her womb from spawning, but what gives me the strength to do this is my love for you, and the knowledge that I must do this for you, and the children you will have one day. Take up the governorship, live well, and think of me sometimes with generosity. I am yours forever.

Julius read it twice, numbed, then cold and calm, as he noticed one small trail she had left him to follow. She had signed the letter with a different name from Calpurnia. The name she used was Zia.

Her Dacian name.

He did not have to struggle to reach a decision. It was made for him. He dismissed the governorship of Scythia from his mind. He called Dio.

'Send someone to the stables and have my best horse made ready. I am going on a journey. I'll pack my own bag.'

Dio looked at him in consternation. 'You're going now?'

'Now.'

'But the sun has set.'

'Now.'

'But what about–?'

Julius looked at him. 'There is no time to lose.'

He went and made ready for his journey, and when he'd finished his horse was saddled and waiting for him. He walked out of his block to the little knot of slaves waiting for him, Dio standing a little apart. Autumn was near, you could feel it in the air.

Julius felt no regret and he felt no fear.

He embraced Dio, mounted his horse, wheeled it round, and rode out of the city, north.